A TOPAZ TENKILLER NOVEL

THE POISONED FRUIT

JULIE COLACCHIO

THE POISONED FRUIT

A TOPAZ TENKILLER NOVEL

JULIE COLACCHIO

Woodhall Press | Norwalk, CT

Woodhall Press, Norwalk, CT 06855
WoodhallPress.com

Cover design: Asha Hossain
Layout artist: L.J. Mucci

Library of Congress Cataloging-in-Publication Data available

ISBN 978-1-960456-21-2 (paper: alk paper)
ISBN 978-1-960456-22-9 (electronic)

First Edition
Distributed by Independent Publishers Group
(800) 888-4741

Printed in the United States of America

To John, for doing everything I was too busy to do.

Chapter One

Mrs. Twoshades burst into Bud's Suds. "Ya better come quick, Topaz, yer sister's on fire."

I inhaled the lightning scent of Matt the Mechanic's coveralls and put them aside to fold later. Tucking a yellow washcloth into my pocket, I followed the old woman to the post office parking lot.

My sister, Coral, set herself on fire in front of the post office. She was only nineteen, but had taken to drinking with mom at The Driftwood Lounge. I had already decided to join them in a few years. Three women from the same family competing for drinks from out-of-work men would be a sick sideshow.

That was Coral's First Death. When we said goodbye to her giggle. My older sister shaped her words out of laughter. She threw herself at life—soap-making, painting, drumming—but forgot it all when she went into the bar. The First Death, the death of her body, set her free, but her family was left to perform the sacred rituals. In accordance with the Old Ways, we had to gather her ashes in a Soul Basket and perform the Witching Hour Chants. Only then, will her magic be released to Canopus.

Mom had a gray tub, the kind used for busing tables, but my father and little brother used red-backed playing cards to gather Coral's still smoking ashes into plastic cups. I used the washcloth to fetch smoldering embers of my sister and put them in Mom's tub. Gray flecks drifted like mourning butterflies. People from town stood on the sidewalk and watched, but nobody helped.

One of the Swiftharts, Merelyn I think, placed the Caesar Soul Basket on the ground and pushed it forward with her foot, fearful of contracting tragedy.

"Thy vessel is empty," Mom murmured.

She smelled like whiskey, but her hands were steady as my mother picked through the gravel. I missed the mom that alcohol stole. My father stood a few feet away from us. Church was his family now. I stood between my parents; the reliable buffer. I motioned to my brother, Malachi, to empty his cup of ashes into the basket.

"In the name of Jesus Christ, amen," Dad whispered.

I hissed, "Don't you dare."

"Sissy," he began, "The Old Ways and Christianity—"

"Don't," I muttered as I moved away. Was I angry that he was praying to Jesus or that he had called me Sissy? He hadn't called me Sissy since he abandoned the Old Ways and my mother.

I squatted next to Malachi. When he looked at me, there were unanswered questions and tears in my tough brother's eyes. "I'm sorry, Mal," I whispered. And I was sorry. Sorry our family was fractured. Sorry he was a prisoner on the croft.

Wind lifted ashes to mingle with the gray sky. The people from town wandered off. There's no spectacle in quiet grief. I thought of the unfolded laundry. Matt needed his coveralls by six.

When my mother sang the Witching Hour Chants for Grandma Fareye, her voice had vibrated with power. The Fareyes were crazy moonshiners, but they followed the Old Ways. Our shout, "May your magic die with you," trailed Grandma's magic to Canopus.

Shifting twilight had mingled ashes and gravel when my mother stood. She bit her lip as she eased the ashes from the tub into the soul basket. She did the same thing when she used to tie my shoes.

Mom said, "Canopus will be up soon." She cradled the basket to her breast and walked toward the woods.

Malachi and I hurried to catch up. My father's sigh and footsteps echoed behind.

She was surefooted. No alcoholic shuffle or stumble as Mom stepped over breached tree roots and jutting rocks. My eyes searched the darkening woods for undulating ribbons of shadow as I followed her. Twilight was Remnant Time. My mother carried a Remnant, amoral motherless magic, in the Soul Basket. Even my beloved sister's ashes were dangerous until we cared for them in the Old Way.

I wiped my ashy hands on my jeans.

Mom stopped at the Final Death Bier. The black rectangle of cement hulked in front of us. The last resting place of Coral's magic. She murmured, "May your magic die with you."

"May your magic die with you," Malachi and I responded. I shivered.

Mom placed the Caesar Soul Basket that contained Coral's ashes on the concrete bier. She drew us close and whispered, "It'll be okay."

I was safe. My mom knew what to do.

Dad stepped away and bowed his head.

"The Old Ways protect us. We do this for the Tenkiller-Fareye Family. For Amber, my eldest child who turned her back on her people; for Coral, who was too beautiful for this world; for Topaz, my strong, talented daughter; and for Malachi, my dear son." Mom's voice trembled, "We await Canopus to reunite her with Coral's Magic."

"Mom," Malachi sounded younger than his thirteen years, "where do we go after the First Death? I mean, we'll release Coral's magic, but what about her?"

Mom's voice was soft, "Honey, when a Canopian dies—"

My father cut her off. "She's in hell. Suicide is an abomination in the eyes of our savior. The 34th Psalm says when the righteous cry for help, the Lord hears and delivers them. The Lord saves the crushed in spirit. He keeps all his bones; not one of them is broken. Coral should have turned to the Lord."

Mom stiffened. Same argument. Same Psalm.

Dad said, "I invited Bishop Allred to offer a proper prayer before you begin your chants."

"We need the Old Ways. Will your God save us from motherless magic?" Mom asked.

"Accept God's love and escape the judgment reserved for the wicked, for those who," he swept his arm toward the Death Bier, "worship false idols."

I eyed the deepening sky. Canopus had risen. When the star beckoned purple, the Witching Hour Chants had to begin. "Mom, Coral wouldn't mind one prayer."

Mom wavered, "But she would. Coral followed the Old Ways."

There was an ahem sound behind us. Dad turned and his face lit up. "Bishop Allred, thank you for coming," He rushed to the pale man in a dark suit.

"I'm sorry for your loss, Henry, children." The Bishop smiled at us. "Mrs. Tenkiller, your husband asked me to say a prayer for Coral. I trust you agree?"

Mom shrank. Was it the suit? The whiteness of his teeth? The word 'Missus'? "Well, I hadn't planned—"

Bishop Allred spoke over her, "Surely one little prayer would not harm the soul of your dear child?"

Mom's face sagged. Her eyes darted around the clearing, looking for an escape. "I can't..I don't...I think I need to go." She stumbled to the path. Mom's heaving breath echoed, then disappeared as she ran back to the safety of The Driftwood Lounge.

Malachi looked from me to Dad. He was thirteen and didn't understand the swirling emotions. My parents gave up on each other and gave in to their vices before he could walk. I put my arm out and he leaned into me. We were a small tower of grief.

Bishop Allred spoke to Dad, "Although your daughter will not pass through the gates of Heaven, prayer will ease her path." He steepled his hands and Dad did the same. The Bishop looked at me and Mal. "Shall we?"

Malachi raised his eyebrows at me. I shrugged. What harm could a prayer do? I bowed my head.

"Dear Heavenly Father, we pray for a lost soul. The Bible tells us every healthy tree bears good fruit, but the diseased tree bears poisoned fruit. A healthy tree cannot bear bad fruit, nor can a diseased tree bear good fruit."

I thought of Mom's attempt to follow the Old Ways. Was Mom the diseased tree? The woman who taught me to bake a cake was diseased? Was Coral the poisoned fruit? Were my little brother and I poisoned fruit?

I lifted my head and looked at the Bishop's doughy face. "No," I said.

"Topaz," Dad hissed at me over his steepled hands.

I stepped close to the Bishop. He smelled like cocoa butter. His eyes popped open and I stared into the blue depths and spoke slowly, "No prayer."

The Bishop's face reddened and the smell of cocoa butter simmered. He murmured, "In the name of Jesus Christ, Amen," and followed the same path as my mother. Maybe they were both going to the Driftwood Lounge.

"Bishop?" My father called, but all that remained was the Bishop's sweet scent. Dad turned on me, "You ruined Coral's Salvation. You are your crazy mother's daughter."

"Are we poisoned fruit, Dad?" Malachi asked. "Is that why you left?"

I stole the fleeting strength of my mother and turned Mal to face the Death Bier, "Prayer won't help. Only the Old Ways and Canopus's Grace will release Coral's magic."

"I won't be part of this heathen ceremony. Only the Lord can save her," Dad said. Instead of alcohol, he used God.

Coral's ashes stirred and I nudged Mal. "Do you see that?" I asked.

Malachi's hand went to his heart, like he was saying the "Pledge of Allegiance," to America.

The smile on my face was in my voice. "That's our big sister's magic; Coral's beautiful magic wants to return home. Canopus beckons."

Mom showed me Canopus when I was five. In a bruised purple twilight, she'd pointed above the ridge line. When I followed her hand, she shook her head. "No, that's Sirius." Mom pulled my hand down a quarter inch and said, "Follow the arc to Arcturus, speed on to Spica, leap like a cat to Canopus. Canopus is close to Earth so she can hear our Witching

Hour Chants. In a long, long time, your body will expire. That is your First Death. Then we will sing the Witching Hour Chants and send your magic, that wonderful fire inside of you, back to Canopus." When I said I didn't want my magic to go, Mom hugged me and said, "May your magic die with you, my love." Even at five, I knew enough to respond, "May your magic die with you, Mommy."

Now, Malachi pointed and asked, "Is that Canopus?"

I pulled his hand down a little. "Canopus is lower so she can hear our chants. Your magic, that fire inside of you, will return to purple Canopus."

"Oh, for God's sake," my father snapped.

Malachi and I glanced at him. I had forgotten he was here.

He shook his head and clomped off through the trees.

I called, "Canopus Grace," to his retreating back and then turned to the Soul Basket. "It's time," I said to Malachi.

"Coral got me high the first time," Malachi said.

Malachi was high a lot these days, but I pretended like I didn't know. "Me too," I said. We laughed. "She and I smoked pot on the merry-go-round and tried to find shapes in the clouds. She told me she wanted six kids. That's what she wanted, to have babies."

"You mean poison fruit," Mal said.

We laughed again and gazed down at the Soul Basket. Coral's ashes whirled in crazy arcs, like the tail of a kite.

After a moment, Malachi said, "She was pregnant once."

I didn't know that. Coral was pregnant and hadn't told me. She was dead, but the rejection still stung. I will never be her confidant.

"She knew she couldn't take care of it and she wasn't sure who the father was, so she went to Justina Twoshades. She was sad. Coral really wanted to be a mom, but...."

I interrupted Malachi, "It's okay. I would've done the same thing." And she'll never know that, I thought.

"Coral's tough. Easy to party with, laugh and stuff, but hard to know," Mal said.

"I'm glad you were there for her," I said. I took a deep breath. "It's time." I had never done the Witching Hour Chants by myself, but I would do my best.

Malachi sniffled next to me. "I don't know the chants."

"I'll teach you, like Mom taught me before..." the lump in my throat stopped the words.

"She started drinking," he finished.

Ashes glowed like white embers in the basket and Canopus shone above the tree line.

I called to the star, *"Purple Canopus hear our cry, accept our Soul Basket offering."*

Coral's ashes lengthened into a serpentine light whirling over itself.

"First Death, Fire Death, May your magic die with you."

The clearing was lit by the sparkle of Coral's ashes as they rose out of the basket.

"May your magic die with you," Malachi repeated.

I pointed up. Canopus pulsed a purple and silver beacon for Coral's magic.

He smiled, "Purple Canopus Calling."

"*Final Death, Home to Canopus,*" I chanted

My brother and I shouted joyously together, *"May your magic die with you."*

Her ashes undulated and ribboned. Malachi's jaw dropped as his eyes followed the streak of light. His image wavered when I wiped away tears.

Coral's magic was a shooting star returning home. A tether of magic connected earth to Canopus. It flared bright, like Coral, then faded.

TOPAZ TENKILLER

Chapter Two

One Year Later

"I got my permit. I'm leaving in the morning," Topaz told her father.

"Leaving right after you turn sixteen, just like Amber," Henry Tenkiller said.

She didn't bother to remind him that, like most Mage children, she had left home when she turned fourteen. He was busy talking to his god, anyway. Her father rested his elbows on the Formica table and lowered his forehead to his knuckles in prayer. She gazed at the loose skin pooled beneath his closed eyes. If she stayed here, that would be her.

After a moment, he murmured, "Amen," and rifled through the jumble of envelopes and newspapers piled next to him. He found a pencil, scrawled a phone number on the back of an envelope, and slid it across the kitchen table to Topaz. "That's Bishop Allred's number. He can help you find your way. You call him when you're ready to accept the love of God."

"That's okay," Topaz said. She wanted to rip the envelope into a million pieces, but did not. This was the last time she would ever see her father. "Dad, I'm going to send money. Will you help Mal? There's a church program off the croft. I think he should go, but it's expensive."

For the first time in a long time, her father looked at her, really looked at her. "I will, Sissy. I know how you both feel about me, but I swear to God, I will help Malachi."

Topaz exhaled breath she did not know she had been holding. "Well, I better—"

"Are you sure you can make it back to town before dark? Martin Swifthart died alone a while back and Sammy Threetree said he saw Swifthart's Remnant up over the ridge last week. You can stay here," Hank offered, but they both knew there were only two livable rooms in the trailer; the kitchen and a combination living room and bedroom. He had an outhouse around back for his needs.

"I'll be okay." Topaz started to rise, but her father waved her down.

"Wait a minute," he called over his shoulder as opened the flimsy accordion door to the other room.

Topaz looked around the kitchen. It had the same brown linoleum as when she left two years ago. Water gathered at the end of the silver faucet and dripped, then gathered and dripped, and then gathered and dripped. The floor in front of the sink had buckled, probably from the leak that produced the maddening dripping sound. Her dad had placed a sheet of plywood to form a bridge connecting the solid floor on each side of the sagging floor. There had been a bigger table when she was young, but it had never been big enough for the six of them. Come to think of it, the four siblings and their parents had rarely lived under the same roof.

The door made a snapping sound when her father returned. "This won't help against Remnants," he placed a black object on the table between them, "but you don't know what you're going to find Offcroft in America. Take it with you."

When Topaz saw what it was, she shook her head. "Dad, I can't take your knife. Grandpa Tenkiller gave that to you."

"Who else am I going to give it to; your mother?" he scoffed. "God will take care of me. The Old Ways won't help you and you'll need protection out there."

Why did he have to take something nice and ruin it? Couldn't he just love his God and allow her to practice the Old Ways like he and Mom had taught her? She wanted to have a nice goodbye.

She got up to leave and hugged him tight, ignoring the sharp pain when her laminated work permit jabbed through her jeans to her thigh. He smelled like tea tree oil. She murmured, "May your magic die with you," into his ear.

"God bless you, Sissy," he said.

Topaz thought of the magic her father had given her when she was twelve, magic that now withered inside of him. He refused to use magic because mediums, necromancers, and sorcerers would not inherit the Kingdom of God. She left the Bishop's number in her father's trailer, but took the beautiful black Gerber Knife and sheath.

When she descended the wobbly cinder block steps, her breath hitched and she swiped at her eyes. He used to give her piggy-back rides, going faster when she slapped him and yelled "Yah, horsey." He taught her to use a knife, making her practice with a marker until she was fast and lethal. Then he bought her the cheap hunting knife that was tucked in her sock.

She stopped to attach the horizontal sheath to a belt loop on the back of her jeans and watched her father through the smudged window. He was on his knees with his face lifted to the water-stained ceiling. What misfortune had his God saved him from? His wife was an alcoholic who would rather sleep rough than with him. His poisoned fruit was true to the name. Amber, his eldest daughter, had left the croft six years ago and never been heard from again. Coral had committed suicide last year. She was leaving the croft forever and Malachi used whatever drugs he could get his hands on.

Topaz took the knife from where her sock nestled it against her leg and placed it on the top cinder block step. She checked on her magic. Topaz's magic was from her mother's side of the family. Her mom's people, the Fareyes, were mostly see-ers and Takers, and all crazy. She did not have her own power, but Topaz took the magic of others, sometimes with permission.

In his day, Henry Tenkiller had been powerful and his raging fire would be useful in America.

When she was twelve, and learned that she was a Taker, not a Fire Mage like her father and siblings, Topaz had run out to the dunes to hide. She crawled inside the crooked limbs of a juniper so her sisters would not see her cry. It wasn't fair. She wanted her own magic. She'd even be a creepy Fareye like mom, rather than some jerk who had to take magic from other Mages. She pulled her legs up to her chin and sobbed.

Her father followed her and knelt outside the tree. "Sissy, the rest of us only have one type of magic. You can be whatever you want."

"I want to be a badass Fire Mage, a Tenkiller," Topaz sobbed into her knee.

"Then that's what you are," Henry said. "Picture a tarp. That's your barrier."

Twelve-year old Topaz pictured the stained tarp that Dad had used when he painted half of their trailer blue before he quit. She wrote the letters H, C, A, C, T, and M in thick black marker in the corner. Her family.

Henry said, "Lift it up, now lower it, practice that."

Topaz practiced lifting and lowering the tarp. She added a strap at the bottom and tied it tightly to lock her stupid sisters out.

"Now, go inside the room on the other side of your tarp and imagine a container."

Topaz lifted the tarp and saw a bright, clean open space. Then she imagined an old-fashioned milk container, like the kind delivered to the front door of the Cunningham house in the TV show, "Happy Days."

Red lava filled the container and cast a campfire glow over her magical chamber. "You have my magic, the Tenkiller Fire. This magic can be a hammer or a scalpel."

"What does that mean?" Topaz asked.

"Someday you'll understand, Sissy," Henry said.

Now, Topaz stilled, clenched the muscle near her heart, and ducked under her tarp. Each Canopian had a space carved out inside of themselves to house their magic; their Magic Chamber. Topaz's was a dazzlingly white room with a single window. Three old-fashioned milk bottles lined the window sill. Two of the bottles were filled and one was empty. One bottle was filled with swirling pink and yellow liquid, magic she had taken from Coral before she died, and the other contained her father's still lava-hot magic. Her sterile Magic Chamber had the order that her life had always lacked.

Topaz's tongue found the empty space where her canine tooth used to be. She whispered, "Bye, Dad," and turned away.

Red dust rose around her as she jogged on the rutted road toward Thatcher Highway, where she could hitch a ride the rest of the way to town. Right about now, she could use some of Merelyn Swifthart's speed, to get to town before it got dark. It got dark and cold fast in the desert and her father said there was a Remnant nearby. When Topaz was young, Remnants were rare, but many Canopians had turned away from the Old Ways and now Remnants wandered the croft. Remnants, the abandoned magic of dead Canopians, were fast and sneaky. In the dark, they were especially dangerous. A Remnant could catch her and invade her Magic Chamber before Topaz even saw the silver ribbon. Remnants did not like electricity, so she would only be safe when she got to town. Luckily, she was used to bipedal locomotion. She broke into a smooth lope, feeling the hard plastic permit shift in her front pocket. Topaz eyed the brush by the road, but Remnants stayed hidden until dark.

She increased her pace, long legs eating up the distance. She needed to see Malachi before she left, to explain why she was leaving. He was her last sibling and she had to help him. Making peace with Coral was not possible, but she could make Mal understand.

Ahead, an indignant bird fluttered above the gray green scrub and Topaz slowed. A slash of red streaked away. Cardinals were good luck for her. If she could speak to animals like Cecilia Trillby, what would she say to a cardinal? She would tell it to get off the croft before somebody ate it.

She hurried past twisted, possibly Remnant-harboring, cedars. A shadow darkened the ground in front of her and Topaz smiled. She had never seen two cardinals in one day. When she looked up, instead of a brilliant red bird, a small figure in a black hooded sweatshirt soared thirty feet above her.

"Canopus' Balls, not Izzy," Topaz said. She ran faster to make herself a smaller target.

Izzy Sparrow was a Jumper and christened Isabella. She stayed a Jumper, but shortened her name to Izzy and changed her gender to him. Magic had no gender, why should people? So, Canopians paid no attention to gender. Izzy was part of a group of Canopians called The Warders. This self-appointed group beat the shit out of any Canopian who left the croft. Topaz liked Izzy. It's a shame she was going to fight him and the rest of the group. Ken and Robbie, maybe other Warders, were nearby. This fight would not be fair and she would get beaten up, but she would fight back. However, as was customary, no weapons.

"Izzy, I don't want to fight you," Topaz called.

In response, Izzy tucked his legs and hurtled toward Topaz.

Topaz opened her own tarp and rushed to Izzy's Magic Chamber. She shouldered open the glass door of Izzy's room and hurried past the posters of galloping horses and flying birds until she reached Izzy's flaming chalice. Topaz inhaled blue fire.

Izzy plummeted to the ground like a broken raven. He lay in the dirt road ahead of Topaz.

His magic would refill, like a well, in a few minutes. Topaz went back to her own Magical Chamber, exhaled Izzy's blue magic into the last empty bottle, and secured her tarp. She had disrupted Izzy's magic, but he would keep coming.

Izzy scrambled to his feet.

Topaz ran off the road into the soft sand and low scrub. She should have been more alert. Sure, she was watching for Remnants, but she had forgotten the more immediate threat of the Warders. Never mind that Topaz worked in a laundromat for room and board, her sister killed herself out of despair, or that Malachi Tenkiller abused drugs. The Warders thought Topaz was a traitor for leaving Caesar Croft.

Topaz scrambled up a hill, away from Izzy. There was a huffing sound behind her and Topaz smelled sweat. She looked back, but nobody was there. At the top of the hill, she looked back to check on Izzy and there was another set of footsteps behind her. The scent of sour sweat intensified, the scent of magic. Damn it, Robbie Skipnot was an Invisible. There was an Invisible Warder behind her and a Jumper Warder above.

Topaz pivoted and flung herself downhill toward the footsteps. She struck something soft and heard a gratifying "oomph." There was a flicker of denim and a man, cradling his midsection, appeared in front of her.

"Come on, Robbie, this is stupid." Topaz staggered to stay upright.

He reached for her, but she pulled him toward her. Robbie tripped and fell forward.

Izzy was, no doubt, circling around to cut her off. Where was Ken? There could be others, but the Warder leader was the one she really had to worry about.

"You're dead," Robbie yelled as he heaved himself upright. "You hear me, Topaz? You're an insult to Caesar Croft and the name Tenkiller!" He spat in the soft sand.

Topaz struggled through sandy dirt, angled toward a stand of Junipers above her. Keep moving. Her dad said still water became stagnant. The twisted trees would block an attack from above and her father's trailer was on the other side of the hill, due west. He was old and redeemed, but he was still a Tenkiller and fire slept beneath his piety.

Robbie huffed along behind her. Maybe he should stop drinking beer at The Driftwood Lounge and get some exercise. When she reached the junipers, Topaz leaned against an angled, gravity-defying tree. She was getting released from this godforsaken place and nobody could stop her. Topaz peered through the branches to check the other side of the hill. Damnit, Ken's putty-colored van was parked between here and Henry's trailer.

She was trapped. Robbie was behind her, Izzy above and blocking the road, and Ken, the owner of that doddering van, was between Topaz and her father's trailer. An invisible hand grabbed the collar of her polo shirt and jerked.

The material of her shirt bunched into a noose around her neck. Topaz gasped, "I'm being Released. Do you have to do this?"

"You'll take some bruises with you," Robbie said. He dragged her backwards through the stand of junipers and out the other side.

Izzy swooped down and kicked Topaz's shoulder. Robbie's grip on her shirt loosened and Topaz fell. She scrambled to get up, but Izzy threw himself on top of her. He used his body to pin Topaz's flailing arms.

"Get her feet, Rob," Izzy said.

Robbie, visible in all his crew-cut florid glory, approached Topaz, but she kicked him.

"For burnt magic's sake, watch your barrier," Robbie said to Izzy. He tried to get Topaz's legs again. "She's a Taker. Don't let her get any of your magic."

"I already got Izzy's magic, you dumbshit," Topaz gasped as she lashed out at his legs.

She heard the screech of an unoiled door. Ken, maybe other Warders. She had to get out of here or they would beat her up and leave her for the Remnants.

Topaz jerked her body back and forth to free her hands from Izzy's grip. She grabbed a handful of sand and threw it in Izzy's face, then sprang up and ran back toward the trees. The sky shifted as Topaz was lifted into the air and thrown to the ground.

Breath escaped her. She could not get air back inside. Darkness swam at the corner of her eyes. Topaz could not breathe. A heavy boot settled onto her back and pressed down, pinning her to the ground.

"Hey there, Topaz."

The voice lazily nestled inside her. The man with the voice, and the boot, was Kenneth Twosongs. A Crooner with a grudge.

Robbie grabbed Topaz's upper arms and hauled her up. She drew in breath. Her shoulders protested, but Topaz bucked her body and kicked at Izzy.

"Back up, Izzy," Ken said from behind Topaz.

The scent of sweat was overpowering. The scent of big magic. No use trying to Take; the Jumper, Invisible, and Crooner were ready for her and would have their magic barriers secured.

Robbie pulled her arms back until her shoulder blades met. Ken patted Topaz down and felt the sheathed knife, but left it there. A Tenkiller would never break the unspoken agreement and fight Warders with a weapon. He reached around Topaz, inserted two fingers into the front pocket of her jeans, and removed her work permit.

"You bastards!" Topaz bucked, but Robbie held her. Without that work permit, she would not be Released.

"Let's tie her up," Robbie suggested.

"Give me my permit," Topaz spat.

"Topaz," Ken said, "calm down. You can have it back after we talk."

Calm down? Talk? Why didn't they just hit her and get it over with? When people left the croft, Warders gave them a beating, not a talk.

"Fine. I'll talk if you give me a ride back to town," Topaz said.

"What?" Robbie asked. "You can't bargain. We beat you." Just like when she beat him at "Rock, Paper, Scissors" in fourth grade, the little weasel always wanted best out of three.

Topaz shrugged as well as she could with her arms behind her. "Give me a ride back and we talk."

"Deal," Ken said.

Topaz suppressed a grin. The Warders had saved her a mile of walking and an hour of hitching and she took some of Izzy's magic. Not a bad day.

Chapter Three

Robbie held both arms and Izzy stayed out of kicking distance as they led her down the hill to the van. She had yet to see him, but she felt Ken behind her. She stretched and rotated her neck, ready to run if necessary. She could take Izzy on the ground. Robbie was big, but soft. Ken was a problem. He was a powerful Crooner and Amber's ex-boyfriend. He had taken it hard when Amber left. In fact, that was when he joined the Warders and shaped a loose group of unemployed Mages into an organized force to punish those who deserted their people.

They stopped at the van and Robbie prodded her in the back, "Get in."

"Nope, we talk out here," Topaz said.

"Fine," Ken said.

Robbie snorted and released Topaz's arms. She sat in the open doorway of the van and folded her arms. The smell of oil and cigarette smoke curled around her shoulders. "So, talk."

Izzy went to the front of the van and looked up at the late afternoon sky. Robbie glowered at Topaz. When Ken sat next to Topaz, the van door shrank to the size of a porthole. Ken Twosongs was large, neither muscular nor fat, but present in a big way. Unusual for a Mage, Ken was swarthy, the skin not covered by his black beard was tan.

"Caesar's losing our best. Your sisters abandoned us and now you're leaving. Do you care about the croft? About your brother? Who will teach Malachi the Old Ways? Who will be left to do the Witching Hour Chants after your parent's First Death?" he asked.

Topaz picked at the threadbare knee of her jeans and remained silent. The only way to help Malachi was to leave.

"You think you're helping your brother, but once you go out the "Giving Up Gate," there's no coming back." His voice was urgent. Ken cared deeply about the croft; sometimes that manifested itself in brutal beatings and sometimes in rhetorical passion.

"Yeah, bitch. You leave, you don't come back," Robbie added.

Topaz jerked her foot up and her sneaker connected with Robbie's shin. He cursed and stepped back.

Ken chuckled, then covered his mouth and coughed. He turned to Robbie and said, "Give us a minute." After Robbie stomped away, Ken asked Topaz, "Why you leaving?"

His voice tickled the small hairs on her neck. Topaz sniffed but the air was clear. Ken was not using his powers.

"Why am I leaving?" She finally met Ken's eyes. A breeze rustled the brush and goosebumped her bare arms. "You know us Tenkiller trash. Mom drinks to kill her sadness and Dad killed his magic because the Bishop told him it's evil. Amber went out the Giving Up Gate and we haven't heard from her since. The best," Topaz shrugged, but her voice broke on bitterness, "was when Coral set herself on fire last year. Malachi's headed down the same path if I don't help him. If I stay here, I'll end up like you and Robbie, drink and make babies or drink and play pool to forget my shitty life. No offense."

Ken shrugged. Robbie had three children by three different women and Ken was the best pool player at The Driftwood Lounge.

"Mages need to stay here and change things." He spoke in a more measured tone, "Or, if you're leaving, maybe you can still help your people. There are

Offcrofters who are sympathetic, but it's hard to connect with them. I could put you in contact with others who want to change things, to help Canopians."

"From what I've seen, our people don't want to change. The fences keep us here, but we're trapped by ignorance and fear," Topaz said.

"I'm trying to save our people. I need help. You've worked hard to become a Master Mage. Why just give it to the Offcrofters, the Americans?"

Topaz's tongue wandered to her missing canine, but she had given up more than a tooth to become a Master Mage. "I'm not giving it. I am selling it to the Offcrofters so I can get Malachi into a program. I'll help my family; you can help our people."

"May your magic die with you," Ken Twosongs was resigned.

"Death and life exists within," Topaz responded. She was a devout practitioner of the Old Ways her mother had taught her. The Old Ways got her through Coral's suicide and Amber's abandonment. "But, I'm leaving tomorrow. I have to go through the Giving Up Gate to save Malachi." She held out her hand, "May I have my permit and a ride?"

Izzy spoke from the front of the van. "I told you not to bother with her. She's just like the rest of the Tenkillers. Leave her here."

"No, we said we'd give her a ride," Ken said.

"We're still going to hit her, right?" Robbie asked.

"Yeah, we'll hit her," Ken said. He appealed to Topaz one last time, "I know you care about the Old Ways. What if I told you that Offcrofters are trying to get rid of our customs, that the Old Ways are already outlawed on Macbeth Croft? On Macbeth, Mages are disappearing after the First Death and Remnants outnumber people. You can help us from the outside. Do you care about our future? Is anything important to you?"

"My brother. Now," she waggled her fingers, "my work permit, please."

Ken slapped her work permit into her hand and she clenched it tightly.

Robbie muttered, "Dick," pushed her back into the van, and climbed in.

Topaz slid away from the door. Metal squealed and the rectangle of sunlight shrank and disappeared as Ken heaved it closed. She pushed herself up into the seat and tucked her permit back into her pocket.

Ken adjusted the rearview mirror and caught Topaz's eyes. "The Old Ways are under attack." He stuck the key in the ignition, "I came here to beat you for betraying us, for working for them. But you look too much like Amber."

As the van skittered in the sand, Robbie leaned down and spoke into her ear, "I told him you're a piece of shit. You think you're anybody's first choice? You're going to the right place and we need your power, but nobody chose you. Tenkillers can't be trusted."

Topaz swayed as the van bumped onto the gravel road. "Doesn't matter. I'm out of here." She didn't say it aloud, but she also had some of Izzy's flight now.

"And turning your back on your people."

Topaz turned her back on Robbie.

Chapter Four

Her heels clacked a one-two warning of impatience as Mayor AnnaLeesa Bennett strode down the corridor of Bloomington Town Hall. Her secretary assumed the mayor took the stairs to preserve her trim figure, but AnnaLeesa Bennett had been claustrophobic since she was a child. She hitched her black briefcase higher on her shoulder and stopped by her secretary's desk.

"Good morning, Mayor." A woman in a plaid pantsuit rose to greet AnnaLeesa. Her spectacles bounced against her bosom, but her shellacked hair stayed in place. "How was the Trade Delegation conference call last night?"

"Morning, Margo, detailed and never-ending. Remind me again why America finds it necessary to trade with other countries? I'll give you my notes. I spoke to Mr. Neil, the inspector's assistant. Now, Inspector Thistlewaite demands a tour of the crofts. I think I can mollify the woman with Bloomington, especially if she is allowed to interact with our mixed Security and Logistics Team and investigate the Canopian living quarters. Please adjust the itinerary to reflect this. Also, in the interest of saving time, please contact the driver and instruct him to skip intake at Cheyenne. We need the last Mage members of the Security Team here ASAP." She patted her briefcase, "Too many meetings, Margo, I did not get a chance to review the Croft Reports from yesterday."

"I guess you don't want these then?" Margo smiled and handed AnnaLeesa a stack of pink messages. "Tea?"

"Oh, god yes." AnnaLeesa read the messages and gave instructions as she handed them back, "Please schedule an introduction with the Security and Logistics Team in one month, some baked goods and coffee. The bus is arriving in two days and we want to give the Canopians time to adjust first. I'll call Undersecretary Durant at the Bureau of Land Management," she looked at her watch, "Right now. Ugh, Ambassador Thistlewaite called again? God save the queen, does that woman ever sleep? It's 4 am in London." Annaleesa paused at the next square of pink paper, "Dr. O'Shea? I will call him after my tea. Margo, where's my tea?"

"Got it, Mayor," Margo hustled off.

Annaleesa entered her office and left the door open. She inhaled deeply as she hung her navy-blue trench coat on the wooden rack in the corner, but all she could smell was Jean Nate, her preferred perfume. Smoothing her powder blue skirt down, she settled at her desk and picked up the phone.

"Mayor Bennett for Undersecretary Durant, please...thank you."

She balanced the receiver between her chin and shoulder as she removed a gray folder from her briefcase. She lined it up to match the corner of her desk, a quarter inch from the front and side, while she waited for her liaison in Washington D.C. to pick up the phone. She and Undersecretary Edward Durant coordinated security for the integrated Town of Bloomington as well as research and development on and for the Canopian people.

"Good morning, Ed. How are you?...How's Deborah? Is her back still acting up?...Yes...uh-huh. You know what they say, nothing heavier than a vacuum...Well, you tell her I said to take it easy."

Careful not to smudge her gleaming desk, AnnaLeesa pulled the Macbeth Croft Reports closer. She unleashed fresh hells on Macbeth Croft whenever she could. Hell on the croft was a learning opportunity for America. The first had been enforced schooling; she persuaded the then Canopian Consultant Edward Durant to mandate church school for every child born on Macbeth Croft. Next, AnnaLeesa Bennett initiated the "Modernize Macbeth" campaign. While Macbeth was still reeling from the loss of its children, AnnaLeesa persuaded Canopian Consultant Durant to ban the Old Ways. Her experiments after the First Death had been interesting.

"The Americans are assembled for the Security and Logistics Team and the three Canopians are leaving their crofts in the morning...should be here in two days...one from Caesar Croft, one from Macbeth Croft, and one from Antony Croft...yes...I know Caesar and Macbeth are problematic, but these are the best and brightest, Ed. Optics are especially important for the Security and Logistics Team." She nodded, although he was on the phone. "We can manage them. The delegation must believe we are uniting *all* Canopians and Americans, not just the cooperative crofts like Antony and Othello, the recalcitrants must be front and center...I understand your misgivings, but you do not understand Canopians."

Margo placed a steaming gold-edged teacup and saucer next to the reports on AnnaLeesa's desk. The Mayor smiled thanks and her secretary left the room.

"Let me stop you right there, Ed," she straightened the teacup, "I've decided that this batch will not stop for intake at Cheyenne. No injections or medication will be administered to the Mages at Bloomington, either...I know the technology is available...I don't care how bad they smell. We will not mask the scent of magic in Bloomington. It is culturally insensitive and a security risk, and, most importantly, Inspector Thistlewaite will know."

The conversation ended pleasantly, but tension in his goodbye reminded AnnaLeesa to tread carefully. As the former Deputy Director of Canopian Culture and Security for the Bureau of Land Management and a recognized authority on Mage issues, AnnaLeesa was powerful, but Edward Durant could shut down her life's work with one phone call.

AnnaLeesa lifted the cup and breathed in bergamot and lemon, but the temperature was not yet right for sipping. She opened the Macbeth Economic and Budget Report. Since she had forbidden the Old Ways, electricity usage for Macbeth Croft had more than tripled.

Mages on Macbeth had disobeyed curfew and performed hidden Witching Hour Chants to care for their dead until AnnaLeesa had ordered the Macbeth Death Bier, a 200-year-old structure, dismantled and seized the Macbeth Soul Basket. A few devout practitioners of the Old Ways had still persisted in performing the Witching Hour Chants in the woods, so the Bureau of Land Management-funded strike team shot the Old Ways adherents and carted their bodies off the croft in an electrified truck. After that, Macbeth Mages stopped trying to reunite the magic of their loved ones with Canopus. In fact, they refused to leave their homes at night.

Maybe she would institute rolling blackouts in the next quarter. AnnaLeesa made a note in the report. This would have the threefold benefit of saving money, conserving energy, and increasing Remnant production. She licked her finger and turned to the next report; the Macbeth Census Report. Births had all but stopped on Macbeth because of the constant stress on the people and the knowledge that all children were taken and sent to the church boarding school. Deaths on Macbeth had outpaced those of other crofts by two to one.

Her eyes skipped down to the "H" section of the alphabetical death list and a gleeful smile split her face. James Heartsnake. There he was. Her father.

She took a sip of tea and leaned back in her chair. Dead. AnnaLeesa Bennett, Victoria Heartsnake in another lifetime, had waited decades for James Heartsnake to die. No cause of death was listed, only that his body was found in his trailer. She knew the unlisted details, the mountain of beer cans, privy trench in back, the way the trailer shook when he stumbled down the small hallway, the scent of urine that clung to him. She knew that Mrs. Twohop, from the liquor store, was the only one who would notice his absence. AnnaLeesa checked the document, and yes, Mrs. Twohop was the one who sent government workers to look for James Heartsnake.

The report was one-dimensional. His last name began with an H, but the "M" section of the report did not state that he had murdered his wife forty years earlier. The Macbeth Economic and Budget report did not show if he had charged sales tax when he sold his daughter to men. Nor did the "W" section reflect that Rebecca Warmhands was the midwife who had helped bring AnnaLeesa Bennett into the world forty-seven-years ago. There was no information next to the Warmhands surname to indicate that Rebecca had fed hungry, almost feral, children. Topaz had been one of the kids Rebecca protected, what they called "extras" on the croft.

This was a welcome surprise. AnnaLeesa's father's death had not appeared on the unofficial report compiled by her Macbeth Team. She received weekly reports via personal courier and reviewed all manifests from the "Magic Milk" trucks. She carefully planned her life, and the life of others, to avoid surprises like this. Maybe surprises weren't always a bad thing. Then why was her throat blocked? What was that childish thickness gathering behind her eyes?

"No tears," she whispered. She repeated the words on the inhale and exhale until they were true. He did not deserve her tears. Macbeth Croft did not deserve her tears. The Canopians who lived on Macbeth deserved exactly what they were getting. She blinked to clear her watery eyes. She could not risk losing one of her blue contacts. The blonde-haired, blue-eyed, Annaleesa Bennett could not be seen in public with a puffy red face and Canopian brown eyes.

What were these tears for? His death ensured that she was safe. The last link between AnnaLeesa Bennett and Tori Heartsnake was dead. The croft was amputated from the mayor.

She had banned the Old Ways on Macbeth Croft, but she could not leave the malignance of James Heartsnake to prey on children. All of Heartsnake had to be eradicated. If she did not rid the croft of her father's contagion, it would infect the entire community. Nobody cared enough about this monster to disobey her injunction against the Old Ways. She had not been on the croft in over twenty years, but as his only living blood relative, AnnaLeesa Bennett had to do the Witching Hour Chants to stop his magic from torturing other defenseless little girls.

She turned to the glass cabinets behind her. Tapestries of elaborately woven hair and grass hung at the back of the smaller cabinet. The shape of a lizard emerged from one and the other showed a star colliding with a purple planet. In front, blue velvet pedestals showcased necklaces of hair and teeth. Mages who worked hard at his or her craft lost parts of themselves. It was said that Laura Yellowsong lost three teeth in one year, a Fareye woman went bald when she was eleven, and that powerful Canopian men were sterile. Colorful Soul Baskets were arranged on the lower glass shelf, each croft a different color and design.

The other cabinet was a celebration of American ingenuity. Not long after Benjamin Franklin flew his kite in the storm, Americans discovered that electricity disabled Canopian's magic. She had a replica of Luigi Galvani's "Galvani's De Viribus Electricitatis in Motu Musculari," the tubes and metal prods that the scientist used to reanimate dead frogs. Tools to oppress her people, electrical cathodes of varying sizes and materials, dotted the cabinet. The largest was two feet long and used in the guard towers that surrounded each of the crofts. Others, less bulky, were used by the guards and border control agents who worked with Mages. Small compact models were used by American policemen in towns that bordered crofts or by those who needed personal protection from Mages. At the front was a 3M, Magic Monitoring Machine. The pride of the American Military. At the back of the cabinet, she had a large, framed reproduction of President Adams' "Mage Imprisonment Order of 1800," ordering that all Mages be confined to crofts to protect the American people from "most pernicious and devilish magick." Adams was an avid fan of Shakespeare so he named the five crofts after his favorite tragedies; *Julius Caesar*, *Macbeth*, *Antony*, *Othello*, and *Lear*. The framed diploma from John Jay College of Criminal Justice to the left of the Mage display cabinet reminded AnnaLeesa Bennett of who and what she had become.

Why should she care about the Canopians of Macbeth? They had not been concerned about an abused little girl. She put the side of her teacup against her cheek and closed her eyes. Rebecca Warmhands had sheltered her until James inevitably came looking for his only child.

AnnaLeesa stuck her head out of her office door, "Margo, hold my calls, please."

"Yes, Mayor."

AnnaLeesa locked the door, turned off the lights in her office, and bent under the desk to turn off the power strip. What she was about to do was practical, she told herself, she could not risk problems right before Inspector Thistlewaite visited to renew the International Trade Agreement.

She stood in front of the glass cabinets and wiped her clammy hands on her skirt. The rituals of conquered people stank of superstition, but they were rooted in necessity. She took a deep breath and opened the cabinet. In the dim room, the black widow spider colors of black and red seemed to scuttle across Macbeth's Soul Basket. It had already been two days since her father died, so she could not wait for Canopus to rise. Annaleesa placed the basket on her desk blotter. She removed a red pack of cigarettes from her briefcase, ripped off the filter, and sprinkled tobacco into the Soul Basket. Tobacco was not a substitute for First Death ashes and her mahogany desk was certainly no Death Bier, but maybe their genetic link and similar magic would be enough for her to send her father's magic to Canopus.

AnnaLeesa Bennett clenched the muscle beneath her heart and entered her gleaming silver and black Magic Chamber. She removed the chalice of blue fire from a mottled and cracked leather trunk in the center of her chamber, knelt and opened the heavy lid. The Mayor of Bloomington whisper-sang the Witching Hour Chants.

"Purple Canopus Calling, May your magic die with you."

She held out her hand.

"First Death, Fire Death, Our Soul Basket Offering. May your magic die with you."

A hand grasped hers and Annaleesa helped a pale girl out of the trunk. Her victim-self, Tori Heartsnake, was not wearing any clothes and each knob of her spine was visible. The child shivered and warmed herself near the chalice as it flamed higher with magic.

In her office, Mayor Annaleesa Bennett continued the breathy chant. She lit the tobacco and the smoke mingled with the smell of sweat that rose from her.

"*Purple Canopus Calling. Song of Final Death, Home to Canopus.*"

At the end of the chant, the child and adult murmured in the same voice, "*May your magic die with you.*"

Inside the Magical Chamber, Annaleesa gently lifted the bruised child and placed her back into the trunk. She ignored the tears leaking from the corners of the child's eyes.

"Daddy's gone," Annaleesa murmured. She prayed to Canopus she was right, but there was no way to know if the spider of James Heartsnake's venomous magic had returned to Canopus. "Death and life exists within."

As AnnaLeesa lowered the lid of the trunk, her child-self whispered, "I wish I died before you were born."

Chapter Five

Topaz felt around on the van floor for something to use as a weapon, but all she found were oily papers and beer cans.

The lone streetlight of Caesar was ahead, in the short part of the u-shaped parking lot. Maybe the Warders let her off easy. The ride had been silent and their chambers locked tight. She eyed Robbie in the sepia of twilight, but he was relaxed. There was a chance she would not get her "Going Through the Giving Up Gate" beating before leaving the croft.

The van slowed. Topaz watched Robbie carefully as she grasped the door handle. "Well, thanks for the—"

Izzy crouched in the front passenger seat and Topaz shifted her body to face him. The small Canopian's fist blurred down. Topaz tried to duck, but there was no room to maneuver in the van. Izzy slammed his fist into Topaz's eye and temple. Blossoms of fireworks sparkled in her eyes.

The van slowed. Through the ringing in her ears, Topaz heard the screech of metal. Then Robbie pushed her out of the open van door. She scrambled to get her feet beneath her body, but the sparklers in her head were distracting. Topaz stumbled and fell to the graveled parking lot of Caesar's town center.

"Assholes," Topaz muttered, though a sucker punch from Izzy was not bad as beatings went.

The van left a trail of dust like a settling parachute. Topaz waited until it accelerated onto Thatcher Highway before she sat up. Her eye throbbed and the skin tightened at the corner as it swelled. She rose, but swayed until the dizziness lifted. She blinked against the light and smiled.

They had dropped her in front of Bud's Suds, home for the last two years when she left home at fourteen. Now, she could save Izzy's flight. The narrow laundromat was crammed between two flag-decorated buildings; the American Government Check Cashing Service and the American Government Liquor Store. Another clump of buildings was down the way on her left; a ramshackle gas station and the American Government Post Office.

Her bag was packed and waiting in the back room of the laundromat, but she needed to say a few more goodbyes. Topaz sighed and went right, toward The Driftwood Lounge, a corrugated silver building that leaned against the Caesar Croft Community Health Center. The parking lot center of town was empty except for a few elderly trucks. The white church stood an aloof distance away while untamed woods lurked beyond. There were a few houses scattered around the town center, owned by Canopians who worked for America, but Topaz had never been inside one. Most Canopian families lived in FEMA trailers out in the cedars. The young and the old slept where they could.

She aimed herself toward the blue neon sign in the window and tried to walk straight. The spatter of gravel echoed inside her own head. She broke the night quiet of the parking lot when she pulled the metal door open.

The onslaught of sound assaulted Topaz. Voices wrapped in smoke rushed to the open door. Topaz slipped into the bar and leaned against the wall to acclimate herself to the noise and light. The Driftwood Lounge was home to her mother and Coral, before Coral died.

The bartender, Danny Nightshade, was her age. Like Topaz, he had left school to work after he fulfilled the mandatory eighth grade education that America required of its Mages. She tried to catch his eye, but he was busy filling glasses with yeasty ale. His muscles flexed as he lifted the heavy earthenware containers. An unlit cigarette dangled from his mouth, but Topaz knew, like most things about Danny, it was for show. He had asthma.

The bar was divided into three groups. Crystal was not part of the first group drooped on the bar, in various stages of alcoholic forgetfulness. It was Friday, so the hushed group of teens in the corner were watching Mr. Roarke and Tattoo welcome guests on the show, "Fantasy Island." There was the loud clack of a solid break and the third group cheered in the back room. Her mother was mostly a member of the raucous third group, although she had briefly joined the first after Coral committed suicide.

Under the sound of balls ricocheting around a pool table, Willie Nelson's wavery voice underscored the hopelessness of The Driftwood Lounge. He sang about blue eyes crying in the rain, but Canopians had brown eyes. Topaz swiped at the corner of her eye and winced. When she looked at her hand, a red streak bisected it. Izzy must've had a roll of pennies in his hand. Topaz waved to try to catch Danny's eye, too dizzy to leave the safety of the wall.

"Topaz," a voice called from the back room. A voice softened and rounded with alcohol. "I've been waiting for you."

In the bar I avoid? Topaz wondered.

Crystal Fareye weaved from the back room, a queen stumbling past derisive subjects. A cobwebby purple scarf wound around her shoulders and trailed past her wrinkled yellow shirt and tight denim skirt. The diaphanous material dragged on the bar floor, netting cigarette butts and peanut shells.

Topaz swallowed the dizziness and faced her mother.

"Honey, I heard you're released. So, I lose another child to the "Giving Up Gate." Oh, purple Canopus, why must the Offcrofters take our best and brightest?"

"Hi, Mom," Topaz murmured.

Crystal threw her arms around Topaz. They swayed for a moment. Why did her mother always smell like ashes?

"Danny, my love," her mother banged her hand on the bar, "mead for my daughter and me, yet another gifted Canopian stolen by the Offcrofters. Life and death exist within."

"No, Mom, please," Topaz murmured, but Crystal had turned away to search blearily for Danny.

Her mother was mostly bald, but the wispy hair floating around her head gave the impression of an infant. Crystal was a powerful Canopian and magic took its toll. She had lost most of her teeth by the time she was forty. Topaz's tongue wandered to the missing canine in the front of her mouth.

"Danny Nightshade! Where is he?" Crystal peered at Danny, who was standing in front of them. "Mead for me and my girl."

"Crystal," Danny began, "no more credit. Unless you have money, I can't—"

Topaz tried to draw Crystal away from the bar to say a quiet goodbye. She regretted entering Crystal's bankrupt kingdom. "Mom, come on."

"No," Crystal shouted. She twisted away from Topaz and pointed at Danny. She swayed and her finger wavered, but Crystal stayed upright. Willie stopped singing. Crystal looked around the quiet bar. "Topaz Tenkiller is released from Caesar Croft tomorrow. Won't someone honor my daughter? For burnt magic's sake, one mead for a warrior?"

The group at the television huddled closer to their Fantasy Island. Couples whispered near the pool table.

"Danny?" Crystal's voice cracked. "Two meads. I'll pay you tomorrow."

Danny Nightshade would not meet Crystal's eyes. Crystal Fareye had long ago used up her, "I'll pay you tomorrows." She would have to wait until the first of the month when her government check came.

Crystal's eyes filled with tears and her shoulders slumped. "I want to do something nice for my last daughter," she mumbled.

Topaz's Mage-pale cheeks were pink bullseyes. She glared at the pitying faces littering the room. They had seen her fetch Crystal from the bar too many times. Had witnessed her family mourn Coral and say goodbye to Amber. The jukebox clicked and broke the spell. When Amy Mann admonished the drinkers to hush and told them that voices carry, the bustle of drinking returned to The Driftwood Lounge.

Topaz touched her mom's shoulder. "I want to thank you for the Old Ways. I love you."

Crystal snuffled into the upside-down V of her arms. "Topaz, you have to do something."

"I know," Topaz said. She avoided Danny's eyes and rubbed her mother's shoulder.

When she touched Crystal, an image overlaid the grimy bar in front of Topaz. Blonde hair swooped over blue eyes. Then, they changed to brown. The blonde woman smiled and a gaping, toothless, abyss opened. Her hair bounced and settled.

Topaz snatched her hand away and the bar was solid again. "Mom, don't do that."

"The Old Ways, Topaz, help me," her mother moaned and sniffled.

"I don't know how to help you, but I'll help Malachi, your son, my brother." She quashed the anger that rose against her mother. Right now, she hated Crystal, hated her alcoholism, her useless visions, and her weakness.

"Amber failed, but you can do it." Crystal rolled her head around and looked at Topaz, "Help your people."

"We don't know what happened to Amber, but I'm helping my little brother." Topaz did not allow herself to say aloud, *Something you should be doing.* She squeezed her mother's shoulders quickly and released her. "I don't care about anyone else."

When she turned to go, Danny Nightshade called her name. He tossed her ice swaddled in a tattered bar towel. Topaz looked at it quizzically and he pointed at her eye. She smiled thanks and went in search of her little brother.

* * *

Although it was probably too late to prevent a black eye, she held the ice to her face and walked around behind The Driftwood Lounge. Since Malachi stopped going to school, he and his pack gathered in the woods out back of the church. The simple white building with the tall steeple comforted Topaz as the Bishop never had.

Her eyes wandered to the side of the church. In the near darkness, there was a jumble of blue and green, tarps and sleeping bags. Her mother and other alcoholic Mages sheltered there. The light illuminating the steeple deterred Remnants, they got an occasional meal from the Community Center, and it was stumbling distance from The Driftwood Lounge. Prime real estate.

Once in a while, a sober Crystal would tap on the door to Bud's Suds. If there were customers, Crystal waved and walked away, but if the laundromat was empty, she and Topaz would share a can of soup or a peanut butter sandwich. Topaz let Crystal use the shower and gave her mom clothing that had been lost or forgotten at the laundromat. If Crystal was sober, they sat and talked about the Old Ways or shared memories of Amber and Coral. What would happen to her mother? Topaz knew Crystal would rather die than ask Hank for help, and she understood.

Topaz put her knuckle in her mouth to contain the sob at the thought of better times with her mom. She thought of the dogs and cats, the parade of pets she had brought home over the years. The Tenkiller family did not have money for basic care, so the animals slunk to the desert to die alone. If a pet was truly suffering, her mother took it to Mrs. Twoshades to end quickly. Lost animals and drunken piggy-back rides were the sum of her happy childhood memories. The last time the Tenkiller family was together was when they placed the teal and yellow, bright like Coral, Soul Basket on the Death Bier. While she and Malachi chanted Coral's ashes to Canopus, Topaz had watched the path, sure that Amber would return to help her family, but nobody came. Now she had to say goodbye to Malachi so she could save him. And she had to do it fast, before twilight faded completely into night.

She followed the sound of drums up ahead, along the path that wound around away from the town center and the church. Here, the trees were taller and fuller. Off to the side, at the base of a slender tree, a zipping streak of light appeared. It slithered into a shadow and disappeared, but Topaz knew it was near. Her father had warned her Remnants were out. This one would likely wait for her. She might be alone, but she was not weak.

Topaz threw the sodden bar towel at the tree where she had seen the Remnant and hurried along the path, scanning recesses of trees and roots. She hurried toward an area ahead that blazed with light. She usually avoided visiting Mal while he was with his friends, but she needed to say goodbye.

She smelled the sweat at the same time that she reached the clearing where Mal and his crew gathered. They had strung wire from the church's electrical pole to their camp and had four lamps set up around their small campsite. Topaz marveled at the young wonders before her. A slender pillar of fire cast a red glare on this spectacle of youth, pulsing light to be absorbed by the tight circle of pine trees. A girl swirled around the fire like an asbestos ribbon. On the ground, a shirtless teen grappled with a hissing bobcat. A boy in a backwards baseball cap dipped and looped his hands in the air and an aluminum can mirrored his movement. Two girls sat cross-legged in the dirt, facing one another and holding hands, eyes scrunched closed. At the edge of the clearing, his back to Topaz, a teen sat on a white plastic lawn chair, banging a drum in a hard soft soft pattern. The column of fire pulsed in time with the heartbeat drum thump.

Topaz smiled at the joyful magic. Goosebumps rose on her arms as she watched them revel in their power. Magic was a beautiful gift, but her mother said that using magic was like being pregnant. A parasite lived inside of you, took what it needed, and you made do with what was left. You loved and nurtured the parasite, but it lived at your expense. Canopians who regularly used their magic were never overweight, and the more they practiced, the leaner they were. One could identify a powerful Mage by patchy hair, a sallow complexion, and missing teeth. Topaz's tongue slipped habitually into the empty spot where her upper canine tooth used to be. She was only sixteen, but she had lost the tooth and stopped having periods this year. It was all worth it, because she had gotten her work permit.

The smell of sweat intensified and concentrated into an eye-searing miasma. The burnt sweat stench of magic overdose.

Where was their Watcher? These kids had to stop doing magic now. Beginning Mages, like her brother and his friends, could only sustain magic for about five minutes. Topaz knew that their hearts were racing, and their bodies were clammy and drenched with sweat. Next, they would get the shakes and, if they did not stop magicking, the seven teens would collapse. The first rule of magic is to have a Watcher. She had seen a Remnant right outside of their camp. Why was nobody keeping watch? What if something went wrong? Who would get help? A Watcher would have stopped the exhausted kids already. Canopus Grace, were they only two years younger than her?

The stench of magic singed Topaz's nostrils. Her brother and his friends were not equipped to deal with the deep depression that accompanied overtraining. Topaz understood the emptiness that descended when she overused magic.

The floating girl dropped to the ground like a dead moth. Topaz could no longer stand silent. She cleared her throat and deliberately scraped her sneakers on the ground as she stepped into the light. Topaz spoke softly to avoid alarming the teens. "Hey guys, good work, but you don't want to overdo it."

The drummer stopped patting the cowhide disc in his hands and let it hang limp from a crooked index finger. The tin can hurtled to the ground and the boy in the baseball hat startled as if awakened from a falling dream. The two girls blinked at one another. Furry bobcat limbs elongated into a young man and he lay recumbent atop the other teen. Last, the pillar of fire shrank and dimmed into the form of Malachi.

Mal staggered in exhaustion, but did not fall. Topaz took a step forward to help him and stopped. He would never forgive her if she made him look weak in front of his crew.

She stooped next to the drummer and whispered into his ear, "Were you supposed to be the Watcher?"

When the kid didn't answer, Topaz grasped his pimply chin and turned it toward her. His eyes were empty. When she released him, the drum clattered to the ground. The others were still. Her eyes searched the clearing. No water. Water restored the electrolytes lost from excessive use of magic. Stupid kids playing with magic.

She tamped down her anger and went to Mal. He refused to lie down like the rest of his group. Out of the Tenkiller children, Malachi and Topaz were most similar. They were both pale, with black hair, slanted cheekbones, and black eyes. Typical and undisguisedly Mage-blooded.

Topaz didn't want to embarrass him in front of his friends, so she did not give him the hug and shoulder to lean on that he needed. "Mal, I have to talk to you."

He blinked, but his eyes remained unfocused. When he did not respond, she put her arm around his skinny shoulders and led him away from the others, near one of the unshaded lamps. Mal was in magic overload, but Topaz needed him to hear her. She didn't have a choice. Topaz had taught herself to enter the Magical Chamber of another Mage and release their pain. This skill was the result of necessity. Topaz's mother had nearly drunk herself to an early First Death in the aftermath of Coral's death. She sighed. Mal was in no condition to listen and Topaz had to make him understand why she was abandoning the croft.

She went to Mal's Magical Chamber. Since she last saw him, it had been reinforced with a chain-link fence barrier. Through the triangular steel holes, Topaz could barely see the tiny bruised fire inside of Mal's pewter chalice. She blew on it gently and it wavered, but did not strengthen. Then she inhaled and Mal's slender birthday candle flame arched through his fence to reach her. Topaz felt his need. His yearning for a knife, the cold steel, the pressure, and then the catch. The red line. Hot blood dripping down her hand. Rather than store his unhealthy used magic, Topaz siphoned and released it to ease her younger brother's pain.

Enough. She rushed back to her own Magical Chamber. Topaz caressed the initials in the corner of her tarp as she fastened it tightly. She stayed there until the beauty of the knife receded. Her little brother frightened her. He needed help. That was why she was leaving.

What seemed like forever was only a few moments. Topaz still had her arm around Mal's skinny shoulders. She could not resist; she pulled him close and rubbed her cheek against his lank hair. He smelled of smoke and the rank sweat of battered magic, not the baby she had carried on her hip. The other teens were scattered around the clearing like wilted petals. Did they do this often? If so, they were killing themselves.

His stiff body was a reproach, so she released him. "Mal, can you hear me?"

"Yeah," Malachi murmured.

"You didn't assign a Watcher; you don't even have water. If one of these kids died, you know who would be blamed? You. You're a Tenkiller. You know how it is on Caesar."

He folded his arms and looked four instead of fourteen years old. This was not the way she planned to say goodbye. She was not abandoning him like everyone else abandoned them; Amber, Coral, their parents. Topaz was leaving to help him. This was the hardest thing she had ever done, but she had to go.

She took a deep breath and then another before she spoke. "I'm sorry. I didn't come here to yell at you."

"Then why?"

Topaz had to smile at the way her baby brother's lip jutted out. Then, the smile faded. There was no easy way to do this. "I got my work permit. I'm going through the "Giving Up Gate" tomorrow." Topaz waited for him to say something. After a moment, she heard a sniffle. Her tough little brother was crying. He was weak from magic and she was weak from absorbing his pain and she wanted to cry too. "Mal, I'm going to send money and Dad will look out for you. I'll write. I promise."

Malachi threw his arms around her and Topaz fell back a few steps. Mal was thin, but he was five inches taller than her.

The teenage bravado was gone. He hid his face in her neck. "Amber promised. She called us the Lil' Killets and said we would always be together. She swore she was going to write, to send for us, but she didn't."

"I will. For burnt magic's sake, what am I supposed to do? Work at Bud's for a room the rest of my life? Watch Mom drink herself to death? Watch you get in trouble? I have to *do* something." Topaz ached to make her baby brother's life better.

He said, "Mrs. Twoshades says Canopus doesn't exist off croft. That's why we never heard from Amber, she died and became a Remnant."

"Mrs. Twoshades fucks shadows." They both laughed.

The others stirred. The Floater moaned and opened her eyes.

Malachi whispered urgently into Topaz's ear, "Please, don't go. You're all I have."

"Sleeping outside is no way to live. I spoke to Bud. You can take my job. Maybe Dad—"

"Dad won't let me practice the Old Ways. You should hear my chants, smooth as shit. Topaz, are you leaving because I stopped going to school? If you stay, I promise I'll—"

"No," she cut him off. She could not hear what her brother was willing to do to make her stay. "I can't die like Coral, or worse, live like Mom or Dad."

Malachi shook off her hand and walked away.

"Please, I love you, Lil' Killet." Topaz tried to pull him back, to talk until she found the right words to make him understand, but her brother was out of reach.

He looked back at Topaz and shook his head, "You only care about yourself. You're all I have and you're running away. I'll be fine without you."

"Hey Mal, let's go get your crew some water." They could talk on the walk to the spigot in back of the church.

He called over his shoulder, "We're fine. I can take care of my crew."

The others blinked up at him as Malachi threaded his way through the prone bodies. His recovery, as a result of Topaz taking his pain, had just cemented his reputation as a Mage and a leader. He patted the drummer on the shoulder and walked past him to the packs piled near another lamp. Mal squatted with his back to Topaz and unzipped a backpack.

He did bring water. It's what a good leader would do. Topaz exhaled. Her brother would be okay without her. Topaz felt better about her decision to abandon Mal for America.

A metallic rattling sound disturbed the drowsy quiet. Malachi turned to face her and Topaz's heart fell. He was holding an aerosol can and a brown paper bag.

The aerosol hissed as he sprayed paint into the bag. He clenched thc bag around his mouth and inhaled deeply. Malachi closed his eyes and his body sagged. When he removed the bag, there was a red ring around his mouth.

He knelt next to the Floater. Mal sprayed aerosol paint into the bag and held it to her face, a nurse administering to a patient. The girl held his hand while she huffed. Then, Malachi knelt next to the Mover in the baseball cap and provided the temporary, addictive relief for Magic Overload.

"Mal, I saw a Remnant earlier. Be careful, okay?" She called, but he ignored her. Topaz did not bother wiping the tears from her cheeks. The croft was built on tears. "May your magic die with you, baby brother."

* * *

It wasn't far to the laundromat, but she was frightened of the Remnant and, after a few drinks, the Warders may have second thoughts about letting her off easy. She went to her Magic Chamber and opened the bottle with Izzy's sky-blue magic. Like an impatient horse, it leaped and jerked her along. It pulled her body up into the sky. She was longer than Izzy and not good at flight so, rather than a cardinal, Topaz looked like a vulture.

She rose above the tree line and looked down. A silver ribbon, a Remnant, zipped from tree to tree on the outskirts of Mal's well-lit clearing. Wind blew past her face as she rose above the church steeple and then even higher, toward Canopus. Below, a series of stars surrounded the moon of the town center. Lights blazed from every house and trailer to protect Caesar families from Remnants.

After a few soaring minutes, Izzy's magic ran low and Topaz grew tired. Controlling the magic of another was difficult. When she landed in the parking lot, Topaz fell in the gravel for the second time that night and wearily made her way back to her pallet behind the dryers.

Chapter Six

"Stand by your bags, Skels." The squat guard's shout rose above the growl of the beige bus. He gestured with the wooden handle of a Galvanizer and his eyes jittered from side to side.

Topaz had only seen Galvanizers from a distance, when armored cars came to collect money from the government businesses or when she looked up at the guard towers. The glass tube was shiny up close, the silver wires inside reflected the sun and scattered sparkles of light around the gravel lot. Another guard stood in front of the bus doors; he held a clipboard and had a Galvanizer holstered at his side. It was safe to assume that the guard in the bus driver's seat had a Galvanizer as well. Through the long line of darkened windows, Topaz could see silhouettes looking out.

There was another Canopian being released from Caesar today. Merelyn Swifthart stood in front of Topaz, her large blue suitcase with a retractable handle all but saluted the guards. Topaz's black garbage bag containing her clothing slumped at her side. She had been in the same class as Merelyn at church school, but town kids did not talk to trailer trash.

"Hey," Topaz whispered to Merelyn. When the other girl turned around, Topaz pointed to her own purple swollen eye, "How come you didn't get one of these?"

"Shut up, Tenkiller," Merelyn hissed.

"All right, then. Screw you, Swifthart," Topaz murmured.

Apparently, going through the "Giving Up Gate" together did not make them friends. If Merelyn wasn't so rude, Topaz may have refrained from taking the other girl's magic, but the Swiftharts were fast and Speed would be nice to have in her Magical Chamber. Topaz loosened her tarp. She had used all of Izzy's magic last night getting her last look at Caesar, so she had space for Merelyn's magic. She ducked out of her chamber and went to Merelyn's.

Topaz pushed the yellow door with mullioned windows and a butterfly-shaped knocker open and went past spindly white furniture to the fire of Merelyn's magic. She inhaled deeply and Merelyn's Speed rushed into Topaz. She zipped behind her tarp, exhaled into the glass jar, and fastened the metal clasps at the side. Taking magic from a placid Swifthart was like taking candy from an Offcrofter baby.

The air smelled of sweat. Merelyn's feathered hair fanned out when she turned to look at Topaz. Topaz shrugged and smiled at her.

"Okay, Skels," only Merelyn and Topaz stood in front of him, but the guard shouted, "Your bags'll be stowed below. When we reach Bloomington Town, they'll be deloused, sanitized, and returned to you. No magic funny business. This here magic bus is equipped with Sine Wave Stimulation. It ain't too accurate, so if you try anything, you'll be fried and likely take another Skel with you. In case you get any ideas now, I got Bright Betty right here." The slender Galvanizer was reflected in his mirrored sunglasses, "She holds enough electricity to zap the magic right outta ya. Probably your memory and a little piss too. Right, Miller?" He turned toward the guard who stood in front of the bus door and they laughed.

Topaz gazed longingly at the sunburned area between the guard's rigidly cut hair and his creased tan uniform. She could push Merelyn out of the way, kick the Galvanizer aside, and slit his throat. But she had wrapped her knife and sheath inside clothes and hidden them inside her trash-bag luggage. She also needed this fat jerk to get her off the croft. Topaz had to accept whatever the Offcrofters gave her so she could give it to Mal.

The guard motioned Topaz forward. For a heart-stopping moment, she thought he smelled the magic. She was a fast Taker, but magic always lingered for a moment. For burnt magic's sake, why did she Take from Merelyn? This wasn't a game. Malachi was going to end up like Coral if Topaz didn't help him.

"Move slow and leave your stuff where it is," the guard ordered.

He did not catch her, this time. Topaz had to stop being childish. She was sixteen, considered an adult on the croft, and had to start acting like it. It was rude to ask, but Topaz wondered what power this guard had. He was a guard, so it was probably a violent magic. Then she remembered, he was an Offcrofter. Offcrofters did not have magic. He had gone his whole life without flexing the muscle that lived just behind the heart.

Topaz stepped over the black garbage bag that held her belongings and stood next to Merelyn to face the guard. She had never been this close to an Offcrofter before. Fat draped over the guard's belt. Were they all this round? She tried to see his eyes, but his sunglasses reflected the post office behind her.

"Name?"

"Topaz Tenkiller."

The guard, a small pin on his left pocket said "Johnson," tapped his Galvanizer against his thigh and asked, "Do you hate all Americans, Tenkiller, or just me?"

The guard standing near the bus door stopped slouching and murmured, "Heads up."

In the reflection of Johnson's sunglasses, Topaz saw her mother lurch toward them. No quiet trip through the "Giving Up Gate" for Topaz. This was like her third-grade chorus concert. Did her mother piss herself this time also? Crystal Fareye Tenkiller was a See-er, but her prophetic visions did not stop her from making bad decisions.

Johnson yelled past Topaz. "Hey Toothless, you're not allowed in this area now. Stop."

"Topaz? What are you doing?" Crystal called.

Why was she here? Topaz had already said goodbye to her mother. Since last night, Crystal had found a red wig to cover her bald head. The wig leaned over one ear so she looked like she was asking a question. Other than that, the same tattered purple cloth hung past her yellow shirt and denim skirt to drag in the dirt behind her.

Merelyn Swifthart giggled.

Johnson turned on Swifthart, "What are you laughing at, Toothless?"

Swifthart pointed at Crystal, then at Topaz, "Look at them, sir. Tenkillers are a joke."

"This whole place is a joke. Get on the bus," he snapped.

Miller checked Merelyn's work permit and banged on the bus door. The driver opened it and Merelyn scurried aboard.

This is not how she wanted to remember her mother. Topaz tried to follow Merelyn, but Johnson blocked her way.

"You," Johnson pointed at Topaz and then Crystal, "are going to get rid of that."

Johnson stepped toward Crystal. He chuckled when the wig slipped and covered one of her eyes.

Crystal peered around him. "Topaz, you don't have to do this." Her visible eye filled with tears, "After Amber and Coral...I can't lose my last daughter."

Topaz stood silent. She had learned long ago to ignore her mother.

Crystal stumbled and reached for Johnson. He raised his hands in the air and backed away. When she fell onto Topaz's bag, her wig flew off and landed on Johnson's shiny boot. He kicked the red tresses toward the other guard. Miller ducked and the wig hit the bus doors and slid to the ground.

Bud looked out of the plate glass window of the laundromat. A fiery First Death crossed Topaz's mind. She could go to her magical chamber right now and stoke her flame. Maybe she could take Johnson with her. She longed for one moment of dignity.

"Why are you taking her? Was Amber not enough?" Crystal's howl was muffled by the black plastic. The bare patches of skin on her head were grotesque in the morning sun.

"Skel, get up," Johnson said.

The gas station door opened and Frank Cedar wiped his hands on a greasy rag while he watched them. A few wide-eyed Mages pressed their faces against the post office window.

"Why?" Crystal wailed.

Topaz wanted to remind Crystal that she was not there for Amber's leaving. She had been sleeping off a three-day hangover. She wanted to ask if she knew where Malachi was. He should not see this.

Johnson hissed at Topaz over Crystal's heaving body, "Get rid of her before these animals," he gestured at the Mages in the surrounding buildings, "get excited."

Crystal rocked back and forth, sniffling. Her denim skirt bunched up and the yellow shirt had come unbuttoned, ceding both battle and war to pale flesh.

Miller looked at his watch and called, "We gotta leave now or we'll be late. We don't wanna go to Macbeth after dark."

Johnson spoke through clenched teeth, "Want to take your shit? Get her off it or we leave it here!"

"Mom, you have to go." Topaz grasped her mother's shoulder to pull her up. Her donated clothes and books, a worn pink giraffe that Amber gave her, were in that bag.

"Topaz," Crystal wailed. She grabbed Topaz's arm.

"Come on, Mom." Topaz grasped her mother's shoulders and tried to pull her up. When Crystal's head lolled against her, Topaz smelled it; the sour sweat scent of magic. Her mother was doing magic. "No, Mom, please don't do this."

A few Mages shuffled out of the Community Center. The church doors opened and pale, thin people trickled toward the bus. When Canopians left the croft, they were loaded on the bus and through the "Giving Up

Gate" quietly, quickly, with no fuss. This scene reminded the residents of Caesar that gifted Mages were leaving the croft and abandoning the Old Ways because they were tired and hungry.

"Johnson, we have a situation," Miller called.

She needed to stop her mom from doing something stupid. Topaz went to the muscle behind her heart and, for the first time ever, entered her mother's Magical Chamber. Even as a child, she had feared her mother's batshit craziness. She eased the fly-stained aluminum door open. Broken bottles, tattered bills, and plump black garbage bags were shoved against the walls to form a clearing. Orange fire raged in the center, frustrated magic. The walls were covered in crayon stick figure drawings and letters in loopy cursive. Disconnected images flickered. A bruised child huddling behind mildewed water pipes ...ashes in a drawer...a smile masking a toothless abyss...menacing Galvanizers pointed at Malachi and Henry, and, finally, Crystal herself, black hair flowing over the back of a rocking chair, nursing a baby and humming, "You Are My Sunshine." Topaz felt love in the rush of sweet milk.

She was brave when Coral died and she had to be brave now. She was never going to see her mother, or any of her family, again. Topaz was grateful that Malachi was not here to see this.

Johnson wrenched Crystal away and flung her on the ground. "Think I don't smell that magic? Get the hell out of here."

Crystal cowered. Her thighs were scraped red and dotted with gravel.

Topaz wanted to go to her mother, but this had gone too far. Johnson was ready to leave her behind. Vagrants who slept out back of The Driftwood Lounge, Crystal's subjects, emerged from the alley and blinked against the morning sun. Pale faces topped with black hair were everywhere. Oh, Canopus, no. Mal and his friends stood on the flat roof of the post office, black cutouts in the morning light.

Crystal howled luxuriously at the heavens. Makeup and flowing tears tattooed lines into her head.

Johnson bellowed, "I'm warning you. Shut up, Toothless." He flicked his Galvanizer on and electricity crackled in the glass tube.

Topaz's stomach clenched into a knot, tightening in time with the Galvanizer and Crystal's wails.

"Please, Mom," Topaz soothed, but Crystal was beyond hearing.

Topaz looked up. Malachi was still on the roof. She rushed to his Magic Chamber. Behind the familiar chain link fence, he had erected a concrete wall and spraypainted "Fuck you" in red paint. She could not reach her brother.

Johnson raised the glowing baton above his head and brought it down on Crystal's skull. Jangly sparks crowned her bald head. Her mouth snapped shut. Her neck whipped against her upper back. Crystal's arms and legs twitched separate from her body. The scent of urine drenched the air.

Topaz started forward, but Miller grabbed her shoulder. She could not take her eyes off the pale creature quivering in the dirt. Mages streamed to the parking lot. The scent of sweat roiled toward the bus.

"Get on the bus!" Miller shoved Topaz backwards and yelled, "Johnson, now!"

Topaz stumbled on the first step into the bus and looked down. A red wig was tangled around her dirty sneaker.

Chapter Seven

There was a thud and the baggage compartment slammed closed. The bus shook as the guards trampled on and the doors whooshed shut.

Topaz leaned over a shocked man to look out of a side window. Crystal was sprawled in the parking lot, still and alone. Caesar Mages rushed toward the bus, but nobody helped her mother.

The bus jerked forward and Miller shouted, "We don't need this crap, Johnson. This is our last trip. Flip the outer S.W.S. lever, will you?" Johnson stared out the front window at the approaching Mages and Miller snapped, "Turn on the Sine Wave Stimulation now, before they use their magic. I don't want to get stuck here with a pack of angry Skels."

Topaz ran down the aisle, toward the back of the bus, to keep her mother in sight. A wispy haired woman yelped as the movement of the bus knocked Topaz into her, but Topaz kept moving. Was her mother alive? Was Malachi going to help her? Was anyone?

Johnson pulled a black lever at the front of the bus and Topaz's chest trembled deep inside. Her stomach fisted and kept clenching until bile rose in her throat.

Over the bus's engine, Topaz could hear Miller harangue Johnson. "Our last trip. We gotta get to Macbeth, pick up one more Skel, take these animals to Bloomington, and Bob's your uncle. It could've been easy, but *no*, you had to mess up a drunk Skel. If that Toothless is dead, I ain't helping you with the 17b110 forms. Nothing."

"Excuse me," Topaz called.

Two pairs of astonished eyes turned to her and two hands caressed their Galvanizers.

Johnson spoke slowly, "Hey Toothless, sit down."

"Please. Stop the bus. I need off. I can't leave her like that," Topaz spoke calmly, but she felt trapped. She had to escape.

Johnson took his Galvanizer out of the holster and said, "Don't they have seats in Caesar? Sit down."

Topaz backed away. The jangly sparks. Oh Canopus, her mother. She turned and ran to the back window. Her forehead bumped against the glass when the bus turned onto Thatcher Highway. She watched the figure in the parking lot soften to a pale blob. She knelt and pressed her cheek against the glass to see if Malachi was still on the roof, but the world was blurry from her tears.

Bile rose in her throat. Her eyeballs jittered.

Then the village of Caesar, where she was born, raised, and abandoned, was a brown smudge on the horizon. A Canopian left the croft. A Canopian did not return.

Topaz whispered, "Death and life exists within," and sank to the floor of the bus. She pulled her legs up to her midsection to protect herself from the soul-rattling vibration. She ground her teeth together to stop them from chattering.

A high-pitched whine and static sounded from above. Topaz looked ahead. Johnson held a small black object in front of his mouth. She knew from watching "American Bandstand" that the black thing was a microphone, but it wasn't staticky when Dick Clark spoke into it.

"Do you feel that? It's Sine Wave Stimulation. Now, if Tenkiller will just find a seat, I can turn it off and y'all's guts can untwist."

Topaz swiped at her eyes. Mourning was for later. Right now, she needed to find a seat. She looked around. Heads dotted the tops of some seats. Pale faces craned into the aisle and grimaced at her.

She rose and sat in the nearest seat and he resumed speaking, "Too bad you all had to witness that. I'd like to commend Othello and Antony Crofts for conducting your release in a civilized manner. Since we all seemed to have calmed down, I can turn off the Prolonged Sine Wave Stimulation." He reached above the driver and flipped the red lever down.

Black hair smoothed and jaws visibly relaxed as Mages unclenched their teeth and Topaz's gut smoothed.

The man in the seat next to her whispered, "You have to move."

"What?" Topaz asked.

"We're not allowed to sit next to each other," he hissed. The man tucked himself into the window and spoke out of the side of his mouth, as if distance would make her disappear. "He'll Galvanize both of us. For burnt magic's sake, move!"

Topaz leaned out of the seat and looked ahead. She could not tell which seats were occupied. If she rose, Johnson would see her.

"We'll reach Macbeth before nightfall. As a reminder for the stupid, this bad boy," Johnson gestured over the driver's head at another red lever, "activates row-specific Prolonged Sine Wave Stimulation." He looked at Topaz. "Which is why you're not allowed to sit next to anyone." He raised an arm toward the switch, "'Course, if you don't mind taking another Toothless down with you..."

Topaz rose and swayed down the aisle, resigned to wander the bus looking for an empty row while Johnson jeered. Merelyn Swifthart leaned into the aisle to stare at her. Topaz hissed and the girl cringed back into her seat.

Ahead, a pale arm topped with cherry red fingernails waved. Topaz hurried to the empty seat behind Cherry Red. She released a breath she didn't know she was holding as she sat.

"When we reach the Caesar border, have your work permit ready for inspection by American Border Control Agents."

Miller, Johnson, and the driver stayed at the front of the bus, a safe distance from the unpredictable animals. Now that the excitement was over and Johnson had relinquished the microphone, Mages reclined in the seats and wadded sweatshirts underneath their heads to go to sleep.

Topaz looked past the reflection of her own pale face at the shifting landscape. White-topped mountains rose in the distance, a backdrop to gray boulders and silver cedars. Did America have boulders and junipers? Did the cicadas come heavy every seventeen years and leave translucent corpses behind? She clenched her eyes closed, but it did not shut out the image of Crystal's still body. Was her mother dead? If she was, Malachi would do the Witching Hour Chants. She had to believe that. He would not let Crystal's Remnant wander the croft, looking for a weak barrier, a Canopian to live inside.

She closed her ears against the sound of Malachi begging her to stay and Ken asking, "Don't you want to help your people?" Could Ken and the Warders give hope to Malachi and his friends? Provide relief to her mother's forgotten, addicted, mentally ill, tribe? Mages were confined to crofts and Tenkillers were feared and vilified. That was the way it was.

The Tenkillers were a proud and powerful family until 1929. The Tenkiller Rebellion was fomented by Topaz's great-grandparents; Joseph and Lucille Tenkiller. A quarter of the population of Caesar (two hundred Mages) died before it ended. Joseph was shot in the rebellion, but Lucille hid in the desert for three weeks with her 3-year-old son, Arthur Tenkiller. Lucille was found and stood trial for treason in Salt Lake City, Utah. Lucille was hanged in 1930 and her son, Topaz's grandfather, was raised in a church orphanage in Utah. When he turned eighteen, Arthur escaped and returned to Caesar. He was a wild young man, but too damaged from the state-run facility to follow in his family's footsteps and mount a revolution. His son, Henry Tenkiller, was a powerful Mage, but when he met the otherworldly, self-destructive Crystal Fareye, a match was tossed into gasoline. Crystal Fareye and Henry Tenkiller had babies and left them where they landed. Topaz and her three siblings were the last of both infamous lines. She was the third of four children and the third that Crystal had lost in as many years. In America, did people spit when they heard the name Tenkiller?

A soft tap on the window drew Topaz's eyes forward. Cherry Red fingernails waggled.

"Hey," a voice whispered to Topaz, "take out your permit. We have to show it soon."

"Thanks," Topaz murmured and dug her permit out of her pocket.

A pixie face peered back at Topaz in the gap between the seat and the window. "What happened in Caesar? Who was that woman?" The girl rolled her eyes.

Topaz hesitated, then shed the translucent husk of her Tenkiller self. She shook her head, "I have no idea."

"I heard that Caesar was crazy about the Old Ways, but didn't believe it until now. I bet you're glad to be leaving. I'm Joy, from Othello. You're Topaz, right?"

"Yes, hello." Topaz leaned forward and shook the red tipped hand between the seats.

"How long until we get to the Caesar border?" Joy asked.

Topaz glanced out the window. "Another couple minutes."

"When we get there, hold out your work permit. Border Control Agents will walk through and check them, they asked a few people questions before. They're not grody like the guards. They're actually kinda cute."

Topaz jerked her chin toward Johnsons and asked, "Are they round?"

"Nope, and they're breath doesn't smell like ass," Joy said.

They both laughed. It was such a relief to laugh. Were all the Canopians from Othello Croft so friendly? She had never met someone from a different croft. Were other magical people as nice as Joy? On Caesar, people were too busy surviving or destroying to think of others.

"This is all so new, right? I've never met anyone from Caesar before. You guys are out in the middle of nowhere. The way America punished the whole croft after the Tenkiller Rebellion of '29 was bogus. Why not just punish the Tenkillers, right? Othello's by a military base so we have two gas stations, a grocery store, and three bars." She sighed, "Oh Canopus, how I love soldiers. Me and my friends helped with training exercises on the base."

As the girl's chatter washed over her, Topaz felt a little less adrift, unmoored from the familiar. She tried to think of a way to keep the girl talking, but she needn't have worried.

"See him? That's Mark, he's totally cute." The red fingernail rose above the seats and pointed at a seat on the left. Topaz's eyes followed the tiny red beacon of Joy's fingernail and, as if sensing attention, the man looked back. He had close cropped hair, a tentative mustache and a broad smile. "He says we're not going to a work center, we're going to a new town, cool, huh?"

Joy was about Topaz's age, maybe older, but her exuberance was young.

"A new town?" Topaz asked. She needed to work. The only reason she applied for a work permit was to earn money for Malachi.

The bus slowed and Topaz felt the vibration that she was beginning to associate with electricity in her stomach again. Ahead was a yellow automated gate, the border between Caesar and America or, what the Canopians called the "Giving Up Gate." It was flanked by towers of criss-crossed dull metal. Atop each tower, a large glass tube buzzed and a chain link fence extended from the towers all around the 400 acres of which comprised Caesar Croft. The fence was shoulder height, but it was electrified. Any Canopian who went within a foot of it would begin convulsing before they touched it.

"Remember to give the pretty boys what they want and you'll be fine," Joy whispered.

Topaz whispered back, "Story of my life," and they both giggled.

The plastic work permit cut into her palm. Was she doing the right thing? It didn't feel like it. Since leaving the croft, Topaz had lost her brother and mother. Her Caesar life was empty, but it was familiar. Amber had left to make a better life for the Lil' Killets, as she called her Tenkiller siblings, but after she went through the "Giving Up Gate" two years ago, the Lil' Killets never heard from her again. Would the same thing happen to Topaz? If she did not return, Topaz would be yet another person abandoning Malachi.

The bus stopped at the gate. Johnson picked up the microphone and continued his stand- up routine, "Toothless trash, do not move. Speak only if, and when, you're spoken to. Any problems, we fry alla you and ask questions later." He pointed to the SWS lever near the driver and went down the stairs where two men in dark blue uniforms waited.

From the front of the bus, Miller narrowed his eyes at the Mages and cradled his Galvanizer until Johnson reboarded the bus with one of the agents in tow.

Miller and Johnson crammed themselves into the narrow space between the driver and front seat to allow the Border Control Agent to pass. Unlike Johnson, Miller, or the driver, this officer was tan, lean, and muscled.

Joy whispered, "Oh, Purple Canopus, look at him."

"I'm Agent Garcia. In preparation for exiting Caesar Croft and entering America, please have your work permits ready for inspection." The agent's low voice carried without the microphone. He turned to Johnson and said, "I understand two Mages boarded in Caesar."

Johnson nodded, "Yes, sir."

Garcia turned back to the Mages. "Please have your permits out and be prepared to answer a few questions."

Agent Garcia glanced at an outstretched work permit and continued down the aisle, a small Galvanizer and large Walkie Talkie swaying on his black tool belt. He glanced at another permit, looked at the pale face behind it, smiled, and moved on.

The agent paused by the "totally cute" Canopian with the close-cropped hair and took his permit. He looked at the laminated card and then at the man in the seat. He asked, "Is the mustache new, Mark?"

Mark stroked the bristle of hair above his lip, "Thought I'd give it a try, sir."

"Keep at it." Agent Garcia smiled and moved on. He examined the next three permits and handed them back with a brusque nod. When he reached Merelyn Swifthart, the agent took her permit and murmured, "Please step off the bus, ma'am. Agent Holder has a few questions."

"But, I didn't do anything," Merelyn protested.

The other Mages studiously looked away. Miller raised his Galvanizer and Johnson's hand inched toward the lever. Agent Garcia stepped back and pointed at the exit.

"Sir, please, what did I do?" Mereleyn pleaded. "Is it because I'm from Caesar? I'm not a Tenkiller. That's her," she pointed at Topaz.

Topaz looked at that finger and wondered about burning witches and imprisoning Mages. About the long history of pointed fingers.

Agent Garcia said, "Step off the bus, please."

Merelyn scurried down the stairs. Topaz smelled the sweat trail left behind; the girl was working hard to suppress her power. Swiftharts always run.

Agent Garcia continued to check work permits, pausing to ask an occasional question, but he mostly glanced at the permit, nodded, and moved on.

Topaz watched Merelyn out the window. Her hand trembled when she handed the other agent her work permit. The agent's back was to Topaz, but he must have asked a question because Merelyn nodded vigorously.

Topaz examined the muscular figure of the Border Control Agent outside the window. These agents were more relaxed than the guards. They treated Mages kindly, almost like they considered them human, rather than something to be feared and slaughtered. Something was odd about the agent speaking to Merelyn. His curly black hair was sprinkled with gray and hovered just above his uniform collar. His dark blue uniform continued in a smooth line down to his boots. Too smooth. He did not have a Galvanizer or a Walkie Talkie. Why would an agent interview a Canopian without a Galvanizer? Then again, Merelyn was visibly shaking and Galvanizer Cannons were pointed at her from the guard tower.

The agent returned Merelyn's work permit. When she got back on the bus, Merelyn sank into her seat with a sniffle.

"Miss Tenkiller?" Agent Garcia stood next to Topaz's seat.

Topaz handed him her work permit. Yes, I'm a Tenkiller, she thought, but kept her eyes on the seat in front of her.

"From Caesar?"

Topaz nodded. Her tongue found the empty spot in her mouth.

"I'm going to ask you to—"

"Right," Topaz snapped as she rose.

Agent Garcia stepped back as he finished speaking, "—step outside and speak to Agent Holder."

Topaz stalked to the front of the bus, jaw tight.

Agent Garcia called from behind her, "Miss?"

Topaz reminded herself that she was doing this to help Mal. She suppressed a sigh and turned. The agent held her work permit out. A few Mages sniggered as Topaz walked back to retrieve it. She met Agent Garcia's eyes and saw a softness, compassion perhaps.

Topaz stepped off the bus and the proximity to the electrical fences intensified that awful vibration inside of her. The glass jars vibrated in her Magic Chamber. How did the guards stand this awful tooth jarring feeling? Then she remembered, they didn't feel this. Electricity didn't affect Offcrofters.

She handed the agent her work permit. Both she and Merelyn, Mages from Caesar, had been pulled from the bus. Was this because of her mother or because she was a Tenkiller?

The agent took her permit. Rather than checking it, he closed his eyes and took a deep breath. The man looked like he was about to make a bad decision and knew it, but he was making it anyway.

He was detaining her. She tasted the dust of Caesar and felt the groping fingers of her future.

The agent said, "Looks like the Warders were gentle."

Topaz touched her puffy eye. She hadn't thought about it since she woke up.

"Ken says there's hope for you," he said.

Topaz's eyes widened. Agent Holder's voice pulled her into the same drowning pool as Kenneth Twosongs. For a moment she felt slick motor oil on her fingers.

"For burnt magic's sake, look beaten. Spies are everywhere."

Topaz looked at the pavement. Her thick black hair fell to shadow her face, but behind the veil, Topaz's mind raced.

"Canopians need your help," he said.

Same thing that Ken had said. Topaz shook her head against that back-arching purr. She would not risk returning to hunger and a pallet in the laundromat to watch her brother destroy himself.

"Just listen."

"No," Topaz said. Maybe he was a spy. She nudged her tarp and reached out.

"Canopus balls, stop," he hissed. "No magic. The bus has a Magic Monitoring Machine, a 3M. I don't have much time, so here it is." He spoke in a rush, "They've forbidden the Old Ways on Macbeth Croft."

How could they forbid the Old Ways? The Old Ways were like changing seasons or chain link fences. Her hair swayed when Topaz looked up at Holder. His face was bleak.

"But, what about Remnants?" she asked. If not for the Old Ways, Remnants would overrun a croft, taking people until there was nothing left, and then discarding the used bodies.

"Do you think America cares if Remnants are loose in Macbeth? They don't allow Fire Death or Witching Hour Chants. They took the Soul Basket and Death Bier. They load Mage bodies on trucks and take them in the middle of the night. We've followed the trucks to America, specifically Bloomington Town. This bus is going to Bloomington. You told Ken no, but I'm asking you again, will you help us?" His voice was a morning murmur, bodies elongating from hip to ankle. "A delegation is visiting Bloomington next month to evaluate America's treatment of Canopians. Once the inspectors are convinced that we are "valued citizens of America," they'll leave. You have to find out why they have forbidden the Old Ways on Macbeth and tell the trade delegation, the world, what's happening." She opened her mouth to say no, but Agent Holder jabbed a finger in her face and growled, "Look upset, please."

He held her work permit next to her face and compared the two images. "This bus will stop for intake in Cheyenne then go to Bloomington. Your contact at intake is a nurse with a scar on her cheek. Ask her if she has a cousin in Caesar and she'll place you under quarantine for some dirty Mage disease. You'll be given a shot to mask the scent of magic and information about your Bloomington contact. Any questions?"

She stared at the ground. Topaz could feel the busload of Mages staring. Her voice contained the bitterness of lost hope, "No, because I won't do it. I'm going to be a model Mage in a model town."

She did not have much to lose, but she did have Malachi. Leaving, working, helping the Offcrofters, was for Mal. Canopians had to take care of themselves.

Topaz reached for her work permit, but Agent Holder pulled it back out of her reach. She clenched her teeth and glared at him. The only thing between her and a new beginning was this Twosong with a badge.

"One last time, Topaz, will you help your people?"

She ground out, "There is absolutely nothing you can say to change my mind. Now give me my work permit."

"Amber," he said.

The word hit Topaz in the gut. Amber, the shortest Tenkiller, but her big sister with the biggest heart. A tiny ball of love and hugs. The one who taught her how to brush her teeth and cheat at "Go Fish."

Topaz asked, "Is she alive?"

"Last I knew," Holder said. "You can't tell anyone. I haven't even told my cousin, Ken."

"Where is she? Is she okay? Why didn't you tell me?" Topaz grasped his arm.

Agent Holder shrugged her hand off. "I didn't want to force you. If you help us figure out what's happening and make contact with the delegation, I'll tell you where Amber is."

The pink giraffe and three books under the bus were gifts from her big sister. The year after Amber left, Topaz had checked the post office every day for a note, some reassurance that she had not forgotten them, but nothing came. That year, Crystal began to have dark visions. Then, she stayed drunk and started sleeping rough out back of The Driftwood Lounge. Henry Tenkiller forgot everyone but Jesus. Topaz tried to take Amber's place, to comfort Coral and Malachi, but she was too angry to lie and say that things were going to be okay. When Coral set herself on fire in front of the post office, the Tenkillers had already stopped being a family. It was too late for the Tenkillers, but maybe Topaz could help Mal and Amber.

"Prove you're not lying," she said.

Agent Holder extended her permit, "You'll make a great agent, Lil Killett."

Only Tenkillers knew that name. He knew Amber, knew her well. The sister who tried to make life on the croft better. When that was impossible, she went to make the world better.

"I'll help you. After that, I get my sister back."

"Deal." He spoke brusquely, "In Cheyenne, they'll switch your permit for an encoded permit that allows you access to protected areas. Now, look grateful. Tears would be nice."

Topaz swiped at her eyes. The order was unnecessary.

Agent Holder banged a fist on the side of the bus and Agent Garcia exited onto the dusty road. The two men exchanged a long look and Holder nodded.

She boarded the bus and took a deep jerky breath. Amber. The bus stuttered forward and she stumbled into her seat.

Johnson chuckled into the microphone, "Watch your step, Tenkiller."

Through shiny eyes, Topaz watched the gates open for the bus. The Giving Up Gates were her way to Amber. They drove past the corrugated guard house and a sign that said "Now Entering America" whizzed by.

The bus had reached a smooth cruising speed when Johnson spoke into the microphone again, "Change a plans, we will not stop at the Cheyenne Intake Center, we will not pass go. This here bus is going to Macbeth Croft and directly to Bloomington where those with more patience than me will train you worthless pieces a shit."

Chapter Eight

The prisoner's suspended body shook in crazy eights. As the officer with the Galvanizer stepped closer, the shaking grew frenetic. When Officer Hansen jabbed the glass tube into the prisoner's back, his skin sizzled. The prisoner screamed and bucked against the ropes. A dance of action reaction.

AnnaLeesa Bennett stood in the hallway and watched through a large viewing window. Her personal assistant, Thomas, stood a discreet distance away. She always watched interrogations from a distance. The police officers of Bloomington Town thought the mayor cared deeply about the town, but did not want to dirty her hands or stain her pastel dresses. Only Thomas knew that she could not be near the Galvanizer. It would cause her to have a seizure as surely as it would the Mage suspended from the ceiling.

When she rapped on the glass, the trim, gray-haired officer holstered his Galvanizer, nodded to the other guard in the room, and left the Interrogation Room. The prisoner's groans could be heard when he opened the door and then faded when he closed it.

"Good morning, Mayor Bennett." The officer smiled.

"Good morning, Officer Hansen, how are you?" Her cheerful voice echoed off the concrete walls and brightened the hallway. Mayor Bennett's yellow heels put her eye level with him.

"Fine, Mayor. Thank you for writing the recommendation letter for Kaitlyn. She was accepted into John Jay College," Office Hansen said. Despite his formidable appearance, the man had a soft earnest voice.

"Oh, that's wonderful. You must be so proud of her."

"Oh, we are," he said.

"Officer Hansen, Bill, you've had Runningbear since last night?" she asked.

"Since 4 pm yesterday, ma'am."

"You have interrogated him with and without the Galvanizer and yet he has said nothing?" she asked.

"Nothing new, Mayor. He claims he and Jeremiah Threetree were the only Resistance soldiers in Bloomington." Hansen was sorrowful. Things always escalated with these Canopians.

"It fits," AnnaLeesa nodded.

Threetree had been captured and killed last week, but not before he gave up the name of this Canopian, Martin Runningbear. The Resistance was careful. Each member only knew the person who contacted them and the person whom they, in turn, contacted. This Mage said he did not have a contact yet and, after the Galvanizer, Mages were honest. Because it was the showpiece of American and Mage collaboration, the security at Bloomington Town was stringent. Once a Mage arrived, they were not allowed contact with the outside world. So, this was a minor problem. One which AnnaLessa knew she could pull out by the root.

"Officer Hansen, why don't you and the other officer go grab a cup of coffee? Thomas will guard Runningbear while I have a talk with him," AnnaLeesa said.

"Yes, Mayor," Officer Hansen said. He rapped on the window and the officer inside the room came to the door.

Thomas exchanged a smile with the other two officers as they left. AnnaLeesa frequently spoke to prisoners, Mage and American. Her soft touch got results.

When the hallway was empty, AnnaLeesa turned to Thomas, "I need more information."

The muscular, square-jawed man smiled and opened the door to the Interrogation Room. With an "after you" motion of his hand, he followed Mayor Bennett in. Once the door was closed, Mayor Bennett closed the shades on the viewing window. Thomas unbuttoned his suit jacket, reached behind him, and extracted a black object. With a flick of his hand, it stretched and made a cracking sound.

Thomas approached the prisoner. Martin Runningbear was suspended from the ceiling by his arms. He was clad only in a pair of gray sweatpants. His back was dotted with burns. Blood stained his face, neck, and chest. Pink frothy liquid oozed from his mouth. Mages frequently bit their tongues during Galvanizer induced convulsions.

"I've told you all I know," the prisoner slurred. Strands of black hair clung like a spiderweb to the blood caked to his face.

Thomas swished the leather tip of the whip back and forth as he approached the Canopian. The Mage scrabbled for purchase on the concrete floor, but the rope prevented him from doing more than spinning in circles.

His voice was low and intimate when Thomas spoke, "I understand the structure of your organization. You are each one link in a chain, but there's something missing, Martin. Jeremiah Threetree was your contact and he gave you up, but who contacts you?"

"My contact is Jeremiah Threetree, that's all I know," Martin gasped.

"Give me a name. Then I can let you down. Can you do that?"

Under Thomas' patient insistence, the Canopian relaxed. "The Board didn't give me a contact yet. Now, he's gone."

Thomas looked over where AnnaLeesa was standing near the wall. She shrugged.

"Tell me about this board, Martin." Thomas said.

Martin Runningbear's head sagged and he spoke to the floor, "There's a Mage that we use to communicate. He posts stuff in my Magical Chamber. Like a bulletin board."

"Go on," Thomas encouraged.

"That's all I know. I don't know who it was and the Board disappeared after Threetree got picked up. I swear to Purple Canopus, I never got a contact."

AnnaLeesa looked at her watch, "Tick Tock, Thomas. I need a name."

"Your back must feel like it's on fire, am I right?" As he spoke to Runningbear, Thomas knotted the long leather strip of the whip. "See what I'm doing? I pride myself on being precise. When this leather hits one of your many burns, and it will, the knot will dig into your wound and catch in your skin something awful." He rotated Runningbear to face AnnaLeesa.

She jutted her chin up and Thomas pulled the prisoner's hair back. His face was streaked with blood and one eye was obscured by puffy skin.

"Tell the lady what she wants to hear and we untie your hands, maybe give you a little water. Or, I continue my work. If you don't give me a name, you're of no use," Thomas said.

"You have to believe me, I don't know," Runningbear groaned. When Thomas raised the whip, the Mage squeezed his eyes closed, but was silent.

The whip cracked and made a sizzling sound when it slashed down into Runningbear's back. He gasped air in through his mouth and his tongue spurted blood down his chin. The mucous breathing of the Mage was the only sound in the room.

After a moment, AnnaLeesa motioned toward the door. "Make sure nobody comes near this room."

"Yes, Boss," Thomas said and left the Interrogation Room.

AnnaLeesa clenched the muscle behind her heart, the secret muscle of her people. Magic was the way she had escaped the croft and the way she would eliminate her people.

She stepped close to the Canopian. The sweaty smell of magic oozed from the mayor, overpowering the prisoner's reek of blood and piss. His eyes widened and he kicked at her. She chuckled at his last act of free will. Fitting for a soldier in a futile rebellion.

"Martin Runningbear, you must not use magic," AnnaLeesa murmured. "I am right in this. You want to be still."

The Mage stopped moving. He tried to close his eyes, but they remained open wide.

"Enough nonsense, you will answer my questions truthfully. Who is your contact?"

Raw vocal cords hoarsened Martin's voice when he responded, "Jeremiah Threetree."

"Good. Who were you to contact?"

He said, "I don't know." His eyes took on a faraway glow.

AnnaLeesa buffed a nail against her yellow tapestry blazer as she spoke, "You will not give yourself a Fire Death. Who is to contact you?"

His chest rose and fell as Martin Runningbear panted locomotive breaths.

"Oh Purple Canopus, you will not give yourself a heart attack, either." She sighed, "What can you tell me about who is to contact you?"

His breathing slowed. "Someone arriving on the bus, I swear," he said.

AnnaLeesa believed him, but she needed something. The sweat smell of her own magic burned her nostrils. She may have to change her suit.

"No need to swear," she smiled and stroked his cheek. "Tell me something, love, I am right in this."

Tears leaked out of the corners of Runningbear's eyes, cleansing a streak of blood and grime on each side of his face. His voice was desolate when he whispered, "A redhead."

"A redhead?" AnnaLeesa asked. "A redheaded Mage? Tell me more. I am right in this."

His head lolled and his breathing deepened. He was unconscious.

AnnaLeesa sighed. After a moment, she said, "Now you will be forever silent. May your magic die with you."

Mayor Bennett ran to the doorway and yelled, "Oh my god, somebody help! I think he's using magic. Hurry."

Hansen rushed in with his Galvanizer drawn and buzzing. AnnaLeesa ducked out of the room, keeping well clear of the Galvanizer. Thomas fell in behind her as her heels clicked down the hallway. She heard the escalating hum and whine of electricity. A scream of agony and then silence.

She went down a flight of stairs, pushed open a steel door, and entered the underground tunnel from the Bloomington Bus Terminal to the Town Hall and her office. She needed to check the manifest of the next bus arriving in Bloomington Town.

Chapter Nine

Johnson dozed. Miller tilted his clipboard to catch the fading sunlight, jotted notes and flipped back and forth between pages.

Topaz shivered in her polo shirt. She leaned forward and whispered between the seat and window, "Why is the bus so cold?"

"Offcrofters need a constant temperature," Joy said, "something to do with their body heat. Like lizards. So, they cool their vehicles."

"How?" Topaz asked.

Joy shrugged, "Magic, probably."

"Do they use their cars for more than transportation? Maybe they live in them."

Joy laughed and muffled it quickly.

Why was that so funny? The seat creaked when Topaz leaned back into familiar solitude. She could no longer see Joy through the space by the window.

"Topaz," Joy whispered.

Topaz ignored her. Joy could find someone else to laugh at.

"Hey, I didn't mean to hurt your feelings."

Topaz said, "I'm going to sleep now." She thought things would be different in America. No Tenkiller legends or barfly mom to embarrass her. No standing in line for government cheese.

Joy whispered and, despite herself, Topaz strained to hear. "I laughed because they use cars for everything. There are big lots just for cars. They don't live in their cars, but stupid Offcrofters build houses for their cars. They sit in their cars on the road, sometimes for hours. There's even a name for waiting in a car, traffic jam."

Topaz smiled. Traffic jam. Cars on toast.

"You know what else, Topaz?" Joy asked. Topaz wanted to know what else, but she refused to answer. "Offcrofters drive to a place, wait in a line with other cars, food is given to them, and they eat it. All in their car. Guess what that's called?" Joy asked.

Topaz would not guess.

"Come on, guess," Joy urged. Her red nails reflected off the window next to her.

The creaking vinyl seat betrayed her when Topaz leaned forward. "Traffic toast?"

Joy giggled, "Nope. A drive thru. They wait at a drive thru." This time Topaz laughed with her.

In front of Joy, a woman with a fountain of black curls on top of her head turned around and spoke through the gap in the seats, "For burnt magic's sake, can you two shut up?" A smile softened her words.

"Sorry, Delta," Joy said.

"Move back, Joy," Delta commanded. Her voice was smoker raspy. Delta's pale square face filled the gap between the seats when she peered past Joy's seat at Topaz. "You're Topaz?" She allowed the last syllable of the last word to linger in the ancient way of those who want to know who your people are.

"I'm Topaz Ten— Topaz from Caesar."

"Topaz Ten," she smiled, "I'm Delta Dawn, from Othello, in Northern California in America. Pleasure to meet a Canopian from Caesar. Never be ashamed of where you come from or your people. We're Mages. Death and life exists within."

When Topaz dutifully responded, "May your magic die with you," she smelled campfire smoke, the smell of the croft.

Delta narrowed her eyes at Joy until Joy dutifully echoed, "May your magic die with you."

The older woman tilted her head toward Joy. "Don't let this modern Antony girl turn you from the Old Ways. In Nevada, they treat Antony Croft like it's part of America. Topaz Ten, we need our wits about us offcroft, so you two shut the hell up and nap."

When Joy murmured, "Sorry," Delta winked and disappeared from view.

"Sorry I laughed, Topaz," Joy whispered.

Joy had apologized twice in the space of a minute. Topaz felt sorry many times in her life, but never apologized. In Caesar, those three words were weak. How could Joy so casually lay herself open in front of another and wait for them to accept or reject her? They were not family. Joy did not need Topaz for anything.

"It's okay, Joy," Topaz said. She sighed, curled her legs beneath her, and closed her eyes.

They had passed a wooden sign that said "Colorado" a while back. Topaz wondered where the mountains were. All she saw was asphalt and the graffitied back walls of strip malls. As the bus gently rocked the Mages to sleep, rabid thoughts slunk close. Her mother's red wig on a white sneaker. Topaz's breath hitched and she put a knuckle to her mouth. Was her mother alive or did she die saying goodbye to Topaz?

Topaz alone, of the Tenkillers, took after her mother's Fareye side of the family. Luckily, she was not a see-er, like Crystal. The Tenkiller magic of fire had skipped Topaz, but so had the self-destructive prophetic ability of the Fareyes. She tried to make sense of her mother's "gift." Why had her mother given her those images? Were those ciphers worth Crystal being Galvanized? The image of Galvanizers being held on her brother and father haunted her, but she could not do anything now. Crystal singing "You Are

My Sunshine" was a memory. Topaz had watched her sing to Malachi when he was a baby. This time, the baby at her breast had been Topaz, but it had also been Amber, Coral, and Malachi. Her mom had also shared the vision of a blonde woman without teeth last night. Was it only last night when she said goodbye? Topaz shifted to relieve the uncomfortable fullness of her bladder.

Why couldn't her mother have a vision of Amber? Of Topaz's destination? Instead, she got a useless inheritance from a failed mother. What use was memory without context? Her mother's mysterious vignettes already happened or would happen in the future, nobody knew.

The empty mouth, Topaz understood. On the croft, Mages tried to pass as offcrofters or even pretended like they were Master Mages. Charlie Smythfield created inserts that looked like teeth. He also pulled healthy teeth from Mages to create ostentatious gaps. Missing teeth were a sign of power. Topaz's tongue absently probed the empty spot in her mouth. It was part of her, like her long straight hair or inability to make friends. She and her sisters had worked for years to perfect their powers. Amber and Coral manipulated streams of fire and Topaz Took from them. A shadowy smile was proof of her work.

It was only late afternoon, but the weight of the day settled like a mantle over her shoulders and the bus rocked soothingly. Topaz gave in to the heaviness of sleep.

* * *

A grinding wheeze and jerking of the bus woke Topaz. She was huddled against the window and a colorful blanket was draped over her. It smelled of campfire smoke. Delta must have covered her. Topaz stretched and looked around. The sky wasted a purple, cloud-strewn sunset on the sleeping Mages. The bus bounced up a narrow road.

Johnson's mic-staticky voice woke the rest of the Mages, "Rise and shine, Skeletons. We gotta stop in Macbeth and it might get dangerous. You will not speak or leave your seat until we re-enter America." He flipped the black lever up. "This will remind you to behave."

The bone-jarring vibration hit her spine and then Topaz's stomach churned. Around her, stretching and yawning Mages grimaced.

Joy poked her face back between the seats. "You get used to it."

Through her mounting nausea, Topaz tried to smile at Joy.

"You know about Macbeth, right?" Joy asked.

Topaz had just learned about Macbeth from Agent Holder. "I heard they aren't allowed to practice the Old Ways, but that can't be true, right?" Topaz had to lean forward to hear Joy's whispered response.

"It's true, no Fire Death, Soul Baskets, Witching Hour Chants, joyous Final Death, nothing," Joy said.

The First Death was what Americans thought of as "death," when a body expires. When Mages die a First Death, their last act on Earth is to give themself a Fire Death. This sets their body on fire to cremate the body. Then, a Mage's family can perform Witching Hour Chants and return his or her magic to Canopus. Canopians avoided the First Death, preferring that their body and magic died at the same time. When a Mage became ill or too old to enjoy life, or wanted to end it at nineteen like Coral, they triggered the Fire Death to consume their own body. The First Death destroyed the host of Canopian Magic, the Fire Death freed the magic from its confines, and the Final Death returned magic to its home on Canopus.

The Old Ways were followed to prevent magic from reanimating its Mage. If the rites were not performed, the Remnant sought another home. Through centuries of evolution, Mages can temporarily harbor and nurture the voracious needs of magic, but it kills any other vessel. Non-Mages die within minutes when a Remnant hollows out the space below their heart to create a Magical Chamber.

Without the Old Ways, the Mages of Macbeth, living and dead, were at the mercy of Remnants. Her great-grandparents started the Tenkiller Rebellion to stop the Bureau of Land Management from taking Canopian children and sending them off croft to church orphanages. They died so their children would learn the Old Ways and be safe from their own magic.

"Then, the dead walk Macbeth?" Topaz asked the question slowly to clarify her thoughts.

Joy said, "They took their Soul Basket and Death Bier."

"Who? Who did this?" Topaz asked.

"America," Joy said.

"Don't they understand that the Final Death is the only way to prevent Remnants?"

Joy sighed and faced forward.

When Coral's magic joined Canopus, it was a beautiful, sacred, Final Death. Her magic was home, not doomed to wander the Earth as an unwanted Remnant.

The bus stuttered to a stop in front of a tall gate. A concrete wall, rather than the barbed wire and chain link fencing to which Topaz was accustomed, extended from the gate. The bus honked its horn and a soldier in fatigues and a blue face mask emerged from a door near the gate.

The driver opened the window and extended papers to the soldier.

Outside air drifted into the bus. Johnson plugged his nose. A Canopian said, "Ugh," and someone made a retching sound. The air coming from outside smelled like death and waste. A life cut short and left to rot in a pail of water. Topaz pulled Delta's blanket over her mouth and nose and inhaled the smoky scent.

The soldier glanced at the papers, handed them back to the driver, and pulled the gate open. The driver slammed the window closed and the bus into gear. Johnson and Miller braced their arms on the ceiling of the bus as it went through the gate.

From behind an overturned truck, two soldiers followed the bus's progress through the scopes of their rifles. Topaz looked back as the guard closed the gates. The words "Welcome to Hell" had been spray painted on them in dripping scarlet letters.

The hills on either side of the rutted road were dotted with corrugated metal trailers and wooden shacks. The deep grinding of gears joined the low buzz of electricity to make Topaz's bones feel like liquid running through her body. The bus slid back, jerked forward, and reluctantly bumped and scraped its way up a steep incline.

Johnson spoke into the microphone. "Macbeth is a pile of garbage. America has done everything to help these backwards people. Hell, the Bureau of Land Management even banned the Old Ways to drag this shithole into the eighties, but there's no helping these people. If pigs are happy rolling in their own shit, best leave them to it." His laugh turned into a phlegmy cough.

That cloying sweet-rot scent was exposed magic. Remnants. Magic needed protection, the shelter of a body. Topaz's family was poor and fractured, but Crystal had taught them the importance of the Old Ways and this place showed it.

Topaz huddled in the colorful blanket and peered out of the window. The purpled gray twilight cloaked twisted skeletons of abandoned vehicles. How many silvery Remnants lurked in those rusting cars? She relaxed her eyelids to unfocus her vision. Silvery streaks slid down the hill toward the bus, like fast-forwarded light. She shifted her unfocused gaze to the side of the road. Ribbons of Remnants slithered at the edge of the light, keeping pace with the bus.

These stupid Offcrofters did not understand that all of them, Canopian and Offcrofter alike, were potential hosts for Remnants. Everyone on this bus would die if the Macbeth Remnants boarded, either immediately or soon. Then she remembered the weapon that captured and confined her people; electricity. The red lever above the driver's head. For burnt magic's sake, they were safe because of Sine Wave Stimulation.

She tried to find Canopus in the darkening sky, but the purple star was behind the bus. Topaz whispered, "First Death, Fire Death, May your magic die with you."

A few seats in front of Topaz, Delta murmured, "May your magic die with you."

She had always loved the Witching Hour Chants, the colorful Soul Basket and the many voices become one. The warmth of the circle as they bid magic farewell. The beauty of an iridescent Remnant ribboning into the sky in the Final Death. Could Witching Hour Chants even be done without a Soul Basket or Final Death Bier?

Up front, Miller and Johnson clutched their Galvanizers and peered out the windshield.

At the top of the hill, Macbeth's church, post office, and bar huddled together, bright lights glared out of every window. A white box truck idled nearby, the words "Magic Milk" emblazoned in gold lettering on the side. The bus stopped in front of the posto office and a tall figure in a faded green military jacket emerged and stood in the light from the plate glass window. Light washed over him, but he was dreadfully alone in his spotlight. The man stood defiant amid the dark isolation of Macbeth.

The silence on the bus was that of stunned grief. Like Topaz, the Mages pressed their faces to the glass, looking for Remnants. The still man in front of the Macbeth post office was the only life. Next to the church, the sawdust covered playground was empty. Nobody entered or left the brightly lit bar. There were no cars parked around the town square.

"Go on out there so we can get this over with." Johnson folded his thick arms.

Miller shook his head. "Do you smell that? I did two crofts today. You go."

"You think Antony and Othello count? I did Caesar and you're doing Macbeth. The sooner you move, the sooner we get out of this hellhole," Johnson said.

"Can one of you please check the Skels papers, already? I don't like this place," a high voice insisted. Topaz had not heard the driver speak before. He sounded like a Muppet.

"Fucking roger that," Miller mumbled. He patted his Galvanizer and picked up his clipboard.

The driver opened the door and the smell of slick sinew gone rancid intensified. The sound of "Don't Stop Believing" by Journey drifted from the bar. Johnson stood at the top of the steps and trained his Galvanizer on the patiently waiting Canopian.

"Permit?" Miller snapped his fingers and the Canopian extended his permit.

Topaz searched the darkness for Remnants. There, by the side of the post office, ribbons of white vapor wriggled in shadow. She turned her head against the glass and, from the corner of her eye, saw Delta's plume of hair also pressed against the window.

The older woman whispered, "Death and life—" and Topaz finished, "exist within."

Miller looked at the work permit proffered by the Canopian and nodded.

Johnson said, "If you have luggage, it's staying here," and moved out of the way.

The Canopian shrugged and the backpack that hung from one shoulder swayed. His face was pallid and purple shadows clung to his eyes. Long black hair was secured at the back of his neck. He dropped into an empty seat and, with barely a ripple, was absorbed into the pond of Canopians.

The driver shoved the bus into gear and turned around. He sped down the rutted hill until they reached the metal fence. A border control agent darted on the bus, nodded at the guards and called, "Franco Lonespirit." The new Canopian extended his permit, she ignored the permit, told Johnson, Miller, and the driver to have a safe trip, and left.

It was possible that the border control agent had a hot cup of coffee waiting for her in the guard house or maybe she was in a hurry because she had seen the malevolent ribbons of magic. The "Welcome to Hell" message disappeared when the guards opened the gates, but Topaz knew that it was there.

When the bus merged onto Interstate 76, Johnson turned off the SWS and passed a bag of Twinkies back. Mages ate and shuffled past Topaz to the bathroom. She gave in to the deep velvet vibration of the bus and slept.

Chapter Ten

The truck beeped as it backed up to the cement loading dock. Gold letters glittered in the gray twilight, spelling "Magic Milk" on the side of the boxy white truck. The corrugated steel roof of the loading dock protected the truck from prying eyes. The location, tucked behind the Bloomington Bus Terminal and surrounded by parking lot and chain link fence, made it unlikely that anyone would stumble onto it accidentally.

The driver climbed stiffly out of the truck, grabbed a clipboard from behind the seat, and paused to rub his knee before limping up the stairs.

He called up to the man standing on the loading dock, "Whiskey Pete, how the hell are you?"

Pete took the clipboard from Bob and said, "Any better and I would be a fucking Leprechaun, Bob. I see that leg's paining you again. Take the edge off?" The man in the white lab coat handed Bob a flask. The driver took a slug and held the flask while Pete flipped through papers on the clipboard.

The door nestled next to the large delivery bay opened and AnnaLeesa Bennet bustled out in a cloud of Jean Nate. Thomas hulked behind her, as usual. Pete turned away and deftly slipped the flask into his pocket.

"Good afternoon, Bob. What do we have today?" AnnaLeesa read the manifest over Pete's shoulder. She was tall, heightened even more by black high heels, not the sexy kind, but the "I am impervious to pain" type of heel. She pretended not to notice when Pete exhaled the other way. The smell of whiskey blended nicely with the lemony Jean Nate` surrounding them.

Bob removed his green and yellow John Deere cap, "Afternoon, Mayor, only two this week. One fresh Container, pronounced DOA after a motorcycle accident, Sine Wave Stimulation immediately, so it should be healthy."

"And the other Container?" AnnaLeesa's voice was sharp. This was the first shipment from Macbeth to Bloomington after her father's body was found. He was on the Deceased Report, so he should be on this truck.

Bob waved his hand below his nose, "Pretty ripe old guy, found in his trailer out by Revival Creek. The Container is barely holding up, but we may be able to extract his magic."

AnnaLeesa concentrated on the pages in front of her, but she could not control the shakiness of her breath. Thomas watched from his slouched position against the wall.

"Any problems?" she asked. AnnaLeesa Bennett received official reports from the Bureau of Land Management and kept in daily contact with her Macbeth Strike Team, but Bob provided valuable insights.

"No, ma'am. The Mages have mostly stopped trying to do the old stuff. I saw the bus come for that Lonespirit Canopian before I hauled ass, I mean, hurried here. Been a long time since anyone was released from Macbeth." He paused and waited for AnnaLeesa to answer the unasked why. When she was silent, he continued, "Anyway, things are calm there. No Tenkiller Rebellion will happen on Macbeth. I think they've given up."

"You made good time. The bus skipped Cheyenne Intake and you still beat it. It won't arrive until tomorrow afternoon, so we'll have the Containers squared away. Do you want a cup of coffee?" AnnaLeesa asked. She reached around Pete and turned a page on the clipboard.

"No, thank you, Mayor. Gonna grab a bite and some shut eye. I have three days off, unless God sends a plague to Macbeth."

"Thank you, I appreciate your dedication." She smiled at Bob.

"Whatever it takes to fight the Russkies." Bob understood that the weapons from this lab could win the Cold War for America.

"A true patriot." AnnaLeesa nodded and Pete signed the top page. She looked over her shoulder, and Thomas left the shadows.

He and Bob donned long leather gloves. If they touched the walls of the truck, they would be electrocuted. In order to safely transport Containers on the long trip from Macbeth Croft in Colorado to Bloomington Town in New York, the SWS was set at 100 volts to eliminate any possibility of Remnants escaping.

"See you next trip, Bob," AnnaLeesa called over her shoulder as she went inside.

The Bloomington Bus Terminal was a clever place to hide her lab. Since Americans and Mages routinely passed through, certain areas were equipped with SWS. She had installed shielded cable under six inches of concrete in case of a power outage. AnnaLeesa steeled herself and hurried through the small anteroom, between the dock and the lab. This was where they kept the Containers, Mage cadavers that held magic. Called "The Buzzer," this area was equipped with 50 volts of SWS and had freezers on either side of the narrow space. 50 volts of electricity was uncomfortable to Americans, but it made Canopians violently ill. Each mortuary freezer could store four cadavers behind the hinged doors. Right now, they only had three residents, so the arriving two kept the lab below the maximum occupancy of eight.

As AnnaLeesa Bennett rushed into the lab, she heard a metallic clank. Thomas, Bob, and Pete were undoubtedly having a drink while they loaded the bodies onto gurneys to bring them into The Buzzer. Pete and Bob thought her squeamish, that AnnaLeesa could not stand the sight or smell of decay. Being underestimated served her well. If she got too close to the truck or lingered in The Buzzer, she would be ill. It would not do for the mayor to have convulsions like a dirty Mage on the loading dock.

In the small lab, AnnaLeesa settled into a rolling office chair and watched one of the two monitors on the table in front of her; one showed the loading dock and the other was linked to the camera in the Research Room. Now, she was only interested in the loading dock. The manifests identified the condition of the cargo and the possible magic within the Container, but rarely included the identity of the Mage.

Sweat prickled her scalp. The ripe corpse must be James Heartsnake, but she had to see it.

The grainy black and white image showed Dr. Peter O'Shea at the edge of the platform, his back to the camera. He was, no doubt, taking a nip while the other men were getting a body from the truck. The covert exercise was unnecessary, as AnnaLeesa knew his nickname was Whiskey Pete and she had a safe full of pictures documenting the coroner's drinking problem.

Bob and Thomas maneuvered the gurney near the door. When Pete unzipped the opaque bag, AnnaLeesa stood and leaned close to the screen. Her chair rolled backwards and clanged into a metal counter. Pale features and black sweeping brows appeared as the bag fell away. The young female could have been sleeping, if not for the deep dent in her forehead. The fresh Container. AnnaLeesa's breath fogged the monitor.

Pete made a notation on his clipboard. AnnaLeesa heard the clatter of the door to The Buzzer before she saw them open it on the screen. She pulled a tissue from a floral-patterned box and wiped the screen. Pete lit a cigarette on the loading dock while he waited for Thomas and Bob to return. Was there any vice the coroner did not have?

She wrapped her finger in tissue to clean the corners of the monitor as she watched Thomas and Bob push the empty gurney into the truck and emerge with the other body. When Pete unzipped the plastic bag, her hand stilled. He turned away from the gurney. Bob stumbled back and Thomas pulled his black turtleneck sweater up to cover his mouth and nose.

The sides of the bag gaped open and AnnaLeesa saw the soft gray profile. His hooked features had collapsed, but it was James Heartsnake. She ran a finger across the small image on the monitor. Had her Witching Hour Chants worked or was his magic still inside the container of that body? If she had not returned his magic to Canopus, she would torture his Remnant.

Just as he had tortured her body and spirit. She shushed the whimpers inside her Magic Chamber.

In a whirl of decision, AnnaLeesa dropped the tissue into the garbage can and rolled the chair under the table. She glanced around the gleaming lab, but nothing was out of place. A long counter ran the length of the room, and modified electronic microscopes, orbitoclasts, and various electricity imaging devices were labeled and arranged in neat rows. Clasps above the counter and below the stainless steel shelves held 3Ms of varying sizes and caliber. Bright blue metal canisters, like those used to hold helium, were the only color in the sterile room. They were perfectly aligned along the steel cabinet above the counter. An Automated External Defibrillator, tucked in the corner, looked more like a jukebox than a Mage Torture device. As Thomas said, a vegetative patient was twice as nice as one who is conscious.

She opened the door to the Research Room and glanced back at the monitor. The men were bringing her father inside the building. She had not been near James Heartsnake since she was fifteen and ran away with an American guard. She closed the door behind her. Had her Witching Hour Chants worked on his diseased magic? She needed to know now.

She went about the comforting procedure of preparing the Research Room for a Container and tried to forget that it was her father. She pushed a button on the Compaq 32-bit state-of-the-art computer and waited for it to power on. The Research Room was originally the repair facility for buses when Bloomington was a real town. It was large enough to accommodate two buses at the same time and still smelled of oil and exhaust. The small row of windows just under the metal roof was designed to vent carbon monoxide, not dispel shadows. The computer beeped. While the monitor slowly brightened to black and green life, AnnaLeesa took a pen from the "Bloomington is Best" mug on the desk and wrote the name "James Heartsnake" at the top.

She went behind the table to check that the sheaf of wires was connected properly to the computer. The monitor facing away from her threw an eerie green light back, but the rest of the lab was dim as she followed the bundle of wires across the concrete floor, past the red generator, until it separated and led to two small structures. A multi-colored umbilicus of cable swaddled each self-contained building. They were officially called Simulated Magical Chambers, or SMCs, but the team referred to them as The Sheds.

At Annaleesa's instruction, Pete had created two buildings big enough to hold a Death Bier, gurney, dedicated Magic Monitoring Machine (3M), surveillance camera, an external computer port, and all the trappings necessary for magic. Each was designed to mimic a Magical Chamber to entice magic out of a Container. There was a War Shed and an Art Shed. Copper covered the exterior of each to conduct electricity and imprison magic, but the interior was paneled with wood to facilitate the extraction of magic. The wood was kept damp at all times, to further shield the magic from electricity. As she checked the connection to the War Shed, her hand brushed an exposed patch of wood. Damp wood. Moldy particle board under a leaky sink.

She put a knuckle to her mouth. The smell of wood rotted by slimy water drifted toward her and she was no longer in the Research Room. AnnaLeesa Bennett, Tori Heartsnake, wedged herself behind silver duct taped pipes and hid while her father drank. He careened from bathroom to refrigerator to the couch to watch television. A worm clinging to rotted wood dropped onto her head. It wriggled into her matted hair. She put her hand tightly over her mouth to stifle a scream. With her other hand, she frantically felt through the tangle of hair to find the worm. It was squirming near her ear, trying to get into her brain. She pulled on it, but the maggot was caught in her hair. She yanked clumps of her hair out. The small girl banged her arm into a metal pipe and whimpered in pain. Lurching footsteps shook the small trailer. She scrambled away from the cabinet door, but she was already up against the rotting particle board at the back of the cabinet. The door opened and she blinked against the bright light.

The door to the lab opened and the tunnel of light startled AnnaLeesa back to the present. She sucked the blood from her knuckle.

"All set, boss," Thomas was a silhouette until he closed the door. "Pete's taking temperatures and measurements. He said we can try to get the fresh

Container in here tomorrow after the bus unloads the new Mages." The computer monitor cast his face in a sickly green light.

AnnaLeesa finished hooking the computer up to the War Shed port and walked back to the table. "No, I want the second one."

"The old guy? Mayor, he's past his expiration date," Thomas said.

"Yes, the old guy. Tell Pete to freeze him, warm him, whatever he has to do to get him ready. I want samples and tests done tonight. We'll try Heartsnake tomorrow morning."

"I don't know if there's even enough of that Container to take out of the body bag."

AnnaLeesa considered using her Charm on Thomas, but she could not face the child in her Magical Chamber right now. She sat on the table and leaned back on her arms. Her peach silk dress shimmered in the shadowy room.

"Are you right in this?" he asked softly.

"Do you want me to be?" She took a breath and her breasts brushed against his sweater.

Chapter Eleven

Topaz's throbbing bladder drew her out of sleep. She shifted to lean against the window, but it did not ease the pressure.

The nightmare memory of Macbeth rushed back. Topaz had learned the dangers of Remnants when she was twelve. Crystal and Henry Tenkiller were at The Driftwood Lounge the night the Tenkiller Children slept with the lights on. Topaz later learned that Justina Twoshades had sent her husband into the desert at dawn to get tincture supplies. She was out of Mad Apple Flower for nausea and tail of Green Collared Lizard used to treat joint pain. When Mr. Twoshades did not return by nightfall, Matthew Swifthart went to the dunes to alert the FEMA trailers that there may be a Remnant on the loose. When Swifthart knocked on the Tenkillers' door to warn them to stay inside, Amber pretended that their parents would be home any minute and Swifthart pretended to believe her.

Amber clapped her hands and challenged the Lil' Killetts to a game tournament. While 3-year-old Malachi fetched spoons and Coral searched the junk drawer for the red-checked playing cards, Amber told Topaz to turn on all the lights. The trailer was ablaze with light and laughter as Amber kept her younger siblings occupied playing Go Fish, Spoons, Old Maid, and the Telephone Game. After Mal drooped to sleep under the kitchen table, Amber dragged a white plastic chair to the window, then told Coral and Topaz to go to sleep. When Topaz awoke from the warm kitten jumble with Malachi and Coral, Amber was still staring out the window. Only later did she understand her sister's vigil and the enormity of their parents' desertion.

She sighed and tried to sit comfortably. The rest of the bus was sleeping. The smell of urine drifted toward her from the full lavatories. Damnit. Joy snored in the seat in front of her, but Topaz would not be able to go back to sleep until she relieved herself.

As she walked quietly back toward the bathroom, she passed Mages whose faces were relaxed and loose with sleep. On the right was the man who would not let her sit with him. Sleep unfurrowed the worry from his brow. Across from him, a tan girl sprawled across two seats. There were few Canopians in the front of the bus because no one wanted to be near the guards. The back was empty because it smelled like piss.

To the right of the glowing red exit sign was a small door. Inside, the tiny bathroom smelled about the same as the back of the bus. Some of the homes on the croft did not have indoor plumbing, yet Offcrofters had it in vehicles. She washed her hands and splashed water on her face. They would reach Bloomington tomorrow. She'd help the Resistance because of Amber, but this bus was not going to Cheyenne. She had no way to find her contact or to be trained now. She was supposed to give proof to an Inspector, but what proof?

When she left the bathroom, the back of the bus was dark. She glanced up. The red exit sign had been covered with tape. Why would someone cover the light?

A hand wrapped around Topaz's face and covered her mouth. She twisted, jerked her neck to free herself, to cry out. A heavy weight slammed into her and Topaz's face and chest were crushed into the wall opposite the bathroom. Wheezing for breath, she tried to push back. A cold object jabbed into her ribs. Topaz froze. A Galvanizer.

Hot air hissed in her ear, "Feel that, bitch?"

He thrust himself against her from behind. The heavy weight crushed Topaz's pelvis into the wall. Hot tears formed in her eyes as she tried to get breath into starved lungs.

"Yeah, you feel that." He ground his body into her.

Topaz could not draw breath. She opened her mouth to scream in agony, but the hand was tight against her nose and mouth.

He nestled his face in her hair. He breathed out and murmured, "Unbutton your jeans."

Topaz thrashed and tried to wriggle away, but felt a cold object pressed into her ribs.

He jabbed the Galvanizer into her side, "Don't move again, filthy Skel."

Through the desperate need to breathe, over the red haze of pain in her side, Topaz heard a throat clearing.

The movements stilled, but he restrained Topaz with his body.

"What is it?" he asked hoarsely.

"Excuse me, Officer Johnson, I need to use the facilities."

That was the smoky voice of Delta, the Canopian from Othello. Her attacker was Johnson. Topaz filed an image of the pudgy guard away. Death and life exist within.

"Not now. It's out of order. Come back," Johnson said hoarsely.

Topaz bucked back against his body and shot her elbow into his side. Johnson squeezed her face, grinding her cheeks into her teeth.

"Would you like some help repairing the light? I can get Officer Miller from up front."

"No, go back to your seat." Johnson snapped, "I'll take care of it."

"Sir, this old bladder can't wait too long. I'd better wait here."

Another voice sounded from behind Delta, "Guess we should have gone before, Miss Dawn. I'll wait here as well."

Johnson released Topaz's face. She saw Delta and the Canopian from Macbeth sit in the seats closest to Johnson.

"Fucking Skels," Johnson spat. He stalked to the front of the bus.

* * *

The bus continued across America, stopping occasionally for food or to change drivers. They passed a weathered sign thanking them for visiting Colorado. The bus splashed water on a bright blue "Welcome to Indiana" billboard and whizzed by a yellow sign that announced that they had entered New York, "The Empire State."

Topaz was trapped by anger and the feeling of Johnson's body. She could not escape the dark back of the bus. She was accustomed to violence; it was currency on the croft, but she had never been violated. Delta covered Topaz with her blanket and quiet talk of the Old Ways. Joy tried to make her laugh, and Franco, in his worn jacket, gazed at her sadly from the front of the bus.

When they arrived at a tan brick building with smoky windows, Johnson spoke into the microphone, "This is the end of the line; Bloomington Bus Terminal. Get the fuck off my bus."

When Topaz disembarked, he shifted his body to block the exit, smiled, and winked. She tried to commit his face to memory, but all she could see was her reflection in his sunglasses.

Chapter Twelve

"Are you sure he's empty?" AnnaLeesa's voice rose and bounced off of the corrugated roof to pelt Whiskey Pete and Thomas. She had rushed from a meeting with the Town Planning Board to find out the results of James Heartsnake's extraction and she was still out of breath. If his Container was empty, either she had returned his magic to Canopus or his Remnant lurked somewhere. She squinted into a dark corner of the lab.

"Nothing inside. I tried the War Shed first," Pete pointed to the structure on the left, "like you said, but nothing happened. The old guy doesn't look like the Art type, but I tried him in there anyways. Nothing." His chair creaked when Pete leaned forward and tapped his pen on the monitor.

The greenish cast of the screen did not do the Art Shed justice. The grainy image did not show the cold white marble of two Death Biers. The cream color of the silky wallpaper, echoed in the plush carpet, was not reflected in the screen. Colorful Van Gogh reproductions spattered the walls in wild abandon. *Starry Night*, *Sunflowers*, *Almond Blossoms*, and *Starry Night Over the Rhone* all looked like Rorschach blots. A built-in corner table held a white chalice, intricately woven with vines and flowers. A slender flame rose from the chalice.

James Heartsnake's mushroom colored corpse spread across one of the Death Biers and the other was empty. Electrodes formed a crown of thorns around his head. Macbeth's red and black Soul Basket stood at the foot of the marble slab. A silver canister, conspicuous in its sleek modern design, rested against the Death Bier.

"No SWS leaked into the shed?" AnnaLeesa went around behind the table as she spoke.

"Mayor Bennet, it was a real long shot. The Container was real old, the Remnant either escaped or took another body on Macbeth." Pete rubbed his hands together, "Now, the other one—"

"You checked the cables? Sometimes, the connections come loose." She traced the wires back to the generator connected to the Art Shed and bent to check that the lever was in the proper position to provide power to the shed.

Pete and Thomas exchanged a look.

"I checked everything. If anything was in the Container, I would've harvested it." Pete's voice was defensive.

She straightened. "Are we certain that there was something in there when James Heartsnake arrived?"

Pete's cheeks reddened, whether from anxiety or the amount of Jameson in his system was uncertain. "I mean, he was marked as a Container on the manifest, but nothing registered on the Electroencephalography last night."

"And you were careful? No chance a Remnant could have escaped?" She looked in the small window of the Simulated Magical Chamber. AnnaLeesa ignored the quivering in her own Magical Chamber and examined her father's corpse. His bloat body was a sacrilege below the lurid brilliance of Van Gogh's paintings. His sharp edges were concave. She scrutinized the shadowy corners of the Art Shed, but could not see a sidling silver ribbon.

AnnaLeesa turned to the men and shouted, "Where is it?"

Pete's eyes widened. Mayor Bennett was the one who bent others to her will, calmly and methodically. She did not shout. "The...the 3Ms didn't register a Remnant, not here in the Research Room, the lab, The Buzzer, anywhere. Macbeth made a mistake, the old guy isn't a Container, it's just an old man. The fresh Container is real promising. She was iced and jolted immediately. The Remnant might be viable in that same hot, young, body if we don't leave her too long."

Thomas glanced at Pete and said, "You know you're talking about a corpse, right?"

Pete smiled. "It's not necrophilia if we reanimate her."

"You are messed up," Thomas said.

AnnaLeesa took a deep breath and released it. Her improvised Witching Hour Chants had to have worked. She knew, more than anyone, how dangerous Heartsnake's paralytic magic was.

She spoke in more measured tones, "You both know that America is falling behind Russia in the Arms Race. We have to find a way to utilize these Remnants. This magic," she tapped on the window, half expecting her father to rise, "will put America back on top."

Chapter Thirteen

"Oh Mickey, you're so fine. You're so fine you blow my mind," Topaz sang.

She listened to the small clock radio on her desk every morning while she wrote to Mal. Topaz had discovered New Wave Music when she came to Bloomington four weeks ago. The jukebox selection at The Driftwood Lounge consisted of Willie Nelson and Patsy Cline, some Elvis Presley and Neil Young. Those were all great, but she fell hard for Depeche Mode and the Smiths. Her guilty pleasure was pop music, like Howard Jones, Brian Adams, and The Psychedelic Furs.

She finished the letter to Malachi, "Life and death exists within, Love, Topaz," and folded it around a one-hundred-dollar bill. She was paid a fair wage at Bloomington and her salary included room and board. Except for the cash she sent to the croft, Topaz deposited all of her checks in the bank to save.

"Hey Mickey! Hey, hey! Hey Mickey!" Topaz sang.

The Old Ways forbade a Canopian asking about another Mage's power, but Topaz had quickly learned that her roommate, Joy of the cherry red fingernails, possessed the power of sleep. Joy could make anyone, including herself, sleep. Although Joy had stumbled in at 2 am this morning, she would not wake up.

"Hey Mickey! Hey, hey! Hey Mickey!" Topaz clapped as she belted out the song. She put the week's letters in an envelope, licked the flap, and addressed it to Henry Tenkiller. Topaz had not heard back, but she trusted her father to get Mal into some sort of program.

Joy and Topaz were ideal roommates. Joy worked at the Bloomington Hospital and sometimes put in overtime at The Bloomington Hotel and Suites. As a member of the Security and Logistics Team, SaLT, Topaz worked and trained from 7am until 5 or 6pm.

She squinted to look at the Molly Ringwald "Pretty in Pink" calendar tacked to the bulletin board above her desk. She had arrived in Bloomington on March 15th, it was now April 20th, and the UN Inspectors would be here next week. The last month was a blur of activity. Topaz was in classes for six hours a day, then Close Combat and Specialty Training for another two. By the time she got home, although her body ached, Topaz studied for a bit and fell asleep, sometimes in her bed, more often at her desk. Joy had an active social life, but Topaz had not made friends, other than Joy. She was here for the fractured Tenkiller Family; to help Mal and find Amber.

On a morning jog last week, Topaz saw a short woman with dark hair leave the pharmacy. Her heart raced as she followed the woman who looked like Amber. She followed her from a distance for two blocks. When the woman stopped to peer into a restaurant window, the sharp features reflected were not Amber's round-cheeked face. Topaz's racing heart sank.

Now that she was here, Topaz knew the truth. Amber had not wanted to write home. Paper was easy to get and a stamp cost 22 cents. Loss was hardening into anger. Would Coral have killed herself if Amber had written? Did Amber know that Coral did her own Fire Death? Did she care about her family? She had chosen the Resistance over the Tenkillers. She searched for Amber in every face she saw. Her life was good in Bloomington. It would be better if she could stop looking for Amber and wondering if her mother was alive.

It was SaLT's job to keep the United Nations Inspector and staff safe while they toured America's first completely integrated community, Bloomington Town. It was understood that SaLT was the face of that community. The three Americans and three Mages that formed SaLT had finally stopped circling one another, stiff-legged, tail-up and their practice missions had improved. Topaz was top of the class in the Security and Logistics Course and she excelled at Close Combat. Other than the "Interpersonal Skills" and "Teamwork Equals Safework" modules, Topaz had earned mastery on all the tests. Truth be told, she was already familiar with some of the information. "Risk Assessment" was the Tenkiller kids deciding whether or not to wake Crystal up before they caught the bus for school. When Topaz visited her father, she conducted "Situational Awareness" to hitch a ride, avoid Remnants, and make it back to town before dark.

Topaz's problem was social. Curtis, the American SaLT leader, said "A close team is an effective team, by god," at least ten times a day. If TL Curtis was to be believed, SaLT was the bridge for unity and cooperation between the Offcrofters and Mages. Topaz had to admit, the Americans were nice; it was the Mages who were the problem. She should have been happy to see Delta Dawn and Franco Lonespirit from the bus on the first day of training. They were both kind and believed in the Old Ways, but their presence embarrassed Topaz. She felt ashamed that she had needed help, like she should have done more to resist Johnson. She had spent the last month proving to them that she was not weak.

Topaz tucked the envelope into the pocket of her gray SaLT sweatshirt and smoothed a few wisps of her thick black hair back into her tight bun. She picked Joy's blue scrubs up off the floor and smiled. The smell of hospital antiseptic and beer rose when Topaz tossed them into the bin in the corner. She enjoyed doing laundry. Topaz had started working at Bud's Suds when she was fourteen because it was safe and quiet, but the scent of detergent made her feel clean. The sound of the churning washers comforted her. The colorful towers of folded laundry filled her with satisfaction.

When she was stacking the blue mats after training last night, Team Leader Curtis had called her into his office. He was less intimidating sitting behind his neat polished desk, but authority made Topaz nervous. She knew that the Tenkillers were not always welcome and fully expected to be asked to leave the team, or even America, as she fidgeted in front of him.

Team Leader Curtis took off his green cap and rubbed his head.

Topaz was surprised to see that he was balding. How old was he? The man never seemed to run out of energy.

"Topaz Tenkiller, what do you think of America?" Curtis asked.

Was this a trick? He had never been unkind, but Curtis was an American. She needed to stay here.

"Fine, um, just fine, sir," she stammered.

The office was silent. She heard the thwack of mats as the rest of the team stacked them. She longed to be out there.

TL Curtis cleared his throat and said, "You're skilled at Security and Logistics, Topaz. Can you remind me of the other part of SaLT?"

"Ummm...team, sir?" she answered tentatively.

"Damn right, team," he boomed and Topaz jumped. "Are you a member of the team?"

"Yes, Team Leader Curtis."

Curtis said, "I don't think you are. Do you know what this team does, Topaz?"

"Security and Logistics, sir," Topaz said with confidence.

"Oh, Topaz," he shook his head in despair, "that's not all a team does. This team eats breakfast at 0700 hours."

Topaz stood silently, dreading what was sure to come next.

"The other six members of this *team*, my damn self, included, have been communicating with one another." Curtis stood. He towered over Topaz. "So, guess what you're going to do at 0700 tomorrow and every day after?"

"Sir, I—"

Curis sighed in deep disappointment and said, "That's an order." He put his cap on and his hands behind his back. "If you want to be a member of the Security and Logistics *Team*, then you damn well better act like it."

"Yes, sir. Thank you, Team Leader Curtis."

That was how Topaz had been voluntold to do something she had never done and did not know how to do, be part of a team.

Topaz shook her head ruefully and said, "Bye, Joy, I'm going to the post office. I'll say hi to Mark for you. Then I have to go be a member of a team."

The other girl curled into the covers and turned to face the wall.

"It's guys like you, Mickey," Toni Basil wailed.

* * *

Topaz checked that her door was locked and walked to the stairway at the end of the hall. Before she let the steel door close behind her, she listened for a moment. Topaz did not hear a sound from the three floors above or the two below. She stepped into the putty gray stairwell and looked both up and down. The fluorescent lights were in working order and the stairway was empty. She had been stupid on the bus; lulled by laughter with Joy and indoor plumbing. She hurried down the stairs. She had time to mail Malachi's letter and arrive at the cafeteria for breakfast. She planned to be there as they were finishing, so that she made an appearance, but did not have to interact with the team for long.

A member of the Bloomington Police Force sat at a gray desk near the Canopian Dormitory exit. She was not sure if there was a lower part to his body. Topaz had heard rumors that he rose and made rounds periodically, but had never seen it. Was he here to protect Mages or imprison them? Boomington was confusing.

Topaz nodded as she passed, but his eyes did not leave the Rolling Stone magazine that obscured his face. He turned a page and the cover picture of Prince seemed to nod at her.

April in upstate New York was chilly, so she pulled the hood of the gray sweatshirt over her head as she jogged down Main Street. She thought of using Merelyn Swifthart's magic just for fun, but magic freaked Americans out, and Bloomington was a compact town. When President Madison established the Caesar Croft, it was larger than some states. Since then, it had gotten smaller and smaller as Offcrofters "reclaimed" land, but Topaz was still used to running miles, rather than blocks.

Topaz nodded as she passed a woman in the type of slender, big-shouldered blazer that spoke of boardrooms managed and shareholders placated. The woman tapped her foot while a small white dog sniffed for the perfect red geranium. It felt good to run. Red sand would feel better, but burning lungs and lonely footsteps were home. Topaz could run for miles and would, if not for the invisible Galvanizer Fence under the green "Welcome to Bloomington" sign. Bloomington had geraniums, not eyesores like fences or guard towers.

She waited at an intersection for a long black car to pass. Although the Inspector was not due to arrive for a week, the town hummed with activity. Official cars containing official people arrived daily. Neat little houses lined the streets that crossed Main Street. Most were white, but the occasional rebellious yellow or blue cottage peeked out. Pert red, white, and blue geraniums were planted in the squares between the sidewalk and the road and in large stone planters. "Bloomington is Best" signs hung in every store front. Topaz had thought of her own slogan, "This is not a real town, but it tries hard and we pretend," but doubted anyone else would like it.

Humming "Hey, Mickey," she turned right at the end of the next block, her usual route. She always jogged down Main Street, then turned on Center Street to pass the Bloomington Bus Terminal, even if it made her late. Topaz knew it was not true or healthy, but she was not safe until she looked for Johnson. The only way to remove the feel of the pudgy guard from her skin was to check the station. Topaz stopped across the street from the corrugated awning where the bus had let her off and arced an arm over her head. She stretched as she examined the bus station in the early morning light.

As the bus sped across America, Topaz had watched, rewound, and rewatched Johnson's attack on a loop. Each time, she found another reason to hate herself. Topaz had been in fights before, but she had never been helpless, so at the mercy of another. She remembered the soft stifling weight of him, his sweat slick hand over her mouth, and the hard Galvanizer against her.

For the rest of the bus ride, Delta stayed near Topaz. Even in her silent isolation, Topaz noticed that when Johnson left the front of the bus to check on things, the Canopian from Macbeth followed him down the aisle. When Topaz got off the bus to stretch her legs, Delta stayed next to her and the Macbeth Mage stayed near Johnson. Joy, Canopus bless her soul, kept up a steady stream of chatter through Iowa, Illinois, Ohio and Pennsylvania.

When Johnson returned to Bloomington, she would be waiting. As a member of SaLT, she excelled at Close Combat Training. When Curtis noted that she was especially good with a knife, he brought in a specialist to work with her on advanced knife skills. He even had her uniforms fitted with a sheath for the Gerber her father had given her.

She had not seen another bus arrive after the one that brought her, so Topaz varied her jogging times past the terminal. She was not sure how things worked in America, but it seemed odd to have a bus terminal that was not used. In Bloomington, people went out at night, so despite her fear of the dark, Topaz began to leave the dorm after dark. She was always vigilant for Remnants. When she realized that there was no motherless magic in Bloomington, Topaz began jogging by the terminal at night. Only once had she seen any signs of use.

Last Friday, as she took an evening jog by the terminal, a white refrigerated truck with the words "Magic Milk" on the side pulled around to the back and stopped at the locked gate. She did not dare stare openly, so Topaz went around the corner and pretended to check her watch. The truck backed into a corrugated shelter built out from the loading dock. It filled the opening so tightly that Topaz could not see what was being loaded or unloaded. Even though it was dark and she still had Merelyn Swifthart's magic, Topaz did not dare go closer to see what was happening. But she could not stop thinking about it.

A few days later, Topaz knocked on Merelyn Swifthart's door to ask about milk deliveries at the bus station. Merelyn, who worked in the Government Reception Center, only rolled her eyes, asked why an empty bus station would possibly have milk delivered, and closed the door on Topaz.

Today was Thursday. Topaz planned to come back tomorrow night, Friday, to check if the "Magic Milk" shipment arrived weekly. This time she would find a place to hide and bring water to hydrate, in case she had to use magic.

She paused and listened to the quiet morning. She looked carefully at her surroundings, but she was alone on the street. Topaz turned away from the deserted station and jogged back to Main Street to mail Mal's letter. One day Jonhson would return and, this time, Topaz would be ready. In the meantime, she planned to figure out why a bus terminal received milk deliveries.

The bell attached to the glass door clanged when she entered the post office. Joy and Mark, the mustached Canopian from the bus and now mustached Mark the Postal Clerk, were dating. Topaz stopped in to chat with Mark even when she did not have a letter to mail. He was a nice guy and his mustache had grown thick and decadent. Topaz hoped her roommate did not break her favorite Postal Clerk's heart. Although she had not checked, Topaz was sure Mark's power was penis-related.

"Hey, Marky, you're so fine. You're so fine you blow my mind," Topaz sang as she entered the empty post office. Going past the bus terminal and thinking about using the Gerber on Johnson always made her cheerful.

Mark stopped sorting mail into the wooden racks attached to the wall and turned to Topaz. "Secret Agent man," Mark sang, "Secret Agent Man."

They had discovered a mutual love of music, although Mark liked classic rock and Topaz like New Wave music.

"Topaz, my favorite secret agent, how are you?"

"Security, Mark. I told you, boring security." She placed the envelope on the counter. The words, "Henry Tenkiller, Rural Route 4, Caesar Croft, USA," were written clearly on the front.

The secret agent reference bothered Topaz. It was too close to one of her possible truths. Ken Twosongs and Agent Holder said she had a contact here; now, Topaz wondered about everyone she met in Bloomington. Every face hid the secret of rebellion, of Amber, but Topaz had no way to seek it. She gauged every conversation, each interaction for some sort of clue.

"Oh yeah, security, totally." Mark winked at her before he put the envelope in a slot in the wall. "How are you?"

"Fine," Topaz said. "You're in a good mood today."

Mark looked puzzled, "Why not?"

"You're not tired? Joy's zonked out, after your late night," Topaz said.

"What late night?" Mark asked.

Oh crap, Joy wasn't with Mark last night? Joy dated a lot, but lately she had seemed to settle on Mark. Topaz had just assumed it was him. "Ummm, well, you know, maybe she wasn't out so late, now I'm not sure..." she trailed off. Oh god, how could she fix this?

Mark laughed and slapped the counter. "Just messing with you. Oh man, you should've seen your face."

"You creep," Topaz said. But she laughed with him. His power was definitely not penis-related, he was too nice to have a magic penis. Maybe he had super eyesight, the writing on those envelopes was pretty small. Maybe his mustache was radioactive. She was dying to know, but the Old Ways required that a Canopian volunteer their power as a sign of trust and Topaz respected Mark too much to enter his Magical Barrier to snoop.

"Yeah, it sucks. Joy and I have opposite schedules, so if I want to see her, I give up a little sleep." He shrugged. "Too noisy to sleep much, anyway."

"Oh, that's right. You're in Hell Heights."

Contrary to the appearance of integration, the Bloomington Town Planners had provided separate living quarters for Canopians and Americans. Mark was in the town worker section at the top of the male Canopian building. He was housed with carpenters, plumbers, electricians, and firefighters. The Canopian men of Hell Heights worked hard, but they played harder. On the weekends, people stayed away from the sidewalks below

Hell Heights because rooftop parties were common, as were experiments with trajectory, vegetables, gravity, and sofas.

Mark drummed his fingers on the counter. The fluorescent lights buzzed above them.

Topaz pushed off the counter, "Well, I've been ordered to eat with my team, so—"

Mark spoke at the same time, "Hey, Topaz, can I ask—"

They both stopped.

"Go ahead," Topaz said.

"No, it's okay. Never mind. You have to go. I'll see you tomorrow."

Topaz smiled. "Okay, then. Goodbye." The bell banged against the door when she left.

Out on the sidewalk, Topaz glanced through the glass door at Mark. He had turned back to his work, but his shoulders drooped. He was nice and she looked forward to his dopey jokes in the morning. She felt the spring sun on her face and the ache of hunger inside her would quiet with breakfast, as much food as she wanted. She could take time for Mark, she might even be able to help.

She opened the door gently so as not to annoy the bell and said, "Hey, everything okay?"

"Nah," Mark said, "it's nothing. You'll think I'm weird."

Topaz went back in and the bell chastised her indecision. "Come on, we're Mages, weird is cloth napkins and garden gnomes. Tell me."

He spoke in a rush, "Topaz, do you think you could stay with a friend Saturday night? I want to surprise Joy with a romantic dinner. We can't go to my room in the Heights, the guys would embarrass her. I know it's asking a lot, but just for one night, do you think you could stay with a friend? Joy and I have never really been alone and..." Mark's face was red.

"Sure," Topaz said. She didn't want to tell Mark that she had no idea where she would sleep, but she had to put him out of his misery. He, Joy, and Delta were her only friends. She would ask Delta, but Merelyn was her roommate. Merelyn would refuse to allow a Tenkiller in her room. It wasn't the first time she had to find a place to stay. She would figure it out.

Mark smiled in relief and said, "Thank you."

"Okay, Bye, Marky." The bell clanked with finality.

Topaz jogged down the sidewalk. She had just agreed to give up her room. How was this going to help her get Malachi safe? Why did she do it? Mark was her friend. That's why.

She passed a restaurant and the smell of bacon reminded Topaz of breakfast and a tall man who had ordered her to join a team.

Chapter Fourteen

Greg gestured with a slice of toast, "When we started fighting the other team, the spectators ran onto the field. Our parents fought each other. Husky parents against Tiger parents, and, unlike the football players, they weren't wearing pads or a helmet."

There were chuckles from the two Mages and two other Offcrofters at the table. The remains of breakfast were in front of them. Topaz planned to arrive at the end of breakfast, just before they left for classes, but the group slouched in their pushed back chairs. As always, her eyes were drawn to Franco Lonespirit. Since arriving at Bloomington, he had cut the long tail of hair that had hung down his back. The crew cut sported by the male members of SaLT highlighted his generous lips, high cheekbones and narrow nose. He wore the gray sweatsuit uniform of SaLT, but the military jacket alienation still clung to him. Franco carried the croft with him into the most American of places; the cafeteria.

Why was the team laughing? They had all heard Greg's story before. Topaz steeled herself and approached the table. When Greg fell silent at her approach, Topaz knew that her late arrival to the team breakfast was noticed. She looked longingly at all of the empty tables in the cafeteria. In fact, the whole room was empty. Wasn't it enough that she worked with the team and trained with them? Why did she have to eat with SaLT? She already had three more friends than she had ever had before. Canopus Balls, she had just given up her room for a friend.

When Delta saw Topaz she smiled and gestured, "Topaz, love, come."

Team Leader, Curtis McGarry, rose and motioned to Greg and Franco, "Boys, grab a chair for the late girl. Now that we're all here, let's do the briefing."

Big bald TL Curtis could hotwire, drive, and repair anything with wheels. He was an equally tough boss on both Mages and Americans.

"Canopus sake, why can't you be on time?" Franco snapped as he and Greg stood. They put a chair for her between them, but it was too tight for them to sit. Franco yanked his chair back from the table, threw himself into it and shoved a triangle of toast in his mouth.

Topaz regretted avoiding breakfast all these weeks, if only not to disappoint Franco. She had long wanted to thank him for looking out for her on the bus, but she was embarrassed. He was grumpy and unapproachable, but Franco had already become an important member of the team. Others looked to him for direction when Curtis was not around.

Curtis said, "Take it easy, Topaz is here now."

Topaz smiled gratefully. Team Leader Curtis always knew what to say.

With a sweep of his arm, Greg gestured at Topaz's chair, "Milady."

Greg told the same long-winded stories over and over and his loud voice sucked the air out of a room, but the Communications Specialist was kind. He did not ignore her like Jamal or snap at her like Franco.

Jamal, their Weapons Specialist, was as reluctant to be a "close team, by god," as Topaz. She got the impression that the dark color of Jamal's skin was a problem between him and other Americans. Also, Jamal felt that the Mages refusal to carry guns weakened SaLT. An important belief of the Old Ways is that death is personal. Yes, guns were lethal, but they were distant and impersonal. Death and life exist within. The Offcrofters called their guns "sweetheart" and "wife," but Topaz, Franco, and Delta relied on close combat, knives, or the power inside of them for protection. When

TL Curtis supported the Mage's belief and did not require them to carry guns, it only solidified Jamal's distrust of the Mages.

Topaz smiled and sat. Delta slid a plate toward her. It was piled with eggs, hash browns, and muffins. In the beginning, the Offcrofters had been shocked at how much Mages ate, but now their ravenous appetites just amused them. Topaz ate a corn muffin in two bites.

The tight circle of the team had widened to an oval to include Topaz. Curtis rubbed his hands together, "If you're finished, Greg?"

"Yeah, sure, TL, it's just...those guys were the best brothers a guy could ever have." Greg cleared his throat. He cried when Bruce Springsteen's "Glory Days" played on the radio and wore his blue and white MHHS Huskies baseball cap everywhere.

Please don't let him cry, Topaz thought.

Greg said, "I know this team will be as close as Mount Haven High School Class of '85. Go Huskies," he kissed his hand and held it above his head. "You'll be my SaLT brothers, and sisters, of course."

Why would anyone want more brothers or sisters? Topaz had already abandoned one family. She was losing focus, no more worries about Mark or SaLT. She had to think about Mal.

"Copy that, Greg." Team Leader Curtis looked at Topaz and then at Jamal, "Topaz, Jamal, this is the status quo. Either of you Go Elvis for breakfast again, I'll personally smoke you. Understood?"

"Yes, sir," Jamal responded.

Topaz did not understand. TL's acronyms and cultural references confused her.

Next to her, Greg whispered, "Gotta be here. Skip breakfast and you get extra work."

"Yes, sir," Topaz said. She had to eat breakfast with SaLT everyday. That was a lot of togetherness.

"Seeing as I already screwed up your social calendar for today, Tenkiller, I might as well tell you the magnificent day I have planned for tomorrow," Curtis said.

Was that a snort of laughter she heard from Franco? She ignored him and focused on TL.

"First, breakfast will be a meet and greet with Mayor Bennett in which you will show your professionalism and charm the shit out of our boss. After that, you princesses are all getting new ball gowns," he smiled when the team groaned.

"Meet and greet" was self-explanatory, but why would Topaz need a "ball gown?"

Greg helpfully whispered, "Uniform."

She thought the gray SaLT-issued sweatsuits *were* their uniforms. They were comfortable and did not get in the way during close combat. She had seven sweatsuits, more clothing than she had ever owned, why did they need new uniforms?

"We'll be prepping for a covert mission on Saturday. It is a practice mission, but this is our chance to show the mayor that we're ready to protect a high stakes principal."

As one, the team leaned forward. Jamal muttered, "Yessss."

"So far, you've done well at individual skills, hypotheticals, and small exercises, but the Inspector will be here next week and the classroom shit will be real." Curtis looked around the table at each of them before continuing, "Here's the deal, this mission is secret. In order to keep it authentic, the mayor's office has designed it, so I don't have all of the details. Our mission is to get a principal to her for questioning. No casualties, nobody knows we were there. We'll use code names for the target and ourselves. The Principal SaLT is tasked to protect codename Cinderella, who is a tall redhead in his twenties needed for questioning by the Mayor. What intel does SaLT need before proceeding?"

"Where is Cinderella?" Greg asked.

"He resides with his parents, codenamed King and Queen, and teenage sister, Prince Charming. The address is 312 Park Lane, here in town. Most nights, he hangs out in the garage with his friends, smoking reefer. The friends will be designated US One, US Two, and so on."

"US, boss?" Greg asked.

Delta grinned and said, "Ugly Stepsister One and Ugly Stepsister Two."

"Correct," Curtis said. "Ugly Stepsister One is a short Italian-looking man and Ugly Stepsister Two is tall, with brown hair."

Jamal asked, "Is this a Black Op, sir?" The group looked uncomfortable until Jamal smiled wryly, and gave them permission to laugh.

"Yes," Curtis responded. "The family cannot know that we were there. Mayor Bennett is concerned about optics when the trade delegation arrives, so we'll show her that we can provide security that doesn't look like security."

"Got it," Jamal said, but he looked unhappy. Jamal liked big guns that made noise.

Delta raised her hand before she spoke, "We using Walkies, sir?"

"Minimal."

"Do they keep extra gas in the garage, Boss?" Franco asked.

"Unknown," Curtis said.

"Are the Principal or Perimeter individuals armed?" Jamal asked.

"Unknown."

Topaz wanted to contribute, but was afraid she would say something stupid.

Franco asked, "Did Cinderella and the USs smoke all the weed?"

There was a pause and Topaz wondered what Curtis would do. Maybe if she joined them for breakfast, she would understand the joking shorthand of this group. Greg chuckled, then Curtis and Delta guffawed. Greg smiled at her and Topaz felt an unfamiliar sense of warmth.

"No intel on that, pothead. Positions as per your training." Curtis rose and asked, "Any more questions?"

Greg asked, "Any Skels in the vicinity?"

He neatly licked two fingers and extinguished the candle of Topaz's belonging. She had not heard that word since the bus. Would the others notice if this Skel used her father's knife to stab Greg? Just a little? Topaz imagined the fresh-faced guy across from her with one hole in his chest with one knife sticking out of it. Franco met her eyes and shook his head, a tiny "TL would notice a stab wound in Greg" message. Topaz pushed the anger down. It fit nicely next to resentment and loneliness.

Referring to Mages by derogatory terms like "Toothless" and "Skel" ran contrary to the Community Integration section of the Bloomington Town Charter. Both names originated as a result of the toll that the use of magic took on a Mage's body. Mages frequently lost teeth and were slender. Racial slurs were forbidden in Bloomington, but prejudice found an escape. Topaz had noticed that Greg avoided close contact with Jamal. He had brought his own prejudices to Bloomington and probably learned new ones.

Jamal's hands played a frenetic jazz song or disassembled a weapon.

"Mage," Curtis dropped the word into the silent circle. He stared at Greg. "Mage presence is unknown."

"That's not the name for," Greg turned to Topaz and Franco, "your people? How should I refer to you? Is Mage okay? Should I use the word Mage?"

She was not sure whether she believed his confusion, but Topaz shook her head and said, "We call ourselves Canopians."

"Most Americans use the word Mage," Franco added, "which is acceptable."

"This mission is good practice because we have to secure the house and the garage. When the Trade Inspector arrives, we will need to secure two locations on the regular. As we practiced, Jamal and Delta, you're Perimeter Support. Keep eyes on the principal and surroundings. Jamal, get your ass on a roof nearby and watch our six. Your tag is Bang. You're only there for "end of days," last resort shit, you hear me?" Jamal nodded regretfully. Curtis gestured to Delta. The heavy woman seated next to him did not wear the gray SaLT sweatsuit. She preferred high waisted jeans and flowing caftans, but she was deadly with a club. "Delta, you're with Jamal on PS, but in the van. Your codename's Sunny. Do what you do and control our environment."

Topaz realized it was no coincidence that the cafeteria was empty. Did they always have strategy discussions at breakfast? SaLT had become a team without Topaz. No wonder Franco was angry at her all the time. Regret lingered in the air along with the sweet scent of syrup.

"Delta, the van's prepped for eyes and a possible ghost if we get in a bag of dicks."

Greg turned to Topaz with raised eyebrows. When she shrugged, he said, "Curtis said the van has all of the equipment for surveillance and ready to move if we get in trouble."

Topaz had the feeling that Curtis was doing this on purpose.

He smiled and continued, "I'll be in the field with Topaz on this one. Code name Tonka."

Tonka, as in Tonka Truck. Topaz looked down and fiddled with the crumbs from her corn muffin, careful to keep her expression neutral. Curtis was in charge of transportation and could hotwire, drive, and repair any sort of vehicle. He was also big and wide, like a Tonka Truck.

"Okay folks, that covers Perimeter Support. Per two location protocol, the garage and the house, Static Protection and Close Protection are working close together. Franco and Greg, you're Static Protection. Your job is—"

The rest of the team finished the sentence, "—Prevention."

Curtis said, "Right. If we have to fight or shoot—"

"—it's too late. SaLT failed," the others finished again.

"All right, wiseasses. Franco, recon and logistics. Code name, Ghost. Also, you're 2iC, second in command. You got big ba—eyes and manage the team well." There were nods of agreement from around the table. Jamal stared morosely at his food, but that did not mean he disapproved. He was morose and food was in front of him. "I go tits up, you're Ops Chief."

"You got it, TL," Franco said. "One more thing, sir. I know you said no casualties, but you want me to distract the Ugly Stepsisters in the garage?" Franco asked.

Topaz smiled down at the table. Franco wanted to fight.

Curtis shook his head, "Negative." He pointed at Greg, the team's communications specialist, "Code name, Talky, run comms from me and Delta. Gem and I are Close Protection. We're the last line for every mission. As a team, we'll get the kid out safely with the Royals none the wiser. Easy out, easy in, just like my second ex-wife. Got it?"

There was a chorus of "Yess!" and a "Hell, yeah," from Greg.

"Okay, team. We spend the next few days prepping and then we do this at 2200 Saturday night. Now, classroom and hand to hand. Dismissed."

Curtis picked up his clipboard as SaLT fell out. Jamal and Topaz followed, carefully creating distance between one another and the others to avoid the expectation of conversation.

Curtis cleared his throat, "Bang, Gem, a moment?"

Gem. That was her. Topaz looked longingly after the others. Franco looked back at her and smirked. Topaz and Jamal sat back down.

His chair squeaked when Curtis leaned back. He rocked back and forth as he leafed through papers. Jamal thrummed his fingers on the table. The noises bounced around Topaz's skull before echoing in the room. She measured her breath to prevent a sigh from escaping.

Topaz hummed a few bars of "Hey Mickey," but felt silly, so she stopped.

Jamal lightly tapped out the melody for "Hey Mickey" with his index and middle fingers. He did not smile or meet Topaz's eyes. Curtis read and wrung tortured screeches from his chair. A white-clad worker poked her head in the doorway, murmured "Sorry," and withdrew.

Curtis scrawled a signature, tucked his pen under the metal clasp on the clipboard, and banged his chair down. "What the hell is wrong with you two?"

Topaz and Jamal flinched and both murmured, "Nothing, sir."

"Do you understand the purpose of Bloomington? Any idea how important SaLT is? We are a mixed, some might say *diverse*," he said the word with a sneer, "group of individuals charged with protecting one of the most important people in the country. The economy of America depends on us and," he leaned over the table and stared into each of their eyes, "I believe in what we're doing. This is bigger than your chip-on-the-shoulder, outsider, victim bullshit." They remained silent. "Bang, what's our job?"

"To protect the Principal at all costs, sir," Jamal said.

"Who's the Principal, Gem?" Curtis asked.

"The Trade Inspector and anyone our C.O. designates, sir."

"Bloomington, especially SaLT, represents what can happen when we put aside our differences. We prove the bigots and separatists wrong. We're more than people with a job to do. We're a team with shit to prove. Everyone on God's green earth is watching. Some want us to succeed, to show the world that Canopians, black people, and women are an integral and respected part of America, but most people, you know what they want?"

Topaz was trying to make sense of what Curtis was saying. He believed in Bloomington, but it was all a facade, a fake community for the benefit of the trade delegation. Could it be real or were there Offcrofters who were duped just as much as the Mages? Did Offcrofters really believe in this place? Curtis said "we." Maybe he wanted to help others.

"This is not rhetorical, Gem, answer me, what do most people want to see?"

"Sir, to see us fail," she said.

"Some people believe this is fake, arranged for the trade delegation, but I believe in Bloomington and in America's willingness to do the right thing. We can hold our noses and get through it, like my first wife when we had sex, or we can show the assholes that doing the right thing is good for America. Bloomington might be an escape for you, but I volunteered for this gig." Topaz looked up in surprise and Curtis continued, "Yeah, Gem, I left a post with the Secret Service in Egypt to head the Security and Logistics Team in Bloomington Town in the Land of the Pilgrims Pride. Go ahead, ask me why?" Topaz opened her mouth to ask but he spoke over her, "Because I love America and Jesus Christ, in that order. The Pledge of Allegiance says, 'One nation under God,' and Jesus told me to love my neighbor. So, it pisses me off when I see you two act like jackasses and squander the god given chance to love your neighbor."

Topaz kept her face neutral. The people that Jesus saved confused her. Hank was so saved that he abandoned his family.

Curtis turned to Jamal, "And you, Bang. Why in Sam Hell are you here? You volunteered. For what? To sit on the sidelines and watch?"

Jamal was silent.

"Well?" Curtis prompted. "Why'd you come to Bloomington?" He jerked his head toward Topaz, "Because, unlike these exploited fuckers, you had a real choice."

The room was silent. Topaz did not breathe, for fear of catching the men's attention.

Jamal met Curtis's eyes and said, "You read my file."

File, Topaz thought, files have information. Her story was in a file. Did the file explain why Crystal Far-Eye Tenkiller drank and slept under Canopus after Coral's death? How was Coral's death listed in the file, spontaneous combustion or suicide? Was Amber's location in a file? What if Topaz's file made sense of her life?

Curtis's voice was gentle as he continued. "Yes, Jamal, I've read your file. You were honorably discharged in 1981, but once a Marine, always a Marine. Unemployed, divorced, food stamp recipient, from Overtown, Florida. Has Miami rebuilt after the riots a few years ago?"

Jamal's hands stilled. "No, sir. We haven't recovered from the protests."

What was the difference between a riot and a protest? What was in Jamal's file? Johnson was America to Topaz. But, what if Curtis was America? What if other Offcrofters wanted to help, like Curtis? Maybe America had wounded others, like Jamal. What if it was unfair to hate every Offcrofter? Learning about individuals was more difficult than hating all Offcrofters.

"Now, that's a shame." Curtis was absorbed in thought for a moment. Banging pans and the sound of water sounded from the kitchen. The boss shook himself and spoke, "You're both to set aside your justified moral outrage and be an active member of this team. I can't yell the racism out of SaLT, but I can tell you two to shape the fuck up. That's an order." He picked up his clipboard. "Dismissed."

Topaz rushed to catch up to Jamal outside the cafeteria. "Hey, Jamal," she called, "wait."

Jamal kept walking, his long strides took him to the exit. Topaz ran to enter his zone of civility, the ten second window of time when it's rude to shut the door on an approaching person. She thought good manners would compel him to hold the door and she was right. Jamal sighed, but waited for Topaz. She had no idea how things worked and needed information.

"Can we talk for a minute?" Topaz asked as she approached.

"Sure," Jamal said, "But I'll tell you right now, I don't date white girls."

"Do you talk to white girls? Exchange words and ideas?" she asked. White girl. Yet another category. She was a Mage and a Tenkiller. She was poor and now she was a white girl. Why did Jamal choose not to date women of a different color? Topaz was not attracted to men without magic, maybe it was like that.

He nodded and jerked his head toward the sidewalk.

She smiled, "Promise you won't run?"

"Just hurry." Topaz went through the doorway and he asked, "What?"

"Does everyone have a file?"

"A file?" he asked.

"Yes, a file. Your story. Does everyone have one?"

"Of course, you have a file," Jamal said.

"So, my story's written? My family's story? Does America know the ending?"

"How would they know the ending?" Jamal laughed "It's not really a story. It's more of a record, a list of what's been done to or for you."

"Like, of places you've been, family members, jobs? You have one, Curtis even read it. How do I get mine?" she asked.

"What's the big deal about your file?" He leaned back against the brick wall. "It already happened. It's history."

"Jamal," Topaz's voice rose in frustration, "I'm not from here. Forget what you think I know and explain it to me."

"Okay, your file has medical records, birth certificates, physicals, psych evals, immunizations, that sort of thing. If you're here, you have a thick one," he said.

"Where is my file? Can I get it?"

"Probably at the Town Center." He turned and pointed down the block at a tan brick building. "Bloomington Government Offices are there. We're military, so you have a file here."

"Do they separate the Canopian and Offcrofter files? Do they separate the files on black and white people? Can I read someone else's file?"

"Now, why would you want to—never mind. I don't want to know." They were silent for a moment, then he said. "You know, I never thought about separating the files like they do people. I think they keep them all together, Topaz."

Two people slowed and looked at Jamal and Topaz as they entered the building. Across the street, a stout man with a cane stared.

"What are you looking at?" Topaz yelled at the man, "I have a work permit." She turned back to Jamal, "Are all files kept at the Town Center, or just people who live in Bloomington?"

Jamal's lips curled up in a smile, "You really don't know, do you?"

"I told you, I don't know anything about my file."

"I mean you don't know about racism, do you?" he asked.

"I've been locked on a croft because of my race. We don't have people of your color, but I've read about slavery, if that's what you mean."

Jamal shook his head and looked down at the sidewalk. He spoke so softly that Topaz had to lean forward to hear. "You don't believe TL, do you? That shit about making things better?"

Topaz leaned back against the brick wall next to him, mimicking his nonchalant pose. "I thought this was a fake place to fool the Inspector, but Curtis means what he says. He's the first Offcrofter I've met who cares about Mages."

Jamal nodded, "Yeah, I've heard it all before. Still...," he let the thought linger.

"Yeah, still," Topaz murmured.

Jamal abruptly pushed off the brick wall and walked away.

Chapter Fifteen

"Enjoy today, ladies and gentlemen, it will be your last chance to dress like a human being. After you receive your formal uniforms, you will be just as uncomfortable as me." Her powder blue suit and light blonde hair were effervescent in the fluorescent classroom lighting. Mayor AnnaLeesa Bennett nodded at the Security and Logistics Team arrayed in front of her.

The group chuckled.

This woman was everything Topaz wanted to be. Gleaming blonde hair, the ruffled shirt that peeked out of her blazer, and the coquettishly crossed heels were all distinctively American. According to a pamphlet Topaz had picked up in the Post Office, AnnaLeesa Bennett was a renowned Mage authority chosen by the Bureau of Land Management to oversee the development of Bloomington, New York. It also said that she was responsible for the successful program to bring various crofts into the Twentieth Century. Did that mean that she was the one who forbade the Old Ways on Macbeth?

"I will paraphrase Team Leader Curtis's colorful description of you because I dare not repeat what he said in front of the camera," she nodded at the videographer standing a short distance away. "Suffice to say that he is proud of you."

Curtis stood off to the side in a blue dress uniform, rather than his usual short sleeved greens. He stood straight, hands tucked behind him, his back precisely one inch from the wall while the mayor addressed his team.

The mayor beamed at them and dimples bookended straight white teeth. The woman had dimples, too? Topaz had never worn heels, but she was sure her rangy figure would not look good in them. How did the Mayor get her hair to bounce like that? Was it VO5? Something nagged at Topaz as Annaleesa Bennett's hair fell to cover one eye. Topaz's tongue strayed to the place where her canine tooth used to be. She had seen the mayor before, but where?

The team's eyes were riveted on the mayor as she continued, "His pride is well placed, because you, SaLT, have been entrusted with a sacred mission, that of protecting Inspector Thistlewaite, the head of the International Trade Federation. As you may or may not know, 1987 has been designated the International Year of Mage People by the United Nations. The Inspector is touring various countries, to ensure that Mages are treated with respect and are fully integrated into society. Once Inspector Thistlewaite certifies that we have complied with the MPR4759, Magical People Resolution 4759, we will renew our membership in the very profitable International Trade Federation. You, ladies and gentlemen, are the "U. S. New Day for American Mages Plan" in action." The mayor beamed at the five people in front of her.

This did not make sense. Topaz looked sideways at Greg. He was nodding at the Mayor. Curtis and Jamal were listening carefully, but Delta's brow was furrowed and Franco's face was tight. They knew Mages were not treated respectfully. They were prisoners on crofts. Glancing at Franco's stony profile, Topaz wanted to sneak behind his barrier. Was he thinking of Macbeth right now?

"At 8 am next Thursday, Inspector Thistlewaite and her staff will arrive and spend two days touring Bloomington. They will be in the capable hands of you, Bloomington's very own Security and Logistics Team. This team shows what is possible when Americans and Mages work together, building a future based on trust rather than fear."

Greg nodded and slapped his fist into his other hand and the Mayor flashed a brighter watt smile at him.

She sounded like Curtis, sincere and passionate, but that smile nudged Topaz back to a dusty parking lot. A fragment of memory, disconnected from experience or context. Her tongue worried the gap in her mouth. She had seen that smile before, but it was different.

"Now, the Inspector may ask you questions, but I ask that you refrain from interacting with the Inspector or her staff. Do your duty, the job for which you were trained, at which each of you excel, and leave the negotiations to the bureaucrats. After all, talking is all we're good at." She chuckled, then Mayor Bennett sought the eyes of each of the six people in the room. "I am right in this."

Everyone leaned forward, eyes focused on the mayor. Topaz nodded. The mayor was right. That memory hid in the horizon of Topaz's thoughts. The bouncing blonde hair and wide blue eyes were right, but the smile was wrong. It was supposed to be different, empty.

"You may respond with brief general responses that focus on the future. Do not discuss past conditions on the crofts. I am right in this." She turned to include TL in her beaming gaze.

The mayor was right. Conditions were primitive on Caesar and Macbeth had been destroyed by the government, but Topaz was not qualified to speak about such things. The mayor wanted Bloomington to be successful and she needed Topaz. She basked in the compelling gaze of AnnaLeesa Bennett. The blue eyes, the grooved dimples, golden hair that fell in big waves to her shoulders.

The memory, a snapshot of an image, approached. The vision from the night at the bar with Crystal, the bouncy hair and empty smile. Topaz's tongue worried the gap in her mouth. Canopus grace, the woman in Crystal's vision was the mayor and she was Canopian. The thought freed Topaz from the tidal pull of the mayor's words. "I am right in this," was a Charm. The mayor had Charmed her and was still Charming the group.

Topaz took a deep breath through her nose and inhaled Delta's campfire scent. She smelled yeasty doughnuts from down the hall and the mayor's strong perfume, but no magic. The mayor did not look like a Canopian and her magic did not smell like magic, but Mayor AnnaLeesa Bennett was a Canopian from a Charmer family. She had Charmed SaLT. Greg was taking notes and Jamal's hands were still.

A strong will tugged at Topaz. How did a Canopian become the Mayor of Bloomington? The mayor was right in this. Topaz should listen to her. The mayor of Bloomington was a Canopian and she wanted what was best for those with magic.

The mouth was empty of teeth, but this woman had straight white teeth. Why pretend to be an American if she wanted to help her people? The blonde hair must be dyed, somehow the mayor made her eyes blue, and dentures restored a Master Mage's smile. Topaz's eyes narrowed.

The mayor benevolently surveyed the group. Her eyes swept past Topaz. Then returned and focused on her.

Topaz blinked and gave the wide-eyed appearance of rapture, but rage whirled inside of her. She had to be sure. It would also be nice to Take some Charm, but Topaz's containers were full. She sidled under her tarp and went to the Mayor's Magical Chamber. She was confronted with a white solid wall. Topaz heard a scuffle and put her ear against the wall. Muffled sobbing. Topaz rushed back behind her tarp. She had never heard magic cry.

"I'm right in this," the mayor repeated. "I know Team Leader Curtis has a rigorous day planned, but I have also heard that Canopians have prodigious appetites."

Mayor Bennett was a priestess and the Security and Logistics Team her acolytes. Greg called out, "You got that right, Mayor."

"To that end, I arranged a mid-morning, productivity boosting snack to compensate for the loss of instructional time," she turned to Curtis, "Team Leader, I hope I did not disrupt your day too much."

Curtis smiled and waved his hand in front of his face, "Not at all. Thank you, Mayor."

* * *

Franco gestured at the empty chair across from Topaz. Yesterday, after speaking to Curtis, Topaz had made an active effort to join the team. When she had eaten lunch with SaLT beneath an oak tree at the training center, rather than on a bench with a book, he had even stopped glowering at her.

Topaz smiled and Franco plopped a heaping plate on top of the red and white checked tablecloth and sat. The mayor's staff had transformed a classroom into a bakery, complete with yellow flowers on each table.

"Franco, do you ever feel—"

"—guilty about all this?" He gestured at the table in front, where muffins overflowed rustic baskets and croissants were arranged in a sunburst pattern.

The memory of her mother sifting worms out of the flour before baking congealed the cheese Danish in Topaz's mouth. She took a drink of coffee to dredge the memories from her throat to her stomach.

Franco said, "Me being hungry won't help Macbeth."

He understood the hopelessness of staying and the guilt of leaving. Topaz had never had a conversation with Franco that did not involve strategy or close combat techniques.

The room buzzed with greetings and conversation as other workers stopped in to take advantage of the mayor's brunch, filling plates, settling at tables, and chatting with colleagues. Were they all Charmed? Did anyone in this room know that Annaleesa Bennett was a Canopian? Topaz searched Franco's eyes. Was he Charmed? At least he remembered Macbeth as it was.

"The mayor's a great speaker, huh?" Topaz ventured.

Franco nodded. "We need to let the talkers do the talking. That's not for me, anyway." He ate half of a glazed doughnut.

"What if the Inspector asks about Macbeth? What will you say?" Topaz asked.

Franco said, "I'm not...talking isn't my..." he stopped chewing and his eyes widened.

The mayor entered the room with Curtis, laughing as they went to the bakery table.

"Will she tell the trade delegation about hunger? That we are born, struggle and starve, and then die on the croft?"

"The Old Ways are forbidden on Macbeth. Now, we have loss and Remnants. But," he lowered his eyes to his overflowing plate, "the future looks great. The mayor is right in this."

Topaz would not be another person telling him that she was right, but Franco had to realize what was happening here. Topaz split a roll in half. Crusty on the outside, soft as cotton inside. She chewed and waited for Franco.

He finally met her eyes. Franco mouthed the word, "Charm," and Topaz nodded.

"Canopus Balls, how'd you know? She's so beautiful. I mean, you know, blonde and—do you know what this means?"

"Canopian," Topaz whispered. "We can't talk here. Don't let her catch you alone."

The mayor and TL stood a few tables away, near Greg and Delta. The mayor spoke and they nodded avidly. Curtis sat down to talk to them, but Mayor Bennett moved on and spoke to a table of technicians from the floor below.

"So," Topaz channeled Joy and spoke brightly, "meeting the Inspector. Exciting, huh?"

"Yes," Franco responded, "although we can't lose sight of the mission."

At the table next to them, the mayor spoke to Jamal. He was reading a thick book with the words "One Shot-One Kill" emblazoned on the front. The mayor laughed and Jamal did the unthinkable, he smiled.

In a cloud of Jean Nate`, the mayor descended on Topaz and Franco. "And here's the rest of SaLT. May I?" She sat before either of them could reply. "How are you adjusting?" She tucked a stem of baby's breath deeper into the glass vase on the table.

She is beautiful, Topaz thought. She understood why the mayor would pretend to be an Offcrofter, look how far she had gotten. Did she know that the Old Ways were forbidden on Macbeth? She had to. Every Canopian understood that the Old Ways were necessary for the survival of the Canopian race.

"Bloomington is wonderful, ma'am," Franco answered.

"Yes, great." Topaz echoed.

"Tell me about yourselves. Where are you from? I'm sure I've been briefed on this, but there are so many details," she smiled conspiratorially at them.

Topaz pushed aside the image of an empty glistening mouth and concentrated on the mayor's full white smile. She had to pretend to be Charmed or the Mayor would be suspicious.

She peeled her lips back into a smile. "I'm Topaz, from Caesar."

Franco said, "I'm Franco, from Macbeth."

She felt a tug; a light pull at her feet. It was easy to recognize the Charm now. The mayor had been dealing with Offcrofters and unsuspecting Mages for so long she had forgotten how to finesse magic. A Tenkiller did not insult others with half-assed spells. Topaz had seen Franco's work, his magic was powerful, probably from necessity. Because of this blonde woman sitting next to them.

"The crofts are isolated, but idyllic," the mayor said.

Sheet-covered windows and the scent of burning garbage were not idyllic. Nor was the apathy that made fences and weapons redundant.

"Tell me about Macbeth Croft," the mayor said to Franco.

"America took the Old Ways, and now we hide," Franco spoke dispassionately

Was he charmed? Why did the mayor want to know about Macbeth?

"The Old Ways are a relic from Canopian history. It is time to leave superstition in the past and embrace the modern. Americans have a microwave in every home and telephones in their cars, yet Canopians still sing to their dead." The mayor stared at Franco as she spoke, "Tell me about Macbeth, then put the past behind you. I am right in this."

It was a small thing, but mayor Bennett used the word, "Canopian," rather than Mage.

Franco said, "We hide from our neighbors and Remnants."

Topaz glanced between Franco and the mayor. He had the slack face of the Charmed and she was engrossed in what he was saying.

The mayor said, "No, start from the beginning."

"The Offcrofters took our Soul Basket and dismantled our Death Bier. We were careful, but there was a First Death. Letitia Notafraid was 90 years old and she had a heart attack. My mother and I tried to give Notafraid a Fire Death, but soldiers threatened to Galvanize us. Mrs. Notafraid was the first Remnant," Franco sighed deeply. "We began to hide in our homes with the lights on. Eventually, Notafraid ambushed Rebecca Warmhands while she was fetching government cheese and powdered milk for the Extras."

"Mrs. Warmhands?" Mayor Bennett asked.

Franco nodded slowly. "She died trying to feed the Extras, what we call abandoned children on Macbeth. Then there were two Remnants, then four, until, desperate for bodies to shelter in, Remnants overran us."

"What about James Heartsnake? Do you know him?"

Why was the mayor so interested in Macbeth? Something rustled at Topaz's barrier. She thought of that empty mouth and tightened her tarp.

"I've heard of him." Franco's eyes were far away. "Heartsnake lives outside of town, by Revival Creek; my mother wouldn't let me swim there with my friends."

The mayor shook her head and spoke in a chipper voice, "America has supported Macbeth Croft during this epidemic of mysterious deaths. You, all the residents of such a backward place, must appreciate America's help. I am right in this."

Topaz met the mayor's blue eyes and steeled herself to prevent her own from rolling. For Burnt Magic's Sake, the epidemic was not a mystery, it was Remnants. No twitching of her lips or narrowing her eyes, she could not allow anything but Charmed to enter her expression.

"Now that I live here, I appreciate what America has done for me. Am I correct in saying that I also value my Mage upbringing?" Franco asked.

He was fooled by her Charm. Franco was better than this, certainly his magic was more powerful than the crap Bennett was pushing.

"The Inspector would expect you to value your heritage," the mayor told Franco, "while expressing your gratitude for America."

"You're right in this," Franco agreed.

The mayor turned her high beam smile on Topaz. Charm stroked her barrier and tried to sneak a finger inside.

"Now, Caesar Croft was a thriving community until the unfortunate Tenkiller Rebellion sixty years ago. Since then, the largesse of America has repaired the infrastructure and provided vital resources to the Mage population after Tenkillers attacked unarmed Americans and turned on their own people. One step in repairing American and Canopian relations is putting this behind us. To that end, I have hired a Tenkiller. I am right in this."

The Charm scratched at Topaz's barrier. Not the pitiful scratch of the cold and desperate, but a wicked slashing at her barrier. Topaz clamped her mouth shut so she did not defend the Old Ways or the honor of the Tenkiller Family. The silence dragged.

When the mayor narrowed her eyes at Topaz, Franco kicked her under the table.

"You are right in this," Topaz muttered, but the mayor's gaze did not ease.

The mayor stood and patted Franco's shoulder, "It was a pleasure speaking with you." AnnaLeesa Bennett raised her chin and looked down at Topaz, "I will follow your career closely, Ms. Tenkiller." She moved to the next table.

Topaz used the tip of her finger to pick up crumbs from the table and deposit them on her plate. Why did it bother her to tell the mayor that she was "right in this"? She had already abandoned her family; it was too late for pride.

"So, the team's going to meet at the Paddock on Wednesday before the delegation arrives." Franco hesitated, "Are you going?"

The mayor was using her cheap charm to rewrite the past, one Mage at a time.

"Yes," Topaz said. She wanted to show Curtis that she was a part of the team.

"Topaz," Franco cleared his throat, "want to go together? To Paddocks?"

"What? Oh, sure," she said.

"Want me to walk you over?"

"It's on Main Street, right? It's okay. I know the way." She could go past the bus terminal to see if there was an off-Friday delivery.

"Maybe we can hang out together? Before or after, I mean," he said.

"We should probably make an early night of it, with the delegation coming the next day."

"Jesus, Tenkiller, you're thick. You want to go together? I'm asking you out."

Franco's dark eyes sought hers. She had never seen him look like he cared about anything before. Could he like her, even after what he had seen on the bus?

She smiled, "Yes, let's go together."

The mayor's Charm must really have affected him. Why else would he ask her out? He had kicked her to make her speak, would a Charmed person do that? On the other hand, he hung on the mayor's every word. The dazzling blonde was lingering at the next table. What were the accountants saying that was so interesting? Topaz wanted to be alone with him to find out if Franco was Charmed.

"You going to eat that?" He pointed at half a croissant on her plate. "The mayor's something. We're lucky to have someone who knows Mage Culture. The croft was exquisite, but we must remember to be suitably grateful for America's bounty. " He winked at her.

Chapter Sixteen

Curtis put them through punishing Close Combat after breakfast with the mayor. They took a brief break before two hours of Special Skills practice, then he dismissed SaLT's "sweaty asses to get their ball gowns." Now, Topaz wanted nothing more than to get out of her new uniform, take a shower, listen to "The Housemartins," and go to sleep, but it was Friday. So, despite the late hour and the heavy wardrobe bag slung over her shoulder, Topaz was trying to look natural when she made the turn off of Main Street to see if Johnson was at the bus station.

Besides the navy pantsuit she wore, two black, a tan, and a gray suit were in the plastic wardrobe bag she carried. There was also a slender burgundy dress and an honest-to-god black satin ball gown in the bulky bag. All with damn shoulder pads. Topaz appreciated the thoughtful design of her "uniforms." The pants had a sheath for her knife sewn into the hip and there were inner pockets sewn inside her blazers to hold a slender thermos and flashlight. SaLT was to accompany the delegation at all times while they were touring Bloomington, so they were each provided with specially designed business attire to blend in with government officials, trade specialists, and corporate executives. She preferred her own uniform of worn jeans and loose fitting polo shirts or even SaLT's gray sweatsuit, but Topaz noticed the way Franco and Greg's eyes widened when she entered the conference room in her form-fitting dress "uniform."

The street was empty in the industrial area behind Main Street. She stopped at her usual spot, a shadowy space between an auto repair shop and a lab that made dental appliances, and set the wardrobe bag down. She wiggled to loosen the stiffness in her shoulders and leaned against the brick wall. The bus station remained dark, the carport where the bus had discharged Topaz thirty-plus days ago was empty. There was no movement behind the smoked glass windows in front. She now enjoyed being outside at night, so she stayed and watched in the dark.

The bus terminal remained empty. Bloomington was a quiet town and very few cars passed. She would try again next Friday. Topaz rotated her neck to loosen the cramp from the wardrobe bag. She picked up the bag, slung it over her other shoulder, and headed back to her room. If Joy was home, maybe she would ask for some magical sleep assistance. Joy did not mind using her power to help, and it was necessary. Topaz had a mission tomorrow night and still had nowhere to sleep.

Headlights from behind Topaz lit the sidewalk, swept right, and then disappeared. Topaz kept walking away from the Bloomington Bus Terminal and the headlights. A vehicle had turned into the station. Was it a bus with Johnson or the "Mothers Milk" truck from last week?

Topaz was passing, "Big Poppa's: No Credit? No Problem," car lot. There was a row of maybe half a dozen cars next to the sidewalk. She ducked and knelt between a Honda CRX and an Oldsmobile Cutlass, hung the wardrobe bag from the stalwart Oldsmobile's side mirror, and peeked over the Honda. She had a good view of the terminal's back parking lot.

No bus. Instead, the white refrigerated truck idled while a chubby man limped over to unlock the gate to the bus terminal's back lot. A month ago, Topaz would have assumed he was Johnson, but she had learned that there were many chubby men in America. The driver, not Johnson, heaved himself back into the truck, drove in, and left the gate unlocked.

Why was that milk truck here again? Something was happening. Her knife was reassuringly snug in its built-in sheath. Topaz drank water and put the flask back into the inner pocket of her blazer. This was the perfect time to use Swifthart's magic. Taken magic was difficult to control, so Topaz probably had about five minutes. She went to the spot near her heart and lifted her tarp. Her Magic Chamber was dusty. The Offcrofters discouraged Mages from using magic unless it was for work, so she had not played in a month. She practiced SaLT skills, rather than magic.

When she tested for her work permit, the officials were pleased with her power. Taking power from another, and using it, was rare. Topaz did not tell them that she could store three powers in her magical chamber. She opened the glass container with Merelyn's stolen speed, but left Henry's simmering red magic and Coral's cotton candy bright power in their uneasy truce on her windowsill.

Topaz inhaled and a frenetic energy rose inside of her. Hurrying was easy now. The sidewalk and road were empty and the darkness hid her from eyes inside the bus station. Loud beeps sounded from the terminal. The truck was backing into the loading dock.

She took a step toward the back gate. The pavement blurred beneath her when she zipped down the road. Topaz shook her head against vertigo and focused on the unlocked gate. Then, she slammed into it. Topaz staggered and caught her breath. Maybe Merelyn wasn't as stupid as she looked.

The driver's door opened and the man got out and stretched. Topaz froze. Although he did not look her way, she was glad she had chosen the navy suit and dark, pinstriped, linen blouse to wear home today. The man said hello to somebody and climbed the three steps to the loading dock. He paused at the top to rub his leg.

She slid through the gate and closed it behind her. This time she chose her stopping place carefully. There was a spot to the side of the raised loading dock, near the truck,where the overhang of the dock hid her from view from inside the terminal. The only risk of being seen was in the passenger side truck mirror. She would be out of sight and able to hear what they were saying. Her feet dragged a little on the pavement of the parking lot as she almost flew to the corner between the loading dock and the terminal. This time she landed perfectly. Merelyn's speed had tired her. She could stay here and listen. Topaz crouched and leaned back against the dock.

Then her intestines twisted into themselves. A humming crescendod in her ears. It cut off when her stomach clenched tight. Topaz grasped her midsection and swallowed the vomit that rushed up. Her jaw clacked shut. She heard herself making gasping noises. Her body started to shake. Topaz grasped Merelyn's magic and looked at the Oldsmobile, but only saw blurred pavement. She slammed into the front of the car and collapsed.

* * *

She woke up curled into a ball between the two cars. Her head pounded and there was a small pool of yellow stomach juice next to her. Sine Wave Stimulation.

Chapter Seventeen

Spandex panels sewn into the black slacks of her suit made it easy to move, but the stockings were strangling her body. Topaz rubbed her back against the exterior wall of Cinderella's garage to ease the nylons out of her butt.

Team Leader Curtis whispered into her ear, "Pull your panty hose outta your ass later."

He must have heard her move against the wall, because it was too dark to see. Delta had arranged for the clouds to loiter in front of the moon.

"Sorry TL, oops, I mean Tonka, my skin's suffocating," Topaz whispered. She had to remember to use code names only on this mission.

Curtis's biggest wardrobe worry was whether to wear the red tie or blue tie. Maybe she should stick one of those ties up his ass and tell him to pull it out later, she thought. Canopus balls, the shoulder pads felt like they covered her ears. While she was listing complaints, her stomach still ached from the SWS last night.

Topaz, Curtis, and Greg crouched in hedges by the side of the detached garage. On the other side of the driveway was a white two-story colonial house. It looked like something from a TV sitcom, with the porch swing and matching terracotta pots full of colorful tulips.

As soon as Franco reported the layout of the garage and confirmed the location of Cinderella and the Ugly Stepsisters, TL would give orders and Greg would relay them to Perimeter Security. She could not see PS, but Delta was watching the area from the van parked a few houses down. She glanced up. It was too dark to see the neighbor's dormered roof, but Jamal was up there somewhere, watching the house through the night scope of his rifle. As in life, observing from a distance.

Franco had been in the garage for three minutes. Five minutes was the top range for magic for most Mages. Why was he taking so long? It should have been a quick recon.

TL turned to Greg and whispered, "Two more minutes, Talky. Then, on my signal, Gem and I are going in. You watch our six here."

"Copy," Greg responded. They were giving Franco two minutes before Topaz and Curtis went into the garage blind. Greg would relay the info to Delta and Bang.

With night vision goggles, all-call Walkie, and 3M, Greg was eyes on the ground for magical and human problems. Her shoulder pads were bulky, but at least Topaz did not have a heavy machine strapped to her back. The 3M was the size of a small vacuum, but heavier. Greg had told her that the prototype was as big as a refrigerator and just as heavy. It did not make sense to have a bulky machine on a protection detail, but the Offcrofters were proud of their technology and frightened of Mages. There was also a 3M in the van, one of the many buttons, levers, and dials that TL proudly pushed, pulled, and turned. However, TL was quick to tell them, the SaLT van was not equipped with Sine Wave Stimulation.

Franco could take care of himself; he had invisibility and was adept at hand-to-hand combat, but he did not have much magic left before he spiraled. What if he was in trouble?

When TL shifted, Topaz lifted her blazer to check that her knife was snugged at her hip, and Greg lifted the Walkie to his lips.

A door at the side of the garage opened and a sliver of light and noise cut into the driveway. Loud male voices drifted out and then quieted when the door closed. Topaz smelled the magic sweat scent and smiled.

TL jumped when Franco appeared on the other side of Topaz. Magic was still relatively new to him, Greg, and Jamal. The Mages avoided using it to conserve energy and because it scared the Offcrofters.

Franco took his flat black thermos from the inner pocket of his suit coat, leaned back against the wall, and drank deeply before speaking.

His whisper was strained, "Cinderella, US One, and US Two in the left corner working on a motorcycle. Garage is 16 by 20, concrete. Station Wagon parked directly in front of the side door, good for single file cover. No visible weapons, but wrenches, hammers, and such. A red container, possibly gas, located under the workbench." Franco took a gulp of water before continuing, "Stairs in the back right corner, third one creaks. Three-room apartment, bathroom to the right of the kitchen. A brunette, we'll call him US Three, taking a shit. One entrance, one egress, fire code violation."

"Damnit. Four men, two locations. Change of plans," Curtis whispered. "All ears, Talky. We gotta get Cinderella out of the garage quietly. Gem, Take juice from Ghost. Talky, you're with me and Gem while Ghost watches our six here. Sunny, weather support and prepare to beat ass out of here. Bang, cover us. No noise or corpses."

Greg said, "Roger," and murmured into the Walkie to convey TL's orders.

Curtis gestured to Franco and Topaz. "I'll ruck up while you do your voodoo." He moved further down the wall to give them privacy and looked around the corner. There was nothing to ruck up, but Curtis was respectful of magic.

Franco gestured toward Topaz's breast. At her shocked expression, he grinned and said, "First thing's first. Drink."

"You were a Watcher, weren't you?" Topaz said. She reached into the inner pocket of her blazer for her thermos and drank deeply.

After she emptied her thermos, Franco took her hand. Normally, Takers required contact with another Canopian in order to acquire their magic. Topaz could do it from short distances, but that was another skill she had not disclosed nor shown on her intake exam. As she held Franco's hand, she was glad. His hand was warm and dry and he had a callus on his thumb. Franco was the first person Topaz had touched since Johnson. This was a job, Franco's warm hand and solemn gaze were work, she reminded herself. Maybe she could Take a little extra Franco Magic to keep a part of him inside her. Topaz blinked and shook her head. Where did that come from?

"Do I have your permission to Take?" she asked.

Franco responded with the customary, "Canopus Grace."

She tapped her index finger against her heart and he did the same. Franco's solemn acceptance of her into his most private place made Topaz ashamed of all of the times she did not ask for permission to Take.

The barrier to his Magic Chamber was battle scarred and solid. The age-sheened oak door was dotted with iron spikes jutting out and the bottom was charred from fire. Thick metal bars extended from a black iron lock in the center. The lock turned and dust thickened the air as the door opened. When was the last time his barrier was breached? Taking from Franco would be impossible, but he was giving.

Heat and the scent of cedar assailed Topaz. An intense red fire raged inside of a black and red Soul Basket in the center of Franco's room. She stood in the doorway. His fierce fire honored the Old Ways. Topaz murmured, "Death and life exists within, " before entering.

There were yellow torn maps on the wall. She leaned against his stone wall and she peered at a familiar map, yes, this was a map of Caesar. Next to it was one labeled "Macbeth." Similar maps of Othello and Antony were on the opposite wall. Near the door to the chamber, a white, unwrinkled map was tacked to the wall. Topaz recognized the post office and bus station. It was a map of Bloomington.

She wanted to linger and explore this hushed chamber, but now was not the time. Topaz did not dare get close to the fire. She inhaled and Franco's sunshine scented magic expanded and filled her. Topaz was accustomed to

Taking, but she had forgotten the fullness of sharing. Magic had not been freely given to her since she was a Lil' Killett.

When she left, the lock clacked the heavy bars back into place behind her. Topaz ducked under her tarp and her Magical Chamber seemed faded, left out on the clothesline too long. She deposited his magic into a container and left her chamber.

"Death and life exists within," Franco said. He released her hand, but cedar lingered.

"Death and life exists within," Topaz whispered. As they slid along the wall to Curtis and Greg, Topaz unobtrusively pulled the stockings out of her backside.

Curtis whispered to both of them, "Gem, use Ghost's juice and keep watch while Talky takes care of the shitter upstairs. Gem and I will separate the principal from the others. Ghost, rest up and watch our six out here. Talky, relay, then comm silence."

Greg, Topaz, and Franco gave Curtis a thumbs up.

She clenched the muscle behind her heart. Franco's magic leapt and Topaz's body disappeared. Magic required sacrifice. Controlling Taken or Given magic was exhausting. She could use Franco's Invisibility for about eight minutes before Magic Overload.

Everything looked the same unless she looked down. She could not see her feet or her arm as it reached for the doorknob. She felt the cold round knob of the garage door beneath her hand and watched it turn, but could not visually connect it to her body.

Topaz eased into the dim, grease-scented room. She left the door open a crack and ducked behind the wood paneled station wagon in front of her. Then she remembered there was no need, she was invisible. Topaz stood tall and raised her fist like Rocky Balboa, because she could.

A hanging bulb spotlighted three men in the back left corner, just as Franco said. A man with dark hair in a blinding white T-shirt and jeans knelt next to a motorcycle, Ugly Stepsister One. Two men in denim jackets stood behind him, watching and passing a joint back and forth. One had blazing red hair, so Topaz figured he was Cinderella and the other was a nondescript blonde, US Two.

All three men laughed at something US One said.

Topaz jumped when a wrench clanged on the concrete floor. She looked down at her hand and concentrated. It reappeared, floated in the air, clearly visible. She poked her hand out through the crack in the door and crooked her index finger. Curtis and Greg came in low and quiet and crouched behind the wagon. Topaz pointed to the back left corner and held up three fingers.

The men were engrossed in what US One was doing. Topaz made a whirling motion with her visible hand and Greg crouched and ran. He disappeared up the stairs without a sound.

"Hand me an Allen wrench," US One ordered.

Cinderella's hair blazed in the light when he leaned over the open silver box on the tool bench. His hand hovered over the tools. "Uh, Henry, which one is that?"

"Help him, Patrick," US One muttered from his spot on the cement floor.

"Sure, Henry," red and blonde heads hovered over the tool box.

Greg was taking care of US Three upstairs. Topaz needed to separate Cinderella from the other men, then she and Curtis could get him to the van.

"Got it, guys?" US One looked up at the other two. "Come on, I can't wait all night."

Topaz stepped around an old lawnmower and ducked under bicycles hanging from the ceiling to get closer to the men. She needed to give Talky time to get upstairs and incapacitate US Three.

"Sure," Cinderella picked up a tool and handed it to US One.

"No, dude, that's a screwdriver."

"You said screwdriver, right?" Cinderella asked.

There was a loud thump from above.

"What the hell?" US One murmured. "Your friend upstairs can't handle his beer. He better not be yakking in my apartment."

"I'll check on him," Cinderealla said, relief in his voice. He started toward the stairs.

Topaz held perfectly still when he walked past her. He burped and giggled. It smelled like beer. She could not allow him to get to the stairs. If Cinderella went up to the apartment, it would be impossible to get him out of here without alerting the others.

"Get me that wrench?" US One was, once again, intent on the gleaming bike.

US Two bit his lip and rummaged in the toolbox.

Cinderella was almost at the stairs when there was a knock on the garage door. He turned and hissed, "Guys, it's my parents. Hide the beer."

Keeping an eye on the door, US Two covered the case of beer with a black jacket. US One rose and flapped his hands to clear the air of the smell of marijuana.

"I'll check," Cinderella said. He walked toward the door, back toward Curtis.

Greg was upstairs taking care of US Three and Curtis had separated Cinderella from the others, now Topaz needed to do her job. Franco's magic was tiring, but she had to distract the Stepsisters.

Topaz ran and tugged at the large silver toolbox. It would not budge. She pulled as hard as she could, grunting with effort. US Two looked in her direction. His eyes widened in confusion when he stared at the empty air.

The box did not move. It was anchored by the weight of the tools inside. There was another thump from upstairs. All three men looked up.

"What is going on up there?" Cinderella asked. "Okay, keep it quiet, I'll try to get rid of my parents."

She had to time this carefully so that the stepsisters were distracted, but Cinderella was on the other side of the station wagon. Topaz slapped both hands on the metal toolbox and pushed one corner with all her might. Finally, it slid toward the edge of the bench. Just as Cinderella rounded to the other side of the station wagon, Topaz gave a mighty push and the tool box flew off the table. It crashed to the floor, scattering silver tools and small oily items.

The Ugly Stepsisters jumped.

The garage door opened and Curtis dragged Cinderella outside.

Topaz steadied herself against the table. Controlling Franco's magic took a lot out of her.

"Damn it! What the hell are you doing?" Us One shouted as he bent to right the toolbox.

"Weirdest thing, something pushed it off the bench," US Two said. He knelt to help pick items up from the floor.

"You did it," US One scolded. "You smoke all my pot and do stupid shit."

Topaz walked to the stairs on trembling legs. Us One continued to harangue US Two and there was the clink of tools behind her.

A thump of footsteps sounded from upstairs. Had US Three gotten away from Greg? A wave of dizziness hit Topaz and she used the rail to pull herself up the stairs. She had the strength to stay invisible for about two more minutes. The third stair creaked as she went up. She froze and looked back. US One grabbed a steel wrench and headed toward the stairs. Behind him, US Two hefted a hammer and followed.

Topaz's head throbbed and her throat was dry. Her job was Close Protection with Curtis, but she could not leave Talky here against three guys.

As the first man entered the narrow stairway, Topaz braced herself using the handrails on either side and kicked down with both feet. She struck US One in the collarbone. Her position from above, and the man's own momentum, flung him back into US Two. Both men fell backward and sprawled at the bottom of the stairs.

"What the hell?" US Two scrambled out from under US One.

US One said, "Someone pushed me, I swear to God."

Topaz could not manage Franco's magic any longer. If this extraction was to be secret, she had to get out of here. She vaulted down the steps over the men and rushed out of the garage.

The night was silent after the echoey garage. Topaz went around to the side and leaned against the wall. The daggers of Magic Overload stabbed her. Franco's magic struck her tarp and fled. Topaz hoped that Curtis had secured Cinderella in the van.

She tried to control her breathing and squinted into the darkness. Her eyes had not yet acclimated, but a round shadow pooled beneath the oak tree. It could be Delta. Topaz looked toward the house. It was quiet and dark. The garage behind her was also silent. What was happening to everyone else?

Without comms, there was no way to know if the dark silence was good or bad. TL had to know that she was out and okay. A faint scent of campfire smoke drifted toward her. Topaz used the last bit of her strength to crouch and run to the tree.

When she got close and saw that it was Delta, Topaz almost cried. She knew it was the approaching Magic Spiral, but homesickness paralyzed her. She released the futile clenched heart muscle and, like an abandoned marionette, collapsed to her knees. Her blazer and slacks were drenched in sweat.

"I'm here, hon," Delta whispered. "I'm here."

"Talky's," Topaz spoke between heaving breaths, "in trouble."

"I'll help him." Delta rubbed Topaz's back. "You okay?"

"Fucking shoulder pads," Topaz murmured.

Delta handed her a thermos and Topaz guzzled greedily. Delta whispered, "I saw when you Took Ghost's magic and when you released it."

Topaz scoffed, "Released? It kicked my butt and escaped."

"Gem, nobody can use Taken magic for that long. Tonka and Ghost have Cinderella in the van. Can you walk?" Topaz nodded and handed Delta the empty thermos. "Okay, I'll help Talky. You get to the van."

The night air chilled her sweat drenched hair and clothes, but it cleared her head. She rose slowly and dragged herself toward the road. When Topaz glanced back to see if Delta was okay, she saw a streak of lightning flash near the garage and branch in jagged directions. The door banged open and the Ugly Stepsisters leaned out to look, mouths open wide. The ground vibrated when a mighty crack of thunder sounded.

Topaz was just passing the house when the porch light came on and spotlighted her. The front door was flung open. Topaz was too exhausted to do more than walk quickly.

A voice behind her said, "Stop, or I'll shoot."

Topaz stopped.

"Now, turn around, slowly," the voice said.

The voice was high, that of a woman. As she turned, Topaz grazed her hands past her hip, palmed her knife, and slid it up the sleeve of her blazer. Turning was an act of will she forced from her magic-overloaded body, but she could find energy to use her knife.

A small woman in a white sweater stood at the top of the stairs. She held a gun.

The woman's face was in shadow, but her size and straight, chin-length black hair looked like Amber's. It was the sister she had missed for two forever-years.

Topaz stepped forward and whispered, "Amber."

The woman ordered, "Stop there! Hands above your head."

Her voice was low, not high like a ringing bell. Her face was pitted, not smooth like Amber's. She was a coarse version of Amber, but not Amber.

She stopped. Topaz felt the knife against her wrist, hilt at hand.

"Now, where's your Commander?" the Amber look-alike asked. "I need him and you're going to get him for me."

Topaz smelled Mage sweat and a tap at her barrier. Someone was trying to get in. It was the woman. She was a Mage.

Topaz nodded toward her pocket and said, "I have to use my Walkie to contact him."

She heard the scuff of a shoe behind her and Franco's voice whispered, "Go right."

"Franco—," Topaz whispered.

"Fucking go right," he said.

Topaz threw herself on the grass to the right.

"Stop!" the woman shouted.

She pointed the pistol at Topaz and fired. Concrete from the sidewalk chipped into the air and a loud bang disrupted the night.

On the porch, one of the ceramic pots filled with tulips rose behind the woman. At the same time, a pop sounded from above and red bloomed on the sleeve of the woman's sweater. The flowerpot slammed down on the woman's head. She staggered back against the wall of the house and slid to the porch.

From behind her, Topaz heard shouts. The Ugly Stepsisters. She froze.

Simultaneously, lightning splintered the sky and shots were fired. Topaz heard a cry of pain. Then, the van jumped the curb and pulled up next to her.

Delta and Greg ran from the side of the garage, heaved Topaz up and dragged her to the open side door. Hands pulled her inside the idling van and she smelled Franco.

Another jagged brilliant of lightning lit the sky as Franco appeared on the seat next to her. Curtis drove the van slowly away as lights flicked on in neighboring houses. A shadowy figure detached itself from a towering oak tree and sprinted to them. Jamal climbed in and closed the side door and the van accelerated away from the quiet neighborhood.

"Well," Curtis said from the front, "that was catfu."

From the back seat, Greg muttered, "Completely and totally fucked up."

Chapter Eighteen

Topaz was tightly sandwiched between Jamal and Franco in the middle seat of the van. She pushed against them to turn and look back. It was hard to find the shadowy profiles of Greg and Delta among the disorienting red light Flash Gordon galactic background of SaLT's weapons and machines. There. Their shadowy profiles were on either side of the zip-tied, hooded Cinderella. The man was silent, so Topaz assumed he was gagged as well as bound.

"Ghost, did you kill her?" She just had the presence of mind to use his code name in front of the prisoner.

"Maybe. I hit her pretty hard with the flowerpot." Franco's voice rose with uncharacteristic excitement.

Topaz knelt in the space between the two front seats and grabbed TL's arm while he drove. "Go back. She asked for you, TL."

"Sit down." Franco pulled at Topaz, but she refused to sit.

She turned and shook Jamal's leg. "Did you kill her? Is she dead?"

Jamal shrugged. "A bullet in the arm won't kill her. Mighta done some nerve damage."

"This is bad enough," Curtis said. "We can't go back."

"We're done," Greg said from behind her. "We got the package."

"Turn around, Tonka. Go back. Now!" Topaz yelled. Loud objections bounced around the van. Dots of red and white light winked at her from the front.

"Gem," Curtis met her eyes in the rearview mirror. Everyone quieted. "We'll figure out what the hell happened and why later. We have to deliver the package now."

"Where is Canopus?" Topaz said. She scrambled over Franco to look out the window.

Delta smoothed a loose strand of hair back behind Topaz's ear. "What's wrong, hon?"

"That woman is a Mage," Topaz said.

"Fuck!" Franco punched the seat in front of him.

Curtis turned around, "Knock it off! I'm trying to drive."

"See, Mages can carry guns," Jamal said smugly.

"No," Greg gestured at the 3M pointed at Cinderella, "I would've known."

"She was in the house, Talky, how could you? For burnt magic's sake," Delta said. "Tonka, we have to go back."

"Copy that," Curtis sighed. "It's a bad idea, but I'm turning around."

Greg said, "Tonka, just because they say to turn around—"

Curtis cut him off, "Trust your team, Talky. Sunny, can you—"

"Roger that," Delta said and a cloud skittered across the moon.

Curtis turned off his headlights, did a K-turn, and accelerated back toward the house in the darkness provided by Delta. Franco handed bottles of water to Topaz and Delta and the Mages drank.

"This exercise was screwed and I'm going to find out why." Curtis looked in the rearview mirror and asked, "If that woman's a Mage, I assume you three have to do voodoo to or for her?"

"If she had the First Death, the woman must have a Fire Death to release her magic. Then we will follow the Old Ways to return her magic to Canopus, from which it came," Delta said.

Franco muttered, "It cannot become a Remnant."

"I don't know what on God's green Earth you just said. She's a Mage and asked for me and had live ammo and Bang used his live ammo and we got fucked with a big dick. Talky, stay with the package. Check for company, monitor channels for info, and be ready to ruck up. Bang, recon the garage. Flash a light when it's secure. Any trouble, use the Walkie, not your gun."

"Wilco," Jamal muttered, then "damn."

"I'll take point with the wizards." Curtis eased behind a car a half a block down from the house and parked. On either side of the street, lights were on and there was the sound of dogs barking inside a few of the houses. Curtis leaned forward and peered through the windshield. "Why's the house and garage dark? Bang didn't kill the garage guys, so they should've alerted first responders. No sirens, nada."

Topaz reached over Jamal to open the door.

Franco pulled her back and whispered, "You're SaLT first and Canopian second now."

Curtis got out of the driver's door of the van and stiff-armed a gun next to his thigh. His head was on a swivel as he came around and opened the van side door. Keeping a watchful eye on the prisoner, road, and house, Jamal eased out of the van. He turned to cover the van while the Mages exited. Greg attached Cinderella's zip-tied hands to a hook in the back and then moved to the driver's seat.

"Fall out and watch your six," Curtis whispered.

They approached the house from the road, staying in the shadows of parked vehicles to shield SaLT from peering eyes. Jamal peeled away from the group and went to the garage. The rest stopped behind a boxy Ford parked near the white colonial house.

Topaz nudged Franco and pointed. A faint purple light glowed near the horizon. Canopus rose, even in America.

"Sunny," Curtis whispered.

"Roger," Delta said and sour magic replaced her campfire scent. Clouds skittered aside, leaving moonlight to illuminate the porch. The broken planter and forlorn yellow tulips were the only signs of a disturbance.

The woman's white sweater gathered the moon's rays. She lay still.

"Ghost," Curtis whispered, "Porch, then report"

"Sir," Franco's response lingered after he disappeared.

"Sunny," Curtis prompted and the moonlight disappeared.

"Tonka, maybe the Canopian's alive. Let's help her," Delta urged.

"We'll know when Ghost gets back."

Delta hmphed. Topaz's tongue worried the empty space in her mouth. What if the Canopian was dead? A Remnant could reanimate her within a few hours.

A throat cleared behind them and Franco appeared. He held a gun between his thumb and forefinger and gingerly handed it to Curtis. "Here, Tonk, she was still holding it. The Mage's alive, but that head wound's bad."

Curtis put the gun in his waistband and said, "Secure the house and flash the porch light when A-OK."

Franco disappeared, and the front door of the house opened and closed.,

They waited quietly. A light flashed on and off from the garage, briefly illuminating a basketball hoop and driveway. Curtis gestured and left the cover of the car. Topaz and Delta followed and joined him under the oak tree between the garage and house.

Jamal ran across the driveway to join them and whispered, "They un-assed it. Garage and apartment are empty."

The woman on the porch groaned.

Curtis asked, "What can you tell me, Gem?"

Topaz clenched the muscle beneath her heart and loosened the tarp. A jagged mirror stood outside her chamber, reflecting shadowy grief. She considered taking some of the Mage woman's magic, but like drugs, it was dangerous to take what you did not understand.

"Some sort of reflecting power," Topaz said. She did not say that the woman had reflected Topaz's dearest desire, to see Amber.

Franco appeared next to them. Curtis jumped and Jamal muttered, "Shit."

"House empty, boss." There was a smile in Franco's voice

"Cover me," Curtis said. "I'm going to find out why the woman was asking for me. Then you all do what you need to do."

"You may want to take Gem with you," Franco murmured, "for the magic."

Curtis motioned to Topaz. Their bodies cut geometric shapes in the moonlight when they left the shadow of the oak. Jamal followed and trained his gun on the woman's head through the porch railing.

Curtis knelt next to the still figure. Topaz stood behind him and took a deep breath. No scent of magic. Up close, the woman looked nothing like Amber.

"Miss?" Curtis said. The Mage remained motionless. "She awake?" He asked Topaz.

"Unknown." Topaz couldn't tell if a Canopian was conscious, only if they had magic.

Curtis lifted the woman's arm, held it above her head, and let it fall toward her face. Her arm swerved and landed on the wooden porch. "She's conscious." He spoke to the woman gently, "Miss, why were you looking for me? Why did you try to shoot my officer?"

The Mage shook her head. Deep grooves of paler skin cut a swath from her nose to her chin. She mumbled, "Watch...Mayor wants you gone...find the Randy bartender...the Board."

The woman's magic swirled wildly. She whispered, "Life and death exist within."

"Boss," Topaz said.

"Answer me." Curtis shook the Mage's injured arm and she groaned.

Topaz grabbed Curtis's shoulder and pulled, but he refused to move. A soft white glow outlined the woman's body. Rising heat cooled and formed a halo of mist.

Curtis pointed, "Look at her. She's like an angel. What's happening?"

"Fire Death, TL. We have to move," Topaz said.

The Mage said, "Go."

Franco vaulted onto the porch and pulled Curtis upright. "Fire Death, Boss."

"What do you mean—" Curtis began.

"Come on!" Topaz shouted.

The panic in their voices reached Curtis and he followed them down the steps to join the team under the oak.

"What the hell are you doing? We should administer CPR," Jamal said.

Yellow orange flames erupted from the middle of the Mage's chest. She screamed once, and then the flames spread and she was silent.

"Sunny, put out the fire," Curtis said.

"No, Boss," Delta murmured. She stepped closer to Topaz and Franco. They murmured, "Canopus shall welcome you," in unison.

Topaz watched the flames rise, striving toward Canopus. Did anyone say those words for Crystal Tenkiller? She thought of the woman her mom was before loss battered her. Her own faith in the Old Ways was because of her mother's lessons. Flames doubled and wavered in the tears that filled Topaz's eyes. Not knowing was harder than mourning the death of her mother.

As suddenly as they began, the flames extinguished. A shroud of ashes lay on the porch. A pulse of red, like a heart, flared in the center of the ashes.

"Thy vessel is empty," Delta spoke in a sigh.

"When they cremated Percy Bysshe Shelly, his heart wouldn't burn either," Curtis said.

They were silent for a moment.

When Delta spoke again, her voice had returned to its low beauty, "Franco, find something to use as a Death Bier. Topaz, figure out a Soul Basket." She looked up as she spoke. "Hurry, Canopus won't be around much longer."

Curtis asked, "How can we help?"

"Watch our six," Delta said.

Topaz walked around the side of the house to find some sort of container. What would work as a Soul Basket? This would be haphazard, but community was the most important ingredient to any ritual and, thanks to Curtis, they had that. Her eyes fell on a clay geranium pot on the porch, a twin to the one Franco had smashed. She tilted the heavy pot and tulips spilled into the hostas alongside the porch. Magic is hell on landscaping. She listened to the murmur of conversation behind her as she scraped dirt out of the pot.

"What the hell?" Jamal asked. "That girl was on fire."

"The Fire Death," Delta said. "I don't think her injuries were fatal. She chose to die rather than tell us what she wanted with Tonka. Her body's finished. Now, we tend to her magic."

"Magic?" Jamal said. "I don't see nothing but ashes."

"Right, why don't we watch and learn," Curtis said. He and Jamal kept a wary eye on the street, but also on the Mages.

Topaz looked for something to use to wipe dirt out of the clay pot. In Caesar, there was laundry on the line, rags and yellowed insulation littered porches, but not here.

Topaz ripped the shoulder pads out of her blazer and cleaned the pot with them. Delta rose and went into the house. Dancing flashlight marked her progress through the building until she returned with a clinking handful of glass jars. Delta hummed a Witching Hour Chant as she scraped a jar along the red embers as she spread them to cool. She groaned as she knelt. Gray ashes puffed into the air.

Franco came back to the porch and said, "There's no goddamn stone here. Why's everything so clean in this town?" At their looks, he said, "I found a wooden bench."

"That's our Death Bier. Set it up for Canopus," Delta said. Franco went back around the house.

Curtis and Jamal divided their attention between the road and the porch as the women used the jars to scoop ashes into their clay pot Soul Basket. A breeze rustled the budding branches of the oak tree and flared embers red. Topaz tried to finesse a rectangular coal into her Mason jar, but it would not fit. She shrugged off her blazer and used it as an improvised pot holder to get the larger pieces of the Mage into the clay pot.

"Dammit, Gem, you're going to pay for that," Curtis called from the bottom of the steps.

Delta and Topaz managed to get most of the ashes and embers of the dead Canopian in their improvised Soul Basket.

"Canopus is low. I'll find Ghost," Topaz said. Delta smiled her assent.

Topaz went into the dark yard and called softly, "Ghost?"

"Over here," his low voice was part of the night.

She followed the sound. He had arranged a small bench in the corner of the backyard, next to a border hedge. She crouched next to the low bench, angled her head up from where the Soul Basket would be, and gazed up at the tiny purple planet. Topaz moved the bench an inch, checked the position again, and knelt next to it.

Franco settled in next to her and peered up. "I can see it now, but I don't know how to find Canopus when it's cloudy. Why are the women in charge of birth and death?

Topaz took his hand and pointed it upward. "Follow the arc to Arcturus, speed on to Spica, leap like a cat to Canopus. I've found that, in America, you go this far below the North Star and this far from the horizon. See, there? Purple Canopus is beckoning."

The murmur of the others grew closer and Topaz dropped his hand. Curtis and Jamal placed the heavy clay flower pot in the center of the bench where Delta directed, then backed up a respectful distance.

"Ready?" Delta asked. She looked at the other Mages and they nodded.

Curtis cleared his throat behind them. "Uh, do you mind if I say a quick prayer? I think, maybe, a kind word to Jesus may ease her way."

Prayer can rip a family apart. Topaz opened her mouth to refuse Curtis's hesitant question. He had no right to pray for a Mage.

As if sensing her thoughts, Curtis hurried on, "I don't want to intrude and if it's not appropriate, I understand. I'm a man of faith."

There was silence. The grass rustled when Jamal shuffled his feet.

Topaz wondered how she would feel if she were denied the Witching Hour Songs.

"Please?" Curtis asked simply.

Franco exhaled, "Yes."

Jamal bowed his head while Curtis spoke quietly. "We commend thee to Almighty God. Ashes to ashes and dust to dust. Lord, shine thy face upon her and give her thy gracious peace. Amen."

Topaz was grateful for the simple beauty of Curtis's words. She turned to look at him. He left his head bowed for a moment. When he raised it, he said, "Thank you."

"No grinding the bones or poisoned fruit?" Topaz asked.

Delta elbowed her in the ribs. She said, "We do this for an honorable Fire Death."

"We do this for the Old Ways and a woman who showed courage when she pointed her gun at me," Topaz added.

"She stood tall until I hit her with a clay pot," Franco said.

A white light rose from the clay pot Soul Basket.

"What the fuck?" Jamal said.

"Purple Canopus Calling, May your magic die with you," Delta sang in her smoke soaked alto. *"First Death, Fire Death, Our Soul Basket Offering."*

The light from the pot stirred.

"*May your magic die with you*," the Mages sang together.

A thread of love spread from Delta, through Topaz, to Franco. Canopus pulsed impatient purple and the ashes skittered in the pot like leaves on a deserted street.

Their voices rose through the heavens to a star. "*May your magic die with you.*"

Silver light swirled above the pot, circled, dipped. A sparkling ribbon shot above their heads and over the trees, a silver string connecting the Earth to Canopus. It faded and SaLT was left in darkness.

* * *

When they returned to the van, Curtis motioned for Greg to drive and climbed in the passenger seat. Topaz and Franco sat in the back on either side of Cinderella, while Jamal and Delta took the middle seats.

Franco grinned, "That's what I'm talking about."

Delta said, "Canopus Grace, I never get tired of a beautiful return."

"What happened, guys? What'd I miss?" Greg asked.

Curtis cleared his throat before he answered Greg. "She used death fire, right?" he turned to look at Delta.

"Fire Death," she supplied. "May your magic die with you."

Topaz and Franco echoed her.

"For real? That's too bad. It would've been cool to take two of them to Barbie," Greg said as he pulled smoothly away from the curb.

Although his hands were secured on the metal loop in front of him, Cinderella threw his body from side to side. He slammed into Topaz and she hit the side of the van before she could brace herself.

"Secure him," Curtis yelled.

There was nowhere he could go, but Cinderella flailed wildly. Franco put his elbow at the other man's throat, but he would not stop moving. Topaz threw herself on the man's legs to stop him from kicking.

"He's going crazy," Greg said from the driver's seat.

Jamal and Delta knelt, reached back, and pushed Cinderella's shoulders against the seat.

Cinderella's struggles weakened and he wheezed for breath beneath the hood.

Delta said, "Franco, hon, he needs air."

"Oops, aw shit," Franco said. He eased his forearm off. Cinderella breathed raggedly, but remained still.

Topaz looked up at Jamal, Delta, and Franco. "What was that about?"

They passed the Town Center and Curtis gave Greg directions to drive around the block. He pointed to a tiny space between two buildings and Greg pulled into a narrow alley. They followed it between two government buildings and stopped next to a stairwell.

Curtis said, "I'll be back," and got out of the van. He walked up the brown metal steps and pushed a silver button next to the door.

Greg looked back at them through the rearview mirror, "Guys, what happened?"

"He was fine, and then he just lost it," Franco said.

Jamal raised his eyebrows, "You didn't say anything or do something to him?"

"Yeah, Bang, I bit the prisoner. That against the rules? Jeez, I'm really sorry," Topaz said.

Franco inserted, "No, we didn't do anything. Just like you and Greg didn't do anything when you were watching him. Because we are professionals, just like— "

Delta cut Franco off and held a hand up when Jamal opened his mouth. "We're the Security and Logistics Team. We are all professionals. He was calm until two minutes ago. Greg's right, something happened. What was it?"

Curtis opened the center doors and said, "Franco, you're with me to make the delivery."

Cinderella allowed himself to be led by Franco and Curtis up the steps. The door opened, an arm pulled Cinderella inside, and closed the door.

Chapter Nineteen

Adrenaline had come and gone. The hush of the conference room was deeper than the 2am quiet of an empty building. People in varying stages of sprawl were on the rectangular conference table.

With a curt, "Settle in," TL went to his office and closed the door. His voice rose and fell. Topaz tried to make out what he was saying, but the door muffled his words.

Delta handed out water, then rolled her caftan into a pillow and dozed. Next to her, at the short end of the table, Greg's head drooped to his chest. Jamal spread a flannel on the table and began to disassemble his gun.

After the phone call, there was silence inside and outside of Team Leader Curtis's office.

Topaz felt a drag on her spirit. She was in the well of overload. The light above her was far away and she was trapped by tiredness. With a great effort, Topaz raised her head from the table and rested her chin on her hand. She thought about the mission. From the moment she pulled her pantyhose out of her behind to the Fire Death of the Mage, her actions had ruined the mission. She should have helped Greg with the Ugly Stepsister in the apartment. She screwed up the whole thing when she thought the Mage was Amber.

Next to her, Franco leaned his chair back against the wall and closed his eyes. He, more than anyone, knew she had messed up, but he seemed less angry than usual. She examined his relaxed face. He was not the haunted man who boarded the bus in Macbeth. His military haircut accentuated dark brows and full lips and his skin had lost its Canopian paleness. Franco's starved ropy muscles had hardened to firm strength. And he was quiet. If he said one nice thing to her, she would cry in front of the team.

Franco mumbled, "You're weak. You need to practice more."

"Pardon me?" she said.

"You should've thrown your knife at her," he said, but he didn't open his eyes. "I've seen how good you are. You choked."

"Yeah, well your pain in the ass magic exhausted me," she retorted.

Franco smiled and murmured, "Dumbass."

How dare he call her weak? Anger replaced despair. If he said something comforting, she would cry, but he didn't.

She shivered in her white button-down shirt. She had shoved her ripped and ash covered blazer under the seat in the van, hoping that Curtis would forget about it. The knees of her slacks had rounds of mud. When did that happen?

When Jamal dropped his gun on the flannel cloth in front of him, Greg's head rose and Franco opened his eyes a crack, then they rested again. Jamal began to bore out his gun.

She had let these people down. For burnt magic's sake, how could she have mistaken that girl for Amber? Everyone in this room had done his or her part to make the mission a success, except her. She had to forget about Amber. Malachi needed help and her team counted on her and she needed this job.

Topaz tapped on the table in front of Franco, "Hey, about that girl..."

Franco shrugged, "I get it. My magic is too much for you. I can go all night. But you? You're just a girl. You'll do better next time."

"What the hell are you even saying? You're like two years older than me. I—" She stopped when a grin tugged the corners of his mouth. "Sure, you can go all night. Right."

She would rather Franco thought he was too much for her to handle than know that Topaz mistook the Mage for her sister. And he was flirting with her. She tucked her hair behind her ears, aware of the long tendrils that escaped the bun.

Franco pushed off the wall and leaned close to Topaz, "You're really a Tenkiller?"

Topaz froze. She went through The Giving Up Gate to make a new start in Bloomington. She wanted to deny her name, but Franco was on the bus. Everything she thought she left behind rushed back at her. Was her mother alive? Did Mal do the Old Ways? She felt Johnson's slick hands on her mouth again. The bus ride and tonight. She could no longer blame her failures on her family. Tonight was all Topaz, no Tenkiller.

"It's not a hard question," he said. "I'm Franco Lonespirit."

"Topaz Fareye Tenkiller," she said.

"Have you seen Memorial Park?" Franco asked. Topaz nodded her head and he continued, "It has a plaque commemorating all who fought in the Tenkiller Rebellion, Mages and Offcrofters. The Old Ways are worth fighting for. The Tenkillers are badass. "

"Really?" Topaz asked. She smiled. There was a plaque to honor her family? There were no plaques in Caesar.

Curtis's office door banged open and the group sat up straight. Delta had a red crease in her cheek from where she rested on her arms.

He yanked a chair out, turned it around backwards, and sat at the head of the rectangular conference table. The flag above him framed and punctuated Curtis's righteous indignation as he looked at each of them in turn. His face was red and a little vein throbbed in his forehead. "Okay, folks, what happened?"

Jamal quietly placed his disassembled gun on the table.

Now was a good time to be a Tenkiller. Topaz took a shaky breath and said, "I ruined the mission, sir."

Greg nodded, "It's true. Everything was fine until the Mage got her."

"You weren't even there, you were in the van," Delta snapped. "I'd like to see you react when someone points a gun at you. You couldn't even handle the one guy in the apartment."

"He's right, though," Jamal.

When Franco turned to yell at Jamal, Topaz ducked to avoid his waving arms. "Why'd you shoot the Mage? What's confusing about "no corpses"? I had it under control."

"With your flower pot?" Jamal scoffed.

"I'm just saying we can't lay this all on Topaz," Franco said. He turned to Topaz, "Although you did shit the bed."

Topaz nodded, "Agreed."

Greg said, "That guy upstairs was a beast. I needed help."

Delta scolded Greg. Franco and Jamal glared at one another. Curtis folded his arms and watched SaLT.

This wasn't a team. Topaz cleared her throat, "I could have..."

The arguments swirled around her. She could have ignored her dead sister. Put the mission first, remembered that Malachi needed her. Her tongue strayed to the gap in the front of her mouth. Her heart thundered in her chest as Topaz stood.

Franco closed his mouth. Delta nudged Greg and Curtis cleared his throat.

"I should not have used Franco's magic for so long. Next time, I will be more honest about my ability." Topaz said.

"That's a start," Curtis looked around the room.

Jamal stood and said, "Shooting the Mage was unnecessary. If I held my fire, we would've gotten out quietly." He shrugged, "I get tired of sitting shit out."

Franco said, "I'm 2iC. When things go bad, I need to be responsive."

"Team Leader Curtis, can we talk about why that Mage asked for you? About the Principal?" Delta asked.

"The woman, not a Mage, was rambling before she died. There's nothing to talk about." Curtis put his hand in front of his chest and pointed up with his index finger as he spoke.

Topaz's eyes followed his finger. Behind and above Curtis, the American Flag hung from a rod secured to the chalkboard. Tucked into the corner, obscured by the cloth, was a small black box. A camera. They were being watched. She did not betray emotion or look at the rest of the team, but their energy shifted. The animosity sank cloudy to the floor and they were united against an outside threat. A team.

"This is the shit, folks. Things went bad and we'll sort it out. Next time, it may be a dignitary or ambassador who gets killed. Our instructions were to extract the principal with no corpses and no noise. The results of this mission, ladies and gentlemen, are one dead woman, one ruined suit, three reported weather anomalies, and six "shots fired" calls to EMS. A team takes responsibility and you did. Tonight was supposed to be an opportunity to demonstrate our readiness to Mayor Bennett. Instead, Topaz shit the bed and you all rolled in it." He took a breath and blew it out hard. "Inspector Thistlewaite arrives in less than a week."

* * *

Topaz stood in front of the low boulder at Memorial Park. A low light shone from a nearby hedge and illuminated the engraved plaque affixed to the boulder. It said, "This simple memorial, raised by the United States Government, stands as a symbol of our admiration for Caesar Croft's sacrifice. In this hallowed ground, we remember the Tenkiller Family, a courageous group who ignited a rebellion to safeguard the cherished traditions and freedoms of the Canopian people. Their unwavering resolve in the face of adversity serves as a timeless testament to the enduring spirit of liberty. Dedicated on this day, Tuesday, September 20th, 1955." This was a memorial to her family and all of those lost in their rebellion. In the 1950s, her family had been honored. Did her father even know about this?

She hefted the paper bag she carried into her arms and slumped on a park bench away from the light. It was 1am and she had nowhere to sleep. She had showered and dressed in a gray sweatsuit at SaLT's gym, but sleeping anywhere at the Training Center would draw unwanted attention.

She rested the back of her neck against the bench and pulled the five-pack of beer close to her hip. It had been a six-pack, until she drank one on the way to the park. Topaz had never been a drinker, too many memories of her slurring, stumbling parents stood in the way. She was going to give drinking a try tonight, maybe then she could forget her longing for Amber. Maybe it would quiet her sorrow for her mother and worry about Mal. Luckily, Americans had difficulty judging the age of Mages, so she had stopped at an all-night convenience store and bought beer.

For some reason, the memorial made her feel worse, not better. The night was black, but little sparks of light punched their way through to shine for her, although she didn't deserve the little brilliants. Canopus was long gone, and the Mage woman's magic with it. One minute of wishful thinking and Topaz had screwed up the mission.

She was glad to give Joy and Mark some space tonight and it was not the first time she had slept outside. If she cocked her head just right, a streetlight across the road illuminated the words, "Tenkiller Rebellion," on the stone. Others had security and dignity, but she had a big rock. Her birthright. A slumberous heavy embraced her. She would never tell him, but Franco's magic left her with the aching chest and wobbly limbs of distance running.

Her body and mind were drained from the events of the night; the mission, the Witching Hour Chants, and antagonistic group discussion afterwards. Hotwash, she corrected herself. Greg said the discussion to clear the air after a mission was called a hotwash. Maybe her family should have a hotwash.

She gave in to self-pity. What had she accomplished while at Bloomington? She had not found Johnson, so he was still alive. She had not been able to do what the Border Control Agent asked. She reached for another beer. She had let her team down and disappointed Curtis, that lovely man.

"For burnt magic's sake," she murmured. "Pull it together."

A spring breeze cooled the damp hair that fell over her shoulders and hung over the wooden slats of the bench. Topaz felt ground, not pavement, under her feet. She patted the beer next to her and checked her knife. Magic curled tiredly inside of her.

Topaz's bolted up straight. She turned her head and sniffed, a rabbit testing the wind for a hawk. Underneath hoppy beer, she smelled magic. She clenched the sore muscle that controlled her magic and reached out. A battle-scarred door and safety. A strong, protective blanket of magic. She pulled a beer from the plastic ring and held it out. "Want one, Franco?"

There was a throaty chuckle and Franco appeared on the bench next to her. "I better save you from getting drunk, Gem." He popped the silver tab and slid it into the beer can.

"What? So I won't screw up another mission?"

Franco sucked the foam from the top of the red and white can. "Ugh, this is bad. Why didn't you ask Delta to cool this shit?"

"It's not always this bad? I'm not really a drinker." Topaz smiled. It was hard to be angry around this angry man. She raised her can, "To failure."

"Mage life," Franco tapped her beer with his own. "Want to talk?"

"Not really," Topaz said. She took a sip. "Do you want to tell me about Macbeth?"

"Nope. What's it like being a Tenkiller?" The stars dimmed a little.

"Nope, I don't want to talk about being a Tenkiller," she said.

"Says the girl drinking in a park honoring her family. Is Caesar a dry croft like Othello?"

"No, drunks don't plot rebellion. They're too busy fighting one another. We have mead at the Driftwood Lounge, but for a real drink you go to Justina Twoshades. Her Cactus Moonshine makes you weep. On the croft, we call it "Hairy Balls."" She finished her beer and grimaced. Topaz pulled another from the plastic holder and fiddled with the silver ring tab, but didn't open it. "I know why I'm out here, what about you?"

"A couple of reasons. I prefer to sleep outside and I wanted to check on you," he said.

"I'm fine." The breeze swayed her hair and chilled her back between the slats of the bench.

He pointed to the beer Topaz was holding, "You going to drink that?"

Topaz said, "I stop and think about each drink. If I really want it, I think again and then I usually don't drink it. Product of crappy alcoholic parents and all that. At least they taught me the Old Ways."

"It's been a year since they banned the Old Ways and Macbeth is shit." He took a deep drink of his beer. His hawk nose and slanted cheekbones seemed to be carved from ancient wood. "When we gathered ashes and sang the Chants to Canopus, guards Galvanized us. Ever been Galvanized?"

Topaz shook her head. "No, but Johnson Galvanized my mother when I left."

"Bastard. It tingles, then the shock travels through your body. By the time it hits your magic, right here," he took her hand and placed it below his heart, "it feels like fire."

Topaz pictured his chamber, the maps and the weapons, then she forgot what was underneath and enjoyed the solid warmth of him.

He continued, "Your heart stutters, maybe stops, from the shock, but that fire eats your magic. You feel it burning inside, but Fire Death is impossible because your magic is paralyzed."

She thought of her mother's contorted body and arc of her back. Her magic was on fire.

"There were only three of us who dared do the Witching Hour Chants for Thomas Redwind. They took our Soul Basket, so we gathered his ashes in a plastic bag and went to a gully, covered it with brush so they couldn't see us from above. Ben watched for soldiers and Remnants while Myra and I sang. They found us. We ran separate ways. I never saw my friends again. People disappear." He smiled wryly, "I guess I do want to talk about Macbeth."

"Only if you want to."

"I think I do," he said. "You know those stories our parents tell us? About the Remnants lurking in the shadows?"

"The one about Albert Bigpants when he doesn't listen to his parents?"

"The one about Naomi Dead-Not-Dead always scared the shit out of me and it's true. I saw it. Letitia Notafraid died of a heart attack and could not do a Fire Death. Her magic reanimated her. Have you seen a body Wasting? Her magic devoured her body within a few days and then we were left with her Remnant."

In the distance an owl hooted, or was it a dove? Topaz never could tell the difference, but it was not a cardinal.

"So, we stayed inside. The electricity kept us safe from Remnants, but it hurt our magic. We stopped caring; for the elderly and the sick, for the Old Ways. No children have been born on the Macbeth since the Old Ways were outlawed. Who wants to risk dying in childbirth or watching the untrained magic of an infant become a Remnant? Friends and family killed themselves from sadness while we hid in the light. The Old Ways tell us how to live and die, how to raise a family, the First Death, Fire Death, Final Death, so much." Franco stared at the monument. The light from the tombstone reflected in his eyes.

Topaz squeezed his hand. "May your magic die with you."

He smiled, a quick merciless smile. "Oh, it fucking will." Franco took a deep breath. "I'm glad to be here. They don't usually take Mages from Macbeth, but they made an exception for me. Turns out, if being Galvanized doesn't kill you, it makes your magic stronger."

She wanted to give Franco something. He had shared so much with her, trusted her with the ugliness he saw and the hope that somehow existed inside him.

"My grandparents are Joseph and Lucille Tenkiller," she said.

"Holy shit!" He looked like a kid who just opened a gift. "I knew it. They started a war to keep the Old Ways on Caesar. Canopus balls, Lucille hid in the desert for three days with her baby until they found her."

She nodded. “My grandparents both died because of the Rebellion they began.”

“Joseph Tenkiller was a visionary, you know? Everything he thought was going to happen, really happened on Macbeth. Mages are separated, from our magic and from other Mages. I never even met anyone from another croft until I came here. Divide and conquer weakened our genes. You notice there are fewer Mages than ten years ago? There'll be even fewer of us in ten more, and so on, until we're extinct.”

How had she thought Franco a quiet angry man? He was angry, but he was thoughtful and angry and vital. She squeezed his hand. “They don't feel that way about Tenkillers on Caesar.”

“Well, the Tenkiller Rebellion didn't get members of my family killed.”

He moved the beer from between them and put it on the ground in front of them. When Franco put his arm along the back of the bench, Topaz slid next to him. He smelled like clean cotton and warm sunshine.

“Topaz,” his voice softened, “what happened tonight? You were fine until you saw that girl. Something got to you. What was it?”

“You can't tell anybody,” she said. She could not risk the rest of the team thinking that she was unstable. When he nodded gravely, Topaz continued, “I thought she was my sister.” His silence did not judge her. She wondered about his family. Her bitterness and anger were a birthday candle to the fire raging on his croft. “Amber went through the Giving Up Gate two years ago and we never heard from her again. I thought that the Canopian woman was Amber. She was a Pleaser. She knew what I wanted and became my sister.”

Franco tightened his arm around her. She heard the hoot again and decided it was a dove. Her pulse quickened and she turned to Franco.

Franco's voice was husky when he spoke, “We have to report in a few hours. Can I walk you back to your room?”

Topaz did not want to be alone, but after what happened with Johnson and her failure tonight, Franco didn't want anything to do with her. The stink of failure followed people, she had lived that. She pulled away from him.

"No, I didn't mean inside. I'll just make sure you get—"

"It's not that. I don't have a room tonight. Joy, my roommate, and her boyfriend wanted to be alone." Topaz shrugged, "I'll find somewhere to sleep."

"Do you want my room? I don't sleep inside. I've had enough electricity for a lifetime."

"Where do you sleep?" Topaz asked.

He shrugged, "Different places. Mostly, here." He stretched his legs out in front of him. "Your name's on the sign. I guess I should let you sleep here with me."

Chapter Twenty

Topaz woke to the sound of birdsong. She opened her eyes slowly and took inventory. It was early dark morning and she had slept on a park bench. She smiled when she saw the paper bag with three unopened beers nearby and the two half-full beers on the ground. She was glad that Franco, like her, was not a drinker. She was warm in the nest of Franco's cottony scent.

The last time she woke up with another person was with Coral. Coral did not like to sleep rough or alone. She lived with Dad, but had a hard time living by his rules. She had to attend Sunday Service with him or he locked her out. He locked her out when she did not make it home because she was too drunk or when she made it home, but was too drunk. On those nights, rather than make the trek out to his trailer, Coral tapped on the glass door of the laundromat until Topaz let her in. She slept on Topaz's pallet in the back, and Coral was a cuddler. What did Coral smell like? All Topaz remembered were dusty ashes in a parking lot. Every time Topaz felt one good true moment, the Tenkillers ruined it.

Waking up next to this man felt good, but she had things to do; check the terminal, run, think about how to be better for her team, and write to Mal. Maybe Mark would loan her a pen and paper.

Topaz rose and Franco blinked up at her. She said, "I have to go for a run. See you later?"

"Hey," Franco murmured and held out his arms.

Topaz leaned down to hug him. She could stay like this all day. Something caressed her tarp and she pulled back.

"I don't know what you're up to," Franco said, "but you might need this."

Invisible Magic rushed into her Chamber and filled the lone empty container. Topaz looked into Franco's black almond eyes and pressed her mouth to his.

* * *

"Thanks for helping me out last night, Topaz. I like Joy so much. I know I'm not her normal type." Mark waited for Topaz to respond.

She signed the note to Malachi. She wrote every day, whether she slept in a bed or on a park bench. Her back hurt from the slats of the bench, but she felt...what was she feeling? Safe? Cared for? Mark eyed her over his Styrofoam cup of coffee until she gave him her full attention. He wanted advice and he was her friend.

She smiled. "No, her normal type is stupid and in a uniform." Her smile broadened as she stared at his blue postman uniform.

Mark leaned on the counter of the empty post office and met Topaz's eyes. "I know I'm not the only one she's seeing, but I want to be. I wanted to be alone with her last night because I like her, the way she laughs, the little mole on her chin, but..."

"But what?" Topaz considered him carefully and took a sip of her coffee before she spoke. "It's the mustache. You know what you have to do now, Mark, you have to shave it. I can help."

She thought of Franco's morning-softness. He looked so young without his sharp edges. Topaz's face still burned from his whiskery cheek. Her morning run past the bus terminal would clear her head.

"Screw you, Topaz. This bad boy is hot." Mark stroked his mustache. "Seriously, what should I do?"

"Okay, Mr. Postman," Topaz used her hand to wipe the smile from her face before she spoke. "Talk to her. Tell her."

"Just like that. Tell Joy I don't want her to see other people." Topaz nodded and Mark asked, "What if she says no?"

"The way I see it, there are three possibilities; things stay the same, you stop seeing her, or she does what you ask."

There was a long silence while Mark considered her advice. Topaz eyed the newest stamp. It had a picture of a young, handsome Elvis Presley on it. Even back on the croft, Topaz had heard about the controversy over which picture of the star to use on the stamp; this one or the bloated, sequined, Elvis that he became before he died at forty-two.

"You're really shitty at this, aren't you?" Mark asked.

"What?"

"Relationships," Mark said.

"I'm trying to be better." She folded the letter for Mal and put it in an envelope as she spoke, "I wasn't a good friend just now? I provided a factual statement of your options."

Mark mocked her, "A factual statement of my options? I want advice."

"Okay, how can I do it better?" She looked at him seriously. Behind the jokes, she wanted to know how to be a friend.

"Have empathy or pretend to. Talk about all I have to offer. Mention what a nice guy I am, how she would be stupid not to date me exclusively." He stroked his mustache, "Remind her how good this fella feels when I—"

She held up her hand, "Going to stop you there, Mister Postman." While she wrote her father's address on the envelope, Topaz sang, "Please, wait a minute, Mister Postman."

"Topaz," Mark said.

His serious tone stilled the Marvelettes' song on her lips. Topaz thought of the way Mark looked when she left him last time. Friends made time for friends, even if they would rather be running and thinking about a Macbeth Mage. She looked at him and asked, "What is it?"

Mark leaned across the counter and spoke quietly, "Not, now, but in a minute, look at the flag." He raised his voice and pointed at the envelope, "Check the zip code."

Topaz had written the zip code to Caesar Croft perfectly, and there was no need to look at the flag. She knew a camera would be nestled where the bracket met the wall, just like in the conference room. Someone wanted to keep a close eye on Mages, or was she being paranoid? Maybe someone wanted to keep a close eye on everyone. That someone was probably a blonde with too-perfect teeth.

When Topaz and Mark lowered their heads to examine the envelope, he whispered, "My coworker, Ruth, called in sick today. So, there's no one in the back. I'm alone. You can't tell anyone what I'm about to say. Promise me on your Soul Basket."

"I swear on the teal and yellow Soul Basket of Caesar," Topaz said. "May your magic die with you."

"May your magic die with you." He tapped the envelope that held the letter to Malachi and said loudly, "Sometimes these numbers are hard to read." He whispered, "This won't be mailed. I'm not allowed to send Mage mail."

Her jaw dropped. "Malachi didn't get any of my letters? Why?"

"Shhh, I'm not supposed to tell, but you're my friend. Every week, when I slot your letters, I feel your love for your brother, the worry for your mother, and hope. Then it goes into a fucking bin in the back that we send to the mayor. I can't keep doing this to you."

Mal thought she had abandoned him, just as they had been abandoned by Coral and Amber. "Why? Why can't we write to the people we love?"

He leaned closer and responded loudly, "Let me show you how to write an address correctly." Mark whispered, "Ruth told me to separate Mage correspondence and a courier picks it up. Ruth watches me because, you know, I'm a Mage, but I can't keep doing this." He raised his head and voice, "Oh my god, I'm so sorry. We don't have a public bathroom, but you look awful. Come on, I'll show you where it is." He motioned her around the counter and to the back.

Her little brother didn't know she was alive or, worse, he thought she was alive and didn't keep her promise. Just like Amber. Topaz's jaw dropped. Maybe Amber didn't abandon the Lil' Killets. Maybe she had written.

Mark turned at the archway that led to the back and beckoned.

She murmured, "Thanks for letting me use the facilities," and followed him.

The back was a wood-paneled room with worktables in the center, bins on rollers around the perimeter, and clear crates with "USPS" stamped in black waiting beneath the wall of wooden slots.

Mark spoke as he leaned over and rifled through one of the bins by the wall, "As long as we're quiet and quick, we can talk back here. I put your first few letters in the bag for the courier, but then I took pity on the loser who likes New Wave Music and started to hide them." He stood up and held a rubber banded stack of envelopes out to Topaz. "I kept these for you. You understand, don't you? We have to do what we're told here."

Topaz took the letters from him. They were All addressed to Malachi Tenkiller, c/o Henry Tenkiller, Rural Route 4, Caesar Croft Post, USA, 84666 in her block handwriting. Was there a stack of letters sitting in a warehouse addressed to Topaz Tenkiller in Amber's loopy writing?

"Or you'll lose your job," she said bitterly.

"No, worse than that. I was going to keep my mouth shut and do my job, but I can't. Do you know my magic?"

"Of course I don't. For burnt magic's sake, I would never—"

"I'm a Clairsentient.," Mark said.

"Canopus Grace," Topaz responded in the traditional way.

Mark continued, "That's why I work here. When I sort letters and bills, I sense the thoughts and feelings of the person who wrote them. Part of my job is to use my ability to keep a log of information about the Mage letters and send it with the courier bag every week. It's wrong and I hate doing it, but if I hadn't, I would never have gotten to know you. Everyone else sees tough, angry Topaz Tenkiller, but I know the Topaz who's trying to save her brother and worries about her mom, and is now my friend. I know you're going to run past the bus terminal like you do every day and I wish you would let him go." He took a deep breath, "I also know that Offcrofters are doing horrible things to Mages. She wants our magic, but not us. It's not my job I'm worried about, Topaz, I'm worried about losing my magic, of disappearing."

They were trapped here just as surely as on the croft. Bloomington was America hurting Mages, but in a different location. It was time to stop being an obedient little Mage and do some hurting of her own.

Topaz plucked a rubber band from around the letters and pulled her thick hair back into a ponytail. "I understand, Mark. I'm not angry with you."

"Are you okay? Don't make me regret telling you about the letters. Some of those envelopes in the bin, are you listening, Topaz? Some of those letters are from dead Mages."

She put the most recent letter to Malachi on the pile and proffered them to Mark, "Keep these for me? I've got to get to work."

He took the letters from her. "Topaz? You were horny last night and woke up next to someone special. Don't ruin it."

"I won't, Mustache Mark." Topaz forced her lips to form a smile.

Mark stashed the letters at the bottom of the bin and led Topaz back to the front.

"Thanks for letting me use the bathroom." She made the bell clang extra hard when she opened the door. "Oh, I almost forgot, do you know where they keep our story, our written record?"

"Our file? Sure, there's even a place in City Hall called the Records Department," he pointed to a paper tacked on the large bulletin board. "People have to go there to get information for passports and such. Why?"

"Just curious. Might be interesting to read the story of my life, huh?" Topaz tightened her ponytail and left the P.O.

Chapter Twenty-One

"You have a date?" Joy asked for the fourth time. She held her freshly polished nails in front of her to examine. Mark was reading a copy of *The Shining* at the other end of the bed.

"It's not a big deal." Topaz spritzed Joy's musky perfume on her wrists.

Mark nudged Joy's thigh with his foot. "Our little girl's growing up."

"Shut up, Mark." Topaz threw the plastic perfume bottle at him and he blocked it with a karate chop. "Don't be here when I get back. I'm sleeping in my own bed tonight."

"Are you going to Paddocks? If Randall is bartending, tell him I said hi. Actually, he's been asking me to bring you by. Says you guys have a friend in common, some nurse with a scar? I don't know. Anyway, you should be able to get a free drink," Joy said.

Topaz's hand stilled, the big brush she was using to apply powder suspended next to her cheek. She looked at Joy in the mirror, but she and Mark were engrossed in one another. "He knows the nurse with the scar?"

"Yeah, she's from Shineanne or somewhere," Joy said.

"Who's this Randall guy, Joy?" Mark asked. He tickled Joy's foot.

"Hey," Joy giggled and waggled her shiny fingernails, "don't make me mess up."

The bartender from Paddocks knew the nurse from Cheyenne. He had to be part of the Resistance. After what Mark told her today, Topaz was ready to resist. She turned from the mirror. "How do I look?"

She had rouged her cheeks and thickened her black eyelashes. She had considered plucking the black slash of her eyebrows, but was afraid of messing up and looking shocked for the next few weeks. She was good with a knife and magic, not makeup. Tonight, she had a date and friends to meet, like a normal person. Now she had a Resistance contact to find. Topaz was dressed in black. Her own jeans and black tank top, and an off-the-shoulder sweatshirt and narrow fringed black boots from Joy.

"You look like a slutty Wednesday Adams," Mark said.

"Your hair is pretty, keep it down. Just leave that at home," Joy pointed to the black scrunchie around Topaz's wrist.

There was a knock at the door. Topaz wiped her hands on her pants and opened it.

Franco was in a black thermal shirt that outlined his muscular torso and blue jeans that hung nicely. "Hey," he said, "you look great."

"You too," Topaz said. And he did.

"Have her back at a reasonable hour," Joy called.

"Or keep her out all night so I can—" The rest of what Mark said was muffled.

Franco raised one eyebrow and Topaz opened the door wide so Franco could see inside. Joy was sitting on Mark's chest holding her hand over his mouth while he tried to buck her off.

"Let's go before this gets gross," Topaz said. "Bye mom, bye Mustache Man," she called as she shut the door.

Topaz and Franco walked side by side on the sidewalk. The May sun was low on the horizon.What did people talk about on dates? Why did he have to call this a date?

"So, you know I'm a Tenkiller. What about your people back on Macbeth?" she asked.

"My mother and I lived with my grandparents until they passed. I'm glad they died before Macbeth changed. Then Mom had her First Death and I applied for my permit to get out."

Okay, Topaz thought. Was death a normal topic for a date? "I'm sorry about your mother. My sister died last year. Nothing helps, but at least their magic returned to Canopus."

"It didn't," he said flatly.

"Canopus Grace," Topaz said. There was a silence as she tried to think of a safe, possibly happy, topic.

Franco's face was impassive as he continued, "My mom and I were close. I'm an only child and my father died when I was a baby." He took Topaz's hand as they crossed the street. When they reached the other side, he did not let go. "I've been alone ever since she died."

"My sister gave herself a Fire Death in front of the post office. She left us with guilt and shame, and a lot of unanswered questions."

"You did Witching Hour Chants? Your sister had a Final Death?" When Topaz nodded, Franco said, "Tell me about it." He stopped by a large stone planter. Red, white, and blue Geraniums shone luminous in the twilight.

Topaz stuck her fingers into the planter and scooped out a handful of dirt. She inhaled the scent of dark earth. The ground in Caesar had a different smell, ancient and bone dry. She had never spoken about Coral's suicide before, but she described the Old Ways because Franco asked. Her eyes filled with tears when she told him how she and Mal had been left to sing alone.

"Coral's ashes sparked to life, like her sparkly self. They whirled like a kitten chasing its tail. Then her magic joined Canopus, a fallen star returning home. I let her down in life, but I like to think the Chants showed her my love."

"You saw Macbeth. There's no peace after the First Death without the Old Ways." He spoke gruffly, "She's not right in this."

"You're right in that," she laughed. Topaz knew he was not Charmed, but it felt good to hear him say it. She leaned over to smell a white blossom. Its softness tickled her nose, but it had no scent. Shouldn't something so beautiful smell lovely? Bloomington was like this flower.

"If you weren't there, if we did not talk right after she left, I would've been Charmed."

"But you weren't." Topaz felt something wet in her hand. She had crushed the white petals. She scattered them around the base of the plant.

"She wants me to forget all the death. All the bodies taken in that goddamn milk truck." He tugged on Topaz's hand, "Come on, we have to meet the others soon."

Topaz's arm stretched as Franco walked away, but she did not move. "A milk truck?"

"Yeah," he tugged again but Topaz pulled him back, "refrigerated so Offcrofters don't smell the rot of our stolen bodies. Says "Magic Milk," on the side. Offcroft assholes."

"Oh, burnt magic. Franco, I've seen that truck."

"Where? Does it go to Caesar, too? Have you had missing bodies? Tell me."

"I won't tell you. I'll show you."

* * *

Topaz and Franco stood outside the chain link fence surrounding the back parking lot of the Bloomington Bus Terminal.

She pointed at the rectangular overhang that jutted out from the back of the building. "Every Friday, a "Magic Milk" truck backs into that spot and blocks the whole opening. I can't see what they're doing, but I hear them unloading something."

"That's gotta be the same truck. Do you think it's bringing bodies from Macbeth?"

"I used some of Merelyn's speed to get closer once. The truck has SWS."

She pulled him around to the other side of the building and pointed at the high windows on this side of the terminal. "I've seen lights on here at night. Why are lights on in a closed bus terminal? Why would they take bodies from Macbeth? It has something to do with the mayor. What's she hiding?"

Franco looked around, "What would she want with bodies from Macbeth? She doesn't seem like the type to mess around with the dead."

"What type messes around with dead bodies? Come on, Franco, she tells us everything is okay on the crofts while Canopian corpses are shipped to Bloomington? She has something to do with it."

Topaz wanted to burn Bloomington to the ground. She came here to help her brother and he thought she had abandoned him. She wanted Franco to feel her rage. Maybe she should tell Franco about the letters, but she had promised Mark.

"You're right. If it weren't for you, I would've bought the mayor's bullshit." His dark eyes sought hers. "How did you resist?"

"My mom gave me visions before Johnson Galvanized her. Probably the last thing she ever did. There was a toothless blonde in one of them. It was the mayor. Once you realize what she's doing, the Charm's easy to resist. Petty and weak magic, actually. Nothing your strong manly magic can't handle."

Franco flexed his arm and patted his muscle. The streetlight above them switched on and spotlighted his muscleman act. They laughed and held hands as Franco led them away from the terminal. The street lights dotted the sidewalk with pockets of light. In Caesar, darkness was velvety complete.

"You don't know whether your mother is alive or dead?"

Topaz shrugged, "No."

"What other visions did she give you?"

"It doesn't matter. Her visions are a joke."

"You're fucked up." Franco lifted her hand to his lips and kissed it to soften his words. "This vision saved your ass, your mom might be dead, and you call her power a joke?"

Her heart beat faster at the feel of his warm lips on the back of her hand. Topaz tried to see his expression, but the streetlights left his profile in shadow. He was romanticizing her mother like he did the Tenkillers. If Crystal was alive, she would not be helping Mal or mourning Coral, she would be at the Driftwood trying to get someone to buy her mead.

When she stayed silent, Franco swung their hands back and forth jauntily. "I want to go and meet some friends with a beautiful girl. Have a couple drinks and gently refuse her when she throws herself at me. Can we please do that?"

Topaz smiled. "Okay, but can you really refuse me?"

The combination of fresh dirt on her hands and Franco's clean cotton scent made her hopeful. A breeze carried the sound of "I Can't Go for That," by Hall and Oates, and the smell of fried food from Paddocks.

"I have to see you naked first." He bumped her shoulder with his, knocked her over a few steps, and pulled her back. "It seems like you go past the terminal a lot and it isn't on the way to work."

"I mail a letter to my brother every day," Topaz said.

"There's no way to see the train station from the post office." When Topaz was silent. Franco continued, "You're watching for that guard, aren't you? The fat prick who attacked you."

Topaz shrugged. This was definitely not a date discussion topic.

"What are you going to do when you find him?"

This time when Topaz shrugged, she could not stop her free hand from checking the knife at her hip.

* * *

Paddocks was a restaurant in a red barn-looking building. There was a grassy outside area with a bar and wooden picnic tables enclosed by a white fence. The patrons dressed more nicely than the Mages who went to The Driftwood, but people making spectacles of themselves look the same everywhere. Although it was a Wednesday, the patio was festooned with people in various stages of inebriation.

"Franco! Hey, Topaz!" Greg's head appeared above the crowd when he stood on top of a bench. He waved at them. "Over here."

Franco wound his way through the throng of people and Topaz let go of his hand. He looked back at her, but she pretended not to see the hurt question in his eyes. She did not want to complicate things with the team. Also, Franco was a good guy, but he would tire of a Tenkiller soon enough. He tightened his lips and stalked through the crowd. She slowed even more to space their entrance. Ahead, there were shouts of "Franco." She waited a moment and approached the table SaLT had commandeered.

Franco was already holding a plastic cup of beer. He spilled a little when he high-fived Jamal and more when he hugged Delta. How was he so quiet, yet so comfortable with people? She carried the big heavy load of Caesar with her, but he had left Macbeth behind.

"Hey, Topaz," Greg gestured with the pitcher of beer in his hands when he spoke.

"Greg!" Curtis shouted. "Stop spilling the beer. Topaz, last to arrive, as usual."

"Hi, everyone," Topaz said.

Greg handed her a cup and held the pitcher high above it. He made a glugging sound and poured. Some beer landed in Topaz's cup, but most of it splashed onto the grass.

Delta took the pitcher away, "Pouring privileges revoked, Greg. You're making a mess." She shook her head and smiled. "Topaz, do you like beer?"

"Not really," Topaz said.

"We have food and iced tea over here. How are you, dear?" Delta led her to a table cluttered with appetizers and drinks.

"Great, excited for tomorrow." Topaz ignored Franco's angry stare. This was supposed to be a date and they had connected, but she screwed it up. He was too well-adjusted, anyway. It was only a matter of time before he realized how broken she was. "How about you, Delta?"

"Anxious to earn my keep. I've written and sent money to my daughter every week. I've not heard back, but I know that it's making her and my grandchildren's lives better." Delta pushed a plate toward Topaz, "Have some fries."

Anger at the mayor rose and Topaz shoved a French fry in her mouth to stop herself from telling Delta that her letters and money were sitting in a bin at the post office.

Jamal said, "So, tomorrow, huh?"

Topaz eyed Franco's back as he spoke to Greg, could it get any stiffer?

"We'll be home and in bed by ten, Team, got it?" Curtis said. The picnic bench tilted as he sat next to Delta.

They all nodded and the conversation stuttered. Topaz turned to Curtis, "Is the van ready? The 3M and ummm...machines running?"

"Yup, smooth," he dipped a fry in ketchup. "Changed the air filter, tires inflated to 51 psi. I know, I know," he raised a hand to forestall an objection that nobody made, "I'm pushing it, but I want to be prepared for any circumstance."

"The van is important. I like that you are so careful." Oh god, what a dumb thing to say? She did not know what to say to Curtis. He was a whiz with machines and loved America. Topaz disliked both, but she respected Curtis.

Somebody jostled her from behind and Topaz rested her hand on the hilt of her knife when she turned.

Greg smiled and slung an arm around her shoulders and said, "Hey, Gem." At a look from Curtis, he amended, "I mean, Topaz. You look hot tonight. You've got a kinda 'Like a Virgin' Madonna vibe." His beery breath surrounded Topaz when he sang, "Touched for the very first time."

She pulled back, but sang, "Papa, Don't Preach," in response. When Topaz and Greg laughed, Franco's back got even straighter.

"No really, though, where's the funeral?" Greg asked.

"Funeral?" Topaz had seen funerals on television, but did not understand them. "What exactly is a funeral?"

"You know, someone dies and you have a funeral." Greg swayed and put a hand on the table.

Delta asked, "Is a funeral after the First Death when the body expires or after the Fire Death when you burn the body? Or is it when you send a spirit to...heaven, is it?"

"We just have one death, and then we burn, or more often, bury the body six feet under. When a body is burned, we call it cremation," Greg said. "A Fire Death is what you did last night, right?"

"Wait a minute, you bury people six feet under, like...in the ground?" Topaz asked. That was pollution, or was it littering? Regardless, a body without a person living in it was grotesque.

"Of course, in the ground. Dead is dead, am I right?" Greg looked at the group. "So, I was in the van. Why did you all do that ceremony last night?"

Topaz and Delta looked at one another. Finally, Delta, with the look of one jumping out of an airplane, spoke. "Magic is a living thing." At the confused looks, she explained, "It's a separate entity that lives inside us. We provide it with sustenance and shelter and, in return, it helps us." A small whirlwind formed above the table, captured a French fry, and carried it to Delta's mouth. She grinned and ate it.

Jamal lifted the pitcher and filled cups, but Topaz and Delta shook their heads. Topaz wished that Delta had been her mother. Then, she felt guilty and took the wish back. She missed Franco next to her. What was she afraid of? Why did it matter so much to him? It's not like anyone had ever been proud of being with her.

"So, when that woman set herself on fire, that was the Fire Death? Why?" Greg asked.

"This isn't really great party conversation." Delta said.

"No, please, if you don't mind," Curtis said. "I always wondered about this."

"Being a home for magic demands a lot from us. Our bodies wear out quickly." Delta paused to take a drink of her ice tea. "When I am no longer able or willing to inhabit this body, I will light it on fire. If my body dies on its own and I am unable to do a Fire Death, my loved ones will do so. They will follow the Old Ways and return my magic to Canopus."

Franco and Topaz murmured, "May your magic die with you."

"What happens if somebody dies in combat and it's not possible to set the body on fire?" Curtis was not asking an idle question; this was a real possibility.

Topaz took over the explanation, "If that Mage woman had died when Jamal shot her, or when Franco hit her with the flowerpot, or if Delta struck her with lightning," the three potential murderers smiled at each other, "her magic would still be alive and living inside of her. We call that a Remnant. If we did not do a Fire Death, cremate as you call it, her magic would have reanimated her body."

"Like a zombie? Cool," Jamal said. They all turned to look at him. "What? *Night of the Living Dead* is a great movie."

"Yeah," Franco agreed, "a Remnant will use up a Mage's body in a few days. The Remnant takes everything it needs from a non-Mage person in a few hours. Then, after it kills them, it moves on to another."

"No shit?" Jamal asked. This was the first time Topaz had seen him excited.

"No shit," Franco agreed. "The First Death is only the beginning. Magic is awesome. The only thing between us and Remnants is the Old—"

"Old people, the old people told us about this stuff," Topaz interrupted before Franco could say, "Old Ways." Maybe if they did not use the exact words the mayor had used, her Charm would not take effect. So far nobody had said, "The mayor is right in this."

Franco glanced at her and looked away, clearly hurt. She had already screwed up her first real attempt at a relationship. She reminded the rising sadness inside of her that she was here to help Mal. Messing up the mayor's plans would be nice too.

"So, what's The Second Death?" Greg asked.

Delta smiled, "There is only the First Death, that of our body, and the Fire Death, that of our magic. The Fire Death prepares our magic to return to Canopus." She raised her plastic cup.

Topaz and Franco raised their cups and murmured, "Death and Life exists within."

After the others lowered their cups, Franco kept his cup raised and smiled at Topaz. She smiled back. He understood. Nobody had repeated any of the mayor's exact phrasing yet, which was a good sign. What would happen if they did use the exact words she used?

Curtis shook his head in bemusement, "That's why you gather the ashes of your dead, to prevent Remnants. What you all did last night was beautiful, but now I understand how efficient it is. Please, tell me more."

"We gather the ashes after the Fire Death," Topaz said, "and put them in a Soul Basket. Each croft has its own. Caesar's is a pretty teal and yellow. Delta's croft, Antony, has a blue and brown Soul Basket, and, Franco, your croft has that ugly red and black Soul Basket, right?"

"Had, but fuck you," Franco murmured without heat.

Topaz thought of Coral and smiled wistfully. "Like last night, we wait until Canopus pulses purple in the night sky."

Delta lifted her arm and said, "Follow the arc to Arcturus, speed on to Spica, leap like a cat to Canopus."

"That's how kids learn the location of Canopus," Topaz explained. "We join hands and sing the Witching Hour Chants. When our voices become one, the magic returns home."

She was surprised to find tears in her eyes. Why? Because of Coral? She longed for the red sandy earth of Caesar. Why was Bloomington's dirt so dark and clumpy? It smelled like worms. And they buried people in it. People should be ash and magic.

Franco's eyes reminded Topaz of the bus. He had watched her then too. In the midst of misery, she felt his compassion.

Delta tugged on Topaz's long hair, a caress in the contact-averse Mage world. The older woman spoke in a soft voice, "Magic enters the sky like a shooting star. The rightful return of magic to Canopus ensures that both Mage and magic are eternally at peace."

"Why don't you just shoot the Remnants?" Jamal asked.

The Mages laughed.

"Only electricity works on magic, as you know," Franco said. "On Macbeth, when the Old Ways—"

"—Old Times, you mean Old Times," Topaz said, but she was too late.

"The Old Ways are a relic of our superstitious past," Delta said.

"The mayor is right in this," Jamal added.

Curtis said, "I had my doubts about the mayor, thought maybe this whole Bloomington stuff was for show, that she didn't really care about you guys, but I feel better after meeting her. This is," he flung his hands out and Delta ducked out of the way, "real progress, not just for Bloomington, but for Mages and America."

Topaz imagined the opening strains of "The Star Spangled Banner" and a rippling flag unfurled behind Curtis. When an eagle eating an apple pie perched on his shoulder, she couldn't take anymore. The Tenkiller fire inside of her ignited at being used by the mayor to dupe nice people like Curtis.

In the ensuing silence, Air Supply's, "All Out of Love," echoed the group's dispirit. The Americans seemed uncomfortable with what they had just expressed. Jamal walked around the table with the pitcher and filled everyone's drink. Delta caught Topaz's eye and they both smiled when he poured beer into their ice tea.

Franco said, "A toast to the Old Times," and they all raised their glasses. He watched Topaz over the rim of his glass and she had no choice but to drink the disgusting mixture in her cup. Was that the ghost of a smile at the corner of Ghost's mouth? It was hard to tell around the edges of his cup.

Greg said, "I don't know if I told you all this story, but one of my brothers, my fraternity brothers, qualified for the Olympics in skiing. We all got together and..."

Topaz had to get out of here before Greg began to toast his frat brothers. That would only end in shots of some fashionably lethal drink. She turned toward the building, maybe she could find a bathroom or a pit to fall into. "Excuse me, I have to go to the ladies room."

Topaz wound through the sea of people crowded around islands of picnic tables, skirted the crush waiting for drinks at the outside bar, and entered the red barn of Paddocks. The inside bar was dim and reverentially quiet.

The muscular man tending bar eyed her appreciatively. He was pale with dark red hair. He stopped washing glasses and asked, "Can I help you, miss?"

"Restroom, please?" Topaz asked. She thought of Joy telling her to say hi to Randall, but this redheaded muscleman could not possibly be named Randall, his name should be Ranger or Colton.

He pointed to an archway at the back of the room. Topaz stepped into the empty low-ceilinged restaurant. Scattered saddles, sepia newspaper stories, and somberly dead animal trophies reminded Topaz of old episodes of "Bonanza." She checked the corners of the room and looked back at the bartender. The room was empty and he was still behind the bar. She walked past the sign with the horns and into the one with a picture of a cow.

Topaz opened each stall door to check that the bathroom was empty. She had too many thoughts swirling through her head. The mayor was keeping her letters. Franco. Offcrofters could be kind. Franco. The Tenkiller kids each had a role in the family and in life. Amber wondered. Coral searched for happiness. Topaz did what needed doing. Mal hadn't found his place. Had she left Caesar to help Malachi? Was coming to Bloomington another form of escape, like running in the dunes or hiding in the back of Bud's Suds with a book? She had ignored Coral's need for love, left her mother for dead, and abandoned her brother on the other side of the country.

She needed to choose. She could walk outside and join her friends, hang out with Franco, get up and do a job she enjoyed. Normalcy. Success for a Tenkiller.

Or, she could do what needed doing and give up normalcy. The Team would notice her absence. She thought of Franco's smile as he drank and Curtis's pleasure in the group.

She had to prepare. She needed water, in case magic was necessary to get into the terminal. Topaz went into a stall, a mini horse paddock, and shut the door behind her.

The heavy bathroom door opened. The air displaced around Topaz as it eased shut. She eased the knife out of her scabbard. She would not be held captive by a Galvanizer ever again.

"Lil Killet?" a male voice called.

Amber's pet name for her. Nobody knew that, except for family and Agent Holder, the border guard who was related to Ken Twosong. The Resistance.

Topaz held her knife near her thigh and eased the stall door open.

The bartender stood in front of the door, his hand behind his back.

Chapter Twenty-Two

He was the same height as Topaz, but his muscle-bound form filled the space between the sink and the door. The mirror behind him showed a small knife, like one used to cut lemons, hidden in his hand. If he meant to harm her, the bartender would have brought a Galvanizer, they weren't that hard to come by in America. He looked strong, but Topaz liked her chances in a knife fight. The bathroom door opened inward so, although he blocked her escape, he was effectively trapped with her.

"Where did you hear that name?" Topaz's low voice was absorbed by the paneling.

Holding Topaz's dark eyes with his own, the bartender drew his hand out from behind his back and dropped his knife. When it clattered into the sink, he exhaled as if he had gotten rid of a nasty insect. The bartender's white button-down shirt tightened against his pectoral muscles when he leaned against the door and crossed his arms.

"I'm no good at this," he said.

Topaz dangled her knife with two fingers, slid it into the scabbard at her belt, and showed her empty palms to him. "Explain Lil Killet now."

His face flushed, but he spoke defiantly, "I'm supposed to make you explain first."

Was this her Resistance contact? Maybe this Randall guy, who Joy knew, was actually her contact? Amber tried to teach her chess, but Topaz had not liked the delayed action and sacrifice required, examining the angles, and thinking three or four moves ahead was not fun. Coral had been surprisingly good at it. Coral and Amber had played chess while Mal and Topaz played "Truth or Dare" or took turns punching each other. Maybe the bartender was Resistance or maybe he worked for Mayor Bennett and this was a trick, but she did not have the patience to work out the long game for each option.

"My older sister, Amber, called us that."

"Thank Canopus. That's what Twosong said you'd say." Somebody pushed against the door, but his body held it closed.

"Just a moment," Topaz called brightly.

"We're not supposed to exchange names, but I'm Randall Foreman and you're Topaz Tenkiller. No more need for secrecy, you and I are all that's left of the Mage Resistance in Bloomington. Twosong and Holder's years of careful planning are wasted."

Topaz had given up on her Resistance contact. Could this musclehead bartender be it? She needed more than a childhood nickname to be sure.

"The Old Ways are backward superstitions. I am right in this."

"Canopus Balls, the mayor's a bitch. You really got screwed, Tenkiller. If you went to Cheyenne, like me, the nurse with the scar would've given you spray to disguise your magic, a modified identification card, and, I don't know, some other shit. They probably woulda done something to make you look...not so Mage-y. Holder thought you were a lost cause, but Twosong said to reach you. You're always with your Security Team, so I told Joy to bring you here, but apparently you don't party. I don't have time to explain everything—"

"You're going to explain a few things. Like, how do you contact Twosongs and Holder? There are no buses and Mage mail doesn't leave Bloomington."

He opened his mouth to speak, but she spoke over him, "Why contact me now? The Inspector will be here tomorrow. What—"

"Listen," Randall snapped, then lowered his voice. "I should be working and your friends will worry soon." He met her eyes and spoke softly, "I'm a Connector. I keep a board for posting information inside my Magic Chamber. That's how I keep in touch with Garcia and Holder. May your magic die with you."

Telling another Canopian what magic he possessed showed a great deal of trust.

"May your magic die with you," Topaz said. "I'm a Taker."

"Oscar Mountain was run over two years ago, Mages were told that Sage Yellowbird returned to Antony Croft, Jeremiah Threetree fell from a scaffolding while he was doing repairs in the Heights, and Martin Runningbear disappeared last month. If there are others, I don't know of them. So," he held his hands out wide and slapped them against his black jeans, "welcome to the Resistance. "

She relaxed. He was really bad at this.

"After the first two deaths, the nurse with the scar told me some names so at least someone in Bloomington knew what was happening. Runningbear and Threetree had evidence of conditions on the crofts. Canopus Balls, they had pictures and government reports about the conditions on the crofts; suicide rates, poverty, lack of medical care, shit like that. The plan was for you to give the Inspector everything. You have access to the Inspector, but no evidence, and we're screwed." He looked at his watch. "I've got to get back soon."

When Topaz leaned back against the wall, the paneling caught at her hair. "How about Plan B? What's next?"

"I'm the messenger, a bartender. I don't have a Plan B. Any ideas?" Randall looked up at the ceiling, "This was a once in a lifetime chance to help our people."

"It won't be government reports or anything, but I might be able to give something to the Inspector. Would that work?" Did she just agree to join a failed rebellion? Topaz really was a Tenkiller.

"I haven't received any orders since Runningbear disappeared, but I could contact Garcia..." he spoke as if it had just occurred to him that action was possible without orders. "We may be able to do something. What are you thinking?"

Malachi thought she had abandoned him, but maybe she could help her people.

Somebody pushed the door and Randall thumped a meaty fist against it. "Closed for cleaning," he shouted. "Use the horns."

"I don't have a plan, but I'll go to the bus terminal tonight and see what I can find, and then tomorrow night when the truck of bodies arrives—"

"The truck of? Never mind, I don't want to know," Randall said.

"What do I do with the info?" Topaz asked.

"I've got to get back to the bar. Stop for your to-go order on your way out," Randall said. He motioned to Topaz and she joined him near the door. He smelled like bleach and beer. "Do I have your permission to Connect?" He held out his left hand.

Topaz grasped his hand and responded with the customary, "Canopus Grace."

He tapped his index finger against his heart and she did the same. Topaz loosened her tarp. The glass containers that held Coral, Henry, and Franco's magic were lined neatly along the window sill. A bulletin board appeared on the wall and a red thumbtack affixed a jagged sheet of lined paper to the cork. Block writing on the paper said, "we will communicate here. i'm connected with others and can pass messages.."

"Burne magic, how many can you Take?" Randall asked.

She took the pen that rested on the metal shelf and wrote, "Three so far, but Offcrofters think i can take one," on the paper.

Randall shook his head in amazement. "Goodbye, Topaz."

Randall retrieved his knife from the sink and waited until Topaz went into a stall before he opened the door. Shrill voices complained about the long wait as they flooded the room.

Topaz balled her left hand into a fist just below her face to protect her neck and ribs. Her right hand was a blur as she reached across her body, pulled the knife out of the scabbard, and held it in a Power Grip. She did it three times. Then, closed her eyes and did it three more times. Topaz checked her barrier and left the stall.

She washed her hands before she left. Her father had told her not to give the Offcrofters a reason, or an excuse, to call her a dirty Mage. The anticipatory drums of "In the Air Tonight," by Phil Collins, thumped in the bar.

Randall placed two shot glasses of clear liquid on the bar and held one of them aloft.

"I don't drink," Topaz said.

"One for clarity," he murmured.

"Two for forgetting," she finished. When he tapped her glass with his, it reminded Topaz of the bell at the post office, then it was drowned out by Phil Collins' thunderous drums. "How do you know Joy?"

"She comes in a lot. That girl is uncomplicated, unlike most Canopians."

"She told me to say hello."

"To Joy," Randall said. They drank. "You know she looks up to you, right? Says you don't care what anyone thinks."

Topaz spoke low, so even a camera hidden in the flag would not pick up her words, "Not that I care what you think, Randall, but should I stay here with my friends or go snoop on the mayor?"

Randall dried beer mugs with a white cloth while he considered. "You mean, should you stay or should you go? Ahh, The Clash." He tilted his head toward the speaker in the corner. Phil Collins could still feel it coming in the air tonight. "A little racy for this crowd, I think."

Topaz said, "If I go there will be trouble."

"And if you stay it will be double," Randall winked. "Here," he passed a heavy black backpack to her over the bar, "you forgot this. There's a service entrance that goes to the back."

Chapter Twenty-Three

Music lingered at Paddocks, but silence accompanied Topaz down the alley as she snuck away from her friends. Would they miss her? Franco would be angry and he was right. Once he got to know her better it would be over anyway.

In Caesar, the night was angular and apt to cut you, but Bloomington's velvety, trusting breeze cheered Topaz. She turned off Main Street onto a lane that would take her around behind the bus terminal. The paint from the houses was more faded and the lawns less green as she left downtown behind. After a block, Topaz had to pick her way carefully over the sidewalk, it buckled where tree roots grew up and through the cement and broken glass was scattered in the craters. The driveways held cars in various forms of disrepair and the windows were covered by sheets, rather than curtains. She turned right and hid near a closed frame store to watch the terminal.

It looked deserted, but there was no way to be sure the building was empty from this distance. Other than the outside SWS that kicked her butt, what kind of security did the building have? Guards? 3Ms? Guards with 3Ms? On the bright side, the mayor was a Mage, so the SWS could not be strong. The bad news was, the mayor was a Mage.

The backpack Randall had given her had a long bottle of water in the side pocket. All she could hear was the occasional whoosh of a car back on Main Street and her own throat gulping water. She opened the pack and found 3 more long bottles of water on top. Underneath, she located a point-and-shoot camera. All she had to do was attach one of the bulky flash cube towers in the bag and then she was ready to take pictures in the dark. She rummaged through and found a small spray bottle of Jean Nate, matches, extra film, a flashlight, and, oddly, an empty red Folgers Coffee can in the pack.

Topaz pushed off from the brick wall and it caught at her loose sweatshirt. She pulled it up over her bare shoulder before shrugging the pack back on. This was entirely the wrong attire for breaking and entering. Maybe the work suits with elastic panels, built-in knife scabbard, and voluminous pockets, weren't so bad. Then she remembered the way Franco's eyes widened when she opened the door in this outfit and smiled.

Staying across the street in the shadows, Topaz checked the long side of the rectangular terminal, but there was no glint of light from the windows. The windows were too high to reach, so she would have to find a different way to get into the building. Both the terminal and the used car dealership directly facing the front of the terminal were closed and quiet. A streetlight above the used car dealership and another at the end of the block illuminated the smoked glass front of the bus terminal. As with the rest of Bloomington City, the facade was smoked glass and foot-high silver lettering, but the private section was tarnished corrugated metal. Like a deep red apple that was mealy on the inside.

The double doors at the front of the bus terminal looked solid and difficult to break into. Only one way to find out, she thought. Topaz walked casually to the car dealership and paused by an orange, round, Honda Civic. She kicked one of the tires. Why did they do that on TV? Yup, it had air in it. She pretended to look at the interior. Yup, there were seats and a steering wheel. Topaz had never driven, her feet worked just fine. She checked the driver's side mirror, but nothing stirred behind her. A few blocks away, she could see the brightly lit Town Center, the tallest building in the city. What was the mayor doing now? Probably not breaking and entering.

This building was not going to break into itself. She walked to the end of the short block until she was out of the brightly lit area, turned left, crossed the road, and jogged along the last side of the terminal. It was like the other side, no doors, just the high windows. The only doors were at the front of the terminal and at the rear. She liked her chances at the back. It had SWS, but for all she knew, the rest of the building was electrified also. At least it was dark back there.

Why would the mayor store bodies here? This street was quiet, but only two blocks from the main thoroughfare of the town. The seat of the town government, with the mayor's office, tax assessor's office, public works, took up a city block, two blocks parallel with this building, one street over. Why not do this, whatever this was, outside of town in a secret lair, like they did in the James Bond movies?

She stepped off the sidewalk and crouched near the chain link fence that surrounded the parking lot. It was not electrified. There was no thrum and resulting gut churning nausea, but there was also no helpful truck driver to leave the gate open this time. The fence was ten-feet high, but not topped with barbed accordion wire like the fences in Caesar. She could climb it.

Topaz took deep breaths to quiet the magic inside of her. The three magics were vying for her attention. Raging heat, scalpel of fire, and nothingness wanted to be of use. Maybe she could let the Macbeth Stallion run free. Franco would like that one. Hold your horses, she told his impatient magic.

She touched the fence. Her brain knew it was not electrified, but that primal fear of every Mage would not be denied. She grabbed a metal diamond and it clanged faintly when she pulled herself up. Joy's boots had narrow toes that fit neatly into the fence. Topaz climbed it quickly and it was only when she was perched on top of the fence that she saw a camera attached to the loading dock overhang.

She froze. How could she have missed that? Topaz waved her arm, but the camera remained pointed at the loading dock. Okay, it was not motion-sensor activated.

Topaz swung over and let go. She landed in a crouch on the other side of the fence. She grabbed a handful of gravel and threw it. The camera didn't move. She threw her empty water bottle high into the air, but the camera remained motionless. It was a fixed camera. Thank Canopus for her Twentieth Century Surveillance course.

Topaz clenched the muscle below her heart, and Franco's Invisibility frothed out of the glass bottle, purposeful and eager. If she had known it was this easy to control his magic, she would have made out with him before the exercise. Her smile faded. The cedar scent of his magic smelled of the Old Ways, like goodbye and regret. She had hurt him tonight and he would not forgive. She looked down and all she could see was the gravel of the parking lot. Again, the sensation of being in her body, but not seeing her body disoriented her.

As she drew closer to the loading dock, Topaz felt the gut crushing ache of SWS. The closer she got the more it intensified. She got as close as she could bear and circled the structure, looking for weaknesses. The ache stopped when she was next to the concrete steps and resumed when the passed them. She went back. Sure enough, there was no SWS at the entrance to the loading dock. She put her foot on the step. Nothing. After each step, she paused, but the crampy nausea induced by SWS did not return. At the top, she paused. She felt fine and the camera had not moved. A red light indicated that the camera was on. Why in the world was there a surveillance camera on the loading dock of an unused bus station? Why did the loading dock have SWS? She couldn't think about that now. Franco's magic was cooperative, but she needed to get into that building, get evidence, and get out in the next ten or fifteen minutes to avoid magic overload. She had no Watcher.

There were two locks on the door, one on the metal door knob and a deadbolt above it. Topaz slipped her knife into the doorknob lock. She jiggled it back and forth, but the lock held. She tried the same thing with the other lock with the same result. She grinned. So much for breaking into a building the Offcrofter way. If you want something done right, do it the Mage Way. There was no way to keep the break-in a secret, but she did not want to leave clues behind.

She looked around. Her eyes had adjusted to the deeper darkness under the shelter, where the streetlights did not reach. A folded metal gurney leaned against the wall. She pushed it over, climbed on top and rotated the camera so it pointed up at the loading dock roof. Whoever monitored or watched the camera footage would see the camera move, but not how.

Topaz was only able to use one magic at a time. She sat on the gurney and released Franco's Invisibility. It had taken all of her strength to restrain it on the mission. Now, it filled her snugly and was reluctant to leave. She refused to read too much into it. She drank another bottle of water. The bright yellow bottle of Jean Nate in the pack caught her eye and she sprayed it. It was the same scent that the mayor wore. When the mayor Charmed them, Topaz did not remember smelling magic. Was it possible that this scent disguised the smell of magic? She spritzed herself with lemony freshness, put the camera and flash in her back pockets, and hefted the pack securely on both shoulders. This may hide her scent from others, but if there was a 3M around, she was in trouble. Topaz took a deep breath. There was no other way.

Now Topaz twisted the rusty metal top off of the container that had not been opened since its creation. Using Hank Tenkiller's Magic would sever her last connection to the father of her childhood. She kept his magic to honor the powerful family legacy that he rejected.

The red magic felt like a too large jacket. She pictured a scalpel of fire and it appeared in her hand. Topaz aimed it between the door and the jamb. After a moment, the steel reddened. Its rusty scent overpowered the lemony Jean Nate. Topaz pushed and the door opened inward. She attached the flash to the top of the camera and tucked it under her arm. She wanted to preserve some memory of her father, so she closed the lid on his container. She turned on the flashlight and stepped inside.

A nauseating thrum of electricity struck her from both sides. Saliva flooded her mouth and she clenched her throat against bile. Topaz forced herself to stay and get her bearings. Shielding the glare of the flashlight, she found that she was in a narrow space lined with steel coolers on either side leading to a door. Sine wave stimulation radiated from the coolers on either side of her. Topaz swallowed the bile and pulled the metal handle of a cooler. A long drawer slid toward her on rollers and cold air rose.

She blinked, unwilling to believe what her brain registered. A frosty shrunken face perched above a saggy column. Below that, gaping emptiness. The corpse's ribs had been snapped off and the sternum to the stomach was a hollowed gourd. Where was his heart? All of his internal organs were missing.

She stumbled back into the other cooler and choked out, "May your magic die with you."

French fries and ice tea rose inside her and Topaz swallowed hard. Vomit would ruin her first foray into crime. Maybe that could be a clue for police, the Mad Hurler strikes again. She took shallow breaths to ease the spasms in her stomach. After a moment, she leveled the camera above the body and took a picture. The flash threw the room in black and white. Blinking against the dots swarming her eyes, she lowered the camera to get a closeup of the cavity in the center of the body and took another picture. She had to get out of this SWS. She could photograph any horrors contained in the other drawers on her way out.

She listened at the door leading further into the terminal. Silence. Topaz turned off the flashlight and opened the door a crack. She peered in the room. It was dark, empty, and had no SWS. She entered and leaned back against the door. Her gut unclenched, but the frozen corpse would join Johnson in her nightmares. Someone had dissected that body. It looked like they had been searching for its internal chamber, the place where a Mage kept his magic. Did they find it? If not, where was his Remnant? Was there a Remnant in here with her?

A panicked fear of Remnants overcame her. Topaz flicked on her flashlight and waved it around the room. No Remnants slithered toward Topaz.

Light bounced off gleaming steel workspaces that formed an "L" to her right, assorted equipment was arranged neatly on top. Various caliber Magic Monitoring Machines hung along the wall, but none were on. Topaz walked around the room, a laboratory, and took pictures of the equipment. She paused by a desk. It was bare and the drawers were locked. Everything here was sterile and compulsively neat.

The body was damning, especially when coupled with the Magic Milk delivery pictures that she planned to get on Friday. She did not have a Watcher. Even hydrating properly and using her family's magic would not prevent a Magic Spiral and Topaz had expended a lot of energy harnessing magic. She would not leave the terminal until she discovered and documented what they were doing with Canopian bodies, so she better hurry.

There was a door next to the desk. Topaz her ear to it and listened. It was silent. There was no thrum of SWS. Her SaLt training instructed Topaz to extinguish her light because it made her a target, but Topaz, the Mage, said, "No way, that's how a Remnant gets you." So, she put the camera in the backpack to free her hands, palmed her flashlight, and went into the other room.

The smell of exhaust and oil greeted her. She ducked to the side and let the door close. Her light only illuminated a few feet ahead, but the echo of her footsteps told Topaz she was in a large room. In addition to her waning energy, if anyone was monitoring the cameras, she was in trouble. She was not sure what was going on here, but Topaz needed to take more pictures and get the hell out of this deadly bus station.

There was a long table with monitors in front of her and wires led to, what was that? She stepped forward. At the other end of the large room there were two outhouses. Why did they need outhouses? Bloomington had indoor plumbing. She stepped carefully to avoid tripping on the thick bundles of cable that connected the buildings to the monitors in front of her and went to look at the outhouses.

They were about twenty feet apart and elevated off of the concrete floor. She approached the closest one and opened the door. Her flashlight shone on walls covered in ivory fabric. Each wall held large colorful paintings, there were two marble Death Biers in the center of the room, both empty, and an unlit ornate chalice in the corner. The room reminded her of a feeling, something just out of reach. It was pristine and empty. Nothing damning, no evidence of wrongdoing. She took a picture from the doorway anyway and left the room as she had found it.

She took a step toward the other building. Her flashlight flickered and went out. The large room was unremittingly dark. Topaz flicked her flashlight on and off, but nothing happened. She whimpered. Darkness was the kingdom of the Remnants.

Chapter Twenty-Four

She banged her flashlight against her palm, but it stayed stubbornly dead.

Amber told Topaz about the rule of three. A Remnant could enter a person's internal chamber in three seconds and three hours was all the time it needed to burrow behind a Mage's heart. Once a Remnant created its own Magical Chamber in a host, a Canopian had three days before he or she died of malnutrition and dehydration.

Sure that a Remnant was in front of her, Topaz scrambled backward until she bumped into the building behind her. She felt it, a Remnant was in this room with her. She banged her flashlight against the building and tried the button again, but it was no use.

She screamed in frustration. Topaz threw the flashlight and heard it hit the concrete floor at the other end of the large room.

She couldn't stand here and wait for a Remnant glow to appear in the darkness. She went to her Magical Chamber. It was a waste of Henry Tenkiller's powerful fire, but Topaz needed light. She opened the container with a dreg of red lava and a birthday candle flame sputtered from her finger. Red flame provided a small circle of safety.

Topaz took hesitant steps, sliding her feet over bumpy bundles of cable. She scanned the room for any hint of luminescence as she took one tiny step after another. Rationally, she knew that Remnants could not hide their appearance, they were long and iridescent white, but her imagination told her that they lurked in front of and behind her, under the building in front of her. She forced herself to breathe evenly and shuffle in the dim light until she reached the other building.

The candle of flame extinguished, as if blown out by a large child, and she was left in the dark again. Topaz hoped the stupid, large child's wish did not come true. The meager gift from her dad was gone and she was trapped.

A wave of dizziness hit her. Topaz leaned against the outside of the building. Magic was pulling her toward a black center.

"Burnt magic," she said. "Where's my salvation, Dad? Doesn't the poisoned fruit mean anything to you? You were never there and you're still not here."

Her tongue stuck to the roof of her mouth. She was bobbing along the surface of despair.

Topaz thought of her mother, probably dead, children abandoned for alcohol. Mal thought Topaz was the last in a long line of Tenkillers to leave him. Then she thought of Franco telling her to be on time. In her mind's eye, Curtis told her he would kick her ass so hard that her children would feel it if she gave up. He chose her to be part of the Close Protection Team because she kept her head. She had panicked on the exercise and swore she never would again.

She ignored the horde of glowing Remnants that her mind's eye conjured and forced air into her tight chest. Topaz felt along the wall with both hands, but could not find a door. She took a step to the left, nothing. Her heart was pounding and she felt herself being pulled under. She whipped her head back and forth to watch for creatures as she slid along the shelter to feel for the door. Four steps over, her shoulder hit into the door knob. She opened the door, darted inside, and slammed it closed. Blue fire flared then subsided inside the room. Safe for the moment.

Topaz turned around. "Oh, shit!" she said and stumbled back into the door.

A Mage's body lay on top of a simple wooden Death Bier. He had not been dead as long as the Canopian in the cooler. His torso was covered in purple bruises and there were round burns on his chest, arms, and legs, but his midsection was intact. His face was criss-crossed with cuts. Long black hair stuck to scabs on his face to hide it in a macabre mask. He had been shown no mercy. The thin nose and length of the black hair reminded Topaz of Malachi.

She moved closer to the pitiful body. His swollen face was vulnerable in death. She bowed her head and murmured, "Death and life exists within."

What had hidden at the edge of her thoughts exploded into understanding. These buildings were imitation Magic Chambers. Every wall of this structure was covered with shields and swords on wooden plaques. There was a large iron chalice on a pedestal in the corner that held blue flame, the source of light. She was in an artificial internal chamber, probably designed to attract warlike magic. The other shelter was an artificial internal chamber also, but for Magic with an affinity for art. An empty Death Bier was next to the one that contained the brutalized body, and hoses draped between them to disappear into the floor. What was happening? Were they taking magic? Had they done it? Was it too late to stop it?

She could not leave him like this. This Canopian deserved a Fire Death and a Final Death and she was going to give it to him. Topaz took the last bottle of water from her pack. Cool water spread across the fields of her parched mouth, throat, and stomach. As she returned the empty bottle to her pack, her hand brushed the camera. She sighed.

"I'm sorry, brother, one last indignity before departure," she said.

Topaz took pictures of the Mage, his bruises, cuts, and burns, as well as the machinery underneath both Death Biers. Then she took a deep breath and rode it to her magic chamber.

In contrast to the small dim shed in which her body existed, her chamber was an open sunny room. It had grown larger and the dusty walls were now a bright white. Had regular meals and clean living changed her Magic Chamber? Or challenging the authority of America? Or was it hope? The container with Franco's magic was still half full and roiling inside the container, Coral's rainbow brightened when Topaz entered, but Hank Tenkiller's magic was a red smear sulking at the bottom of the container. She tilted it and the red lava did not move. The birthday candle light had used the last of it. There was none left to provide a Fire Death for the dead Mage. She was probably too weak to use magic, anyway. This poor man had been through enough, he deserved a dignified Fire Death.

She had matches, but needed a flame to burn through flesh and bone. Her eyes settled on the chalice in the corner. She grinned. Oh yeah, that would make a glorious fire. The chalice was burning, so there had to be something flammable inside it. On closer examination, Topaz found a hose that extended from the bottom of the vessel down into the floor. Propane chalice. That's why the fire was blue. Such a lazy Offcrofter trick, but it would work.

She dragged the heavy chalice a few feet closer to the wooden Death Biers. The hose stretched and tightened, but did not reach close enough to set the Mage's body on fire. She shrugged out of Joy's sweatshirt, the one that Franco liked. It was hot as Canopus's Balls in the shelter, so it felt good to be in the black tank top. She dangled her sweatshirt above the chalice until it caught fire and then placed it on the dead Mage, atop his Magic Chamber.

His skin charred and the fire dipped down to where his Magic Chamber would be if it was a physical entity. Blue flames changed to red devoured his chest.

Topaz backed out of the Shed. While she waited for Fire Death to take his Magical Chamber, she rummaged through the pack and took out the Folgers Coffee container. That Randy boy was one smart bartender. The last words of the Mage woman at the exercise came back to her. Randy bartender. Oh purple Canopus, she had told Topaz about Randall.

Somebody would see the flames soon. She didn't have time to wait for the Mage's Fire Death to be complete. She pulled her tank top up over her mouth to filter out the smoke and went back into the shelter. The center of the Mage's chest was gray and red with ash and ember.

She took her knife from the scabbard at her hip and said, "May your magic die with you, my friend."

She murmured the Witching Hour Chants as she used her knife to transfer the ashes from the Mage's Magic Chamber into the red Folgers container. "First Death, Fire Death, May your magic die with you." She dug until she retrieved all that burned, then snapped the lid on the can and put it in her pack.

"Your magic will return to Canopus," she said to the dead Mage.

Topaz kicked the chalice over and flames hungrily licked at the two Death Biers. The gap where her canine tooth used to be was a dark hole in her sunny smile. She left the door open to feed the flame and used blue fire to navigate the long room.

Chapter Twenty-Five

The pack bounced against her back as she ran. The magic she carried needed to be returned and Canopus sparkled purple perfect above her. She needed someone to do the Witching Hour Chants with. They were rarely successful without fellowship.

Besides, she wanted to talk to somebody, not just to anybody, to Franco. Is this what it felt like to care? She wanted to tell him everything and get his advice. Topaz shook her head to dislodge the sight of the defaced corpse from her mind and ran as fast as she could.

Franco was sitting on the bench when she got to Memorial Park. He snapped, "the fuck you want?"

Topaz panted for a moment before she could speak. "I need your help."

"Oh, yeah?" he challenged. "You ditch me the first chance you get and now you need my help? I don't think so, Tenkiller."

"Listen, I'll explain everything, but right now, I need you to do the Witching Hour Chants with me before Canopus leaves the sky." Topaz dropped her backpack on the bench and unzipped it.

"Witching Hour Chants? Why?"

She held the red coffee container up, "This. A Canopian needs us."

He took the container from her. "Why's it hot?"

"I had to give him a Fire Death at the bus station." Topaz walked around the grassy area in case a croft basket was nestled in the geraniums. "What am I going to use as a Soul Basket?"

"Topaz, where's your shirt? Canopus Balls, you stink like smoke. Why were you at the bus station giving a Fire Death?" There was now more curiosity than anger in Franco's voice.

"I broke in and found Canopian corpses. He looked like my brother. I," her voice broke, "I couldn't leave him again, Franco. My brother's alone and my mom's probably dead, and I'm here worrying about making you mad and trying to fit in with Offcrofters."

Franco grabbed Topaz to halt her frantic search. He said, "Let's fix this and then you'll explain what the hell you're talking about. What do you need right now?"

She rubbed her cheek against his soft gray sweatshirt. He had changed from the clothes he wore earlier into a SaLT sweatsuit. She spoke into his chest, "A Soul Basket for the ashes. Oh, and a Death Bier. Burnt magic, this'll never work." How could they release this Canopian without a proper vessel? They were backwards. After all she went through tonight, she was defeated by a red coffee can.

"Come," Franco kept one arm around her and walked over to the rock with the Tenkiller plaque. There was a shallow depression in its craggy top. He took the coffee can from Topaz. "This could work. A Soul Basket is just a sacred place to hold the ashes until we send them to Canopus, right?"

"It's too bright," she said. She pointed at the light that was angled up from the ground to highlight the plaque embedded in the stone.

Franco stomped on the light. There was a crunch and a tinkle of glass and it was dark. "How's that?" he asked.

"But, I'm afraid of the dark," she said.

"Come on, dumbass, let's do the Witching Hour Chants," Franco said.

* * *

After the Mage's magic arced back to Canopus, Topaz checked her Magic Chamber. Randall had posted Aok??? on the message board. She responded, Got pics.

She sat on the bench and told Franco everything. "So, I think she's trying to take our magic," Topaz finished.

"They're using Macbeth Mages as science experiments. My croft. How many lives..." Franco shook his head, struck beyond his habitual anger. "What do we do?"

"I don't know. I can't think right now."

"Go home and get some sleep. I'll see you at work tomorrow, right?"

"Yeah, I have to give the film to the Inspector. What if the pictures are blurry or something? So much can go wrong and Randall said this is our only chance. Can I stay here and sleep?" Topaz had never wanted to be near someone so badly before.

"You pissed me off. And you snore and smell like smoke," he nudged her to the other end of the bench. "Go home and sleep."

"Are you punishing me for not taking you to break into the terminal? I didn't want to get you in trouble," Topaz tried to remain in place, but he was too strong and she slid down the bench.

"I like to commit crimes. Find your own park to sleep in," he said, but his lips lifted.

"Franco, you were essentially there. I used your Invisibility." She slid close to him again and said, "This is kind of my park, anyway."

He poked her in the ribs. Topaz laughed, but she refused to move away from him. He wrapped his arms around her and pulled her close.

"I can't say no to you, but if you pull this shit again, it's over. You don't shut me out, you talk to me, got it?"

Topaz smiled and snuggled closer to him. She had never known anyone who could not say no to her, everyone could say no to her.

* * *

The asphalt on the tarmac drew the sun. Topaz's eyes ached and sweat prickled her brow. Next to her, Curtis looked comfortable in his Aviator glasses as they waited for the Inspector to disembark from her plane. Topaz refused to wear sunglasses and had to remind herself that Curtis was not Johnson every time she looked at him.

Mayor AnnaLeesa Bennett, her secretary Margo, and the ever-present Thomas also waited to welcome Inspector Thistlewaite to Bloomington Town. The rest of SaLT was in their customary positions, Jamal on a nearby roof and Delta in the van as Perimeter Support. Franco and Greg were Static Protection, dressed to look like airport maintenance; posted on the runway and at the entrance to the Bloomington Airport.

Air from the small white plane pulled wisps of hair from Topaz's careful bun. She had washed it three times this morning, but the scent of smoke lingered. She mimicked Team Leader Curtis's erect bearing and impassive gaze and resisted the urge to straighten her hair or check the small container of film in her blazer pocket. She needed to get it to the Inspector as soon as possible. They were unsure of SaLT's work schedule with the arrival of the Inspector, but either Topaz or Franco should be able to get the pictures of the Magic Milk delivery.

She watched people disembark and descend the stairs to the tarmac. The Inspector's security detail seemed similar to SaLT, but Topaz could not tell who was Canopian and who was not. Would Canopians from other countries have the same features as those who lived in America? Was the frail man in a banker's suit a Mage? Or the woman with almond eyes and long black hair who bounded down the steps? An elderly redheaded woman slapped the hand of a tall blonde lady who tried to help her. Then, she descended the steps painstakingly, one at a time, slowly. Was the old redhead or the tall blonde a Canopian? A heavyset, light-skinned black woman with a sprinkle of freckles across her nose and a short snappily dressed man rounded out the group.

With such a variety of features, how were Mages identified? Topaz knew that Mages in other countries were not confined to crofts; some countries required them to register and some countries treated them like normal citizens. Any one of these people could be a Mage. Was the Inspector a Mage? Curtis had shown her that good people existed offcroft. A few months ago, she slept on a lonely pallet and lived on peanut butter sandwiches and canned soup. Now, she was watching a dignitary deplane and preparing to give her pictures of dead Mages.

Chapter Twenty-Six

Sweat trickled out from under the mayor's wig and the smell of jet fuel made her head ache. She should be dealing with the mess in her lab, instead of waiting on the hot tarmac like a tour guide.

Mayor Bennett turned to Margo, "Are you sure I have to wait here? I have work to do."

"The UN Protocol Office's explicit instructions are that you meet Inspector Thistlewaite at the airport, make yourself available for the entirety of her stay, and provide a reception in her honor before she leaves in two days, Mayor," Margo said.

The old woman had not even reached the bottom of the steps yet. How long did it take to walk down a few stairs? Yesterday, she had looked forward to this visit as a chance to prove to the Director of Bureau and Land Management that America could be accepted by the international community and still pursue its Mage Defense Program. Now, she needed to get back to the lab to salvage what data she could and supervise the installation of new computers. Her War Shed was beyond saving, but luckily, the Research Room sprinkler system stopped the fire from spreading to the Art Shed and lab.

Things had been quiet at Bloomington Town for the last six months while they planned and prepared for this visit and, right before the UN Inspector arrived, all hell broke loose. A Canopian broke into her lab last night and gave Martin Runningbear his Final Death. When she found out who it was, she would finally have a live Mage to use for her experiments. She was right in this.

Mayor Bennett's smile at the disembarking passengers was wide. After she, well, America, passed this damn inspection, the UN Delegation would certify that the country complied with MPR4759. Then Mayor Bennett's Mage Defense Program would finally move forward, no oversight or interference from well-meaning activists. Passing this inspection bought them two years, two years to develop an effective way to channel magic. Two years to end the stalemate with Russia.

She shook the Inspector's hand and motioned the delegation away from the noise and heat, into the small white building that served as the Bloomington Airport's terminal. AnnaLeesa Bennett's entourage consisted of Thomas, SaLT Team Leader Curtis, and that sneaky Tenkiller girl. The group accompanying Inspector Thistlewaite consisted of six people, all dressed in plain business attire.

Once they were in the cool and relatively quiet building, she said, "Welcome to Bloomington Town, Inspector. I'm Mayor AnnaLeesa Bennett. I hope you had a pleasant flight."

"Good afternoon, Mayor Bennett. It was pleasant enough, thank you." The woman's British accent was clipped. She turned and looked up at the pale man to her right, "This is my Chief of Staff, Andrew Neil." He inclined his head in acknowledgement. "And this," she gestured toward a peaches and cream blonde in a big-shouldered yellow blazer, "is my personal assistant, Kathleen Roberts." The short man and black woman scanned the small airport. Their alert stance marked them as Inspector Thistlewaite's Close Protection Team.

"Nice to meet you," the mayor said as each person was introduced. "Margo Hoskins is my personal assistant, Thomas March my chief of staff and two members of my Logistics Team, Team Leader Curtis and Agent Tenkiller. We have a small reception planned at the hotel later, after you rest."

"It will not do. I did not come to America to rest, Mayor Bennett. Mr. Neil will accompany me to the Canopian Temple in Bloomington and the remainder of my team will proceed to the hotel. Now," Inspector Thistlewaite grasped a large beige pocketbook to her large beige bosom and looked around, "where is our transportation?"

"Bloomington does not have a Canopian Temple, per se. Why don't we discuss this over tea?" AnnaLessa suggested. The last inspector had been more interested in American bagels than American Mages. Why had she not anticipated this inspector could be different? Make this woman happy, say goodbye, repair the lab, and finish her experiments so Reagan could win the Cold War, she reminded herself. You don't have to see the whole staircase, just one step.

"Where do Canopians worship, dear? Practice the Old Ways? Surely you understand the proper procedure? After the Fire Death, magic must be returned to Canopus?"

AnnaLeesa thought quickly and said, "The Canopians in Bloomington prefer to worship outside as they do on the crofts. There is sacred land, Memorial Park, dedicated to one of the bravest Canopian Families in America, the Tenkillers. In fact, one of their descendants," the mayor looked around and located Topaz near the entrance to the terminal. She pointed to her and said, "Topaz Tenkiller is a member of my personal security team."

It was about time the Tenkiller girl was of use.

Inspector Thistlewaite narrowed her eyes at Topaz. "She shall accompany us to this Memorial Park," her tone indicated her doubt of the park's existence. "The Tenkiller Canopian can tell me about the odd custom of worshiping at a park."

This messy woman thought she was an expert. If only she knew to whom she was speaking. For Canopus' Sake, she knew that a new inspector was arriving, but AnnaLeesa had expected some tact in a diplomatic mission. She had always charmed others, with or without magic, but she was unprepared for the way the old woman took charge of the meeting. She did not dare use magic in such a public place; who knew what types of Canopians the Inspector had brought with her. AnnaLeesa felt off balance, she was normally in control of every situation.

"Of course, Inspector, shall we?" AnnaLeesa pointed to the glass terminal entry doors, then turned to Curtis, "Notify Tenkiller that she will ride with me and the Inspector."

He nodded and stepped away to speak into his walkie talkie.

"No need to accompany us, Mayor. I'll not take more of your time. The Canopian and I shall be fine. We will meet you for tea, by and by." Thistlewaite nodded at her Chief of Staff and they moved toward the door.

"I'll meet you at the Park," AnnaLeesa hated the sullen sound of her own voice. This woman was insufferable.

She, Thomas, and Margo followed the Inspector meekly, with the ever-vigilant Curtis trailing. Leaving Inspector Thistlewaite alone with a Canopian was a risk, but AnnaLeesa had thoroughly Charmed SaLT to follow instructions and she had no choice. Mages looked older than their biological age, but AnnaLeesa had difficulty reconciling the Tenkiller girl's slender, hard-eyed appearance with her biological age of sixteen. If she did speak, she would tell the Inspector that the crofts were "isolated, but idyllic."

She did not dare use magic to Charm her, but when Tenkiller held the door open for the group, AnnaLeesa murmured, "What a wonderful opportunity to discuss the isolated, but idyllic Canopian culture with Inspector Thistlewaite."

Tenkiller smiled and said, "You are right in this."

AnnaLeesa turned to smile at the girl. There was no need to worry. Her Charm had always been unbreakable and this was no exception.

As she released the door, Tenkiller's beige blazer rode up her outstretched arm. She jerked her sleeve back down, but it was too late.

AnnaLeesa Bennett carefully maintained a neutral expression, but her jaw tightened at the glistening red burn tracing a line across Topaz Tenkiller's wrist.

* * *

After the limousine carrying Inspector Thistlewaite and Topaz Tenkiller pulled away, Mayor Bennett turned to Curtis, "Apparently, the Security and Logistics Team has expanded to the tour guide business."

"Ma'am?" Curtis responded.

"Is Miss Tenkiller part of the Close Protection Team for the remainder of today?"

"Yes, ma'am. She has a two-hour dinner break from 5 to 7 before the Welcome Reception," Curtis kept a close eye on the road that looped in front of the terminal as he spoke.

Mayor Bennett said tartly, "Well, she seems to have made quite an impression on the Inspector. Tell Tenkiller to report to my office to debrief immediately after Inspector Thistlewaite finishes with her. She will be unavailable for the remainder of the day." Curtis opened the limousine door. There was a long silence as he waited for an explanation that did not come. "I am right in this, is that understood, Team Leader Curtis?"

Finally, he said, "Yes, Ma'am."

"Please see that Margo has a ride back to my office. Thomas and I will ride to Memorial Park alone. You may rejoin your team." Mayor Bennett closed the door in Curtis's face.

Inside, behind tinted windows, she jerked the wig off and flung it aside. "Well, that went splendidly."

Thomas rubbed her head with a soft towel. "Nothing you can't fix, Leesa."

"Oh really, Thomas? What should I fix first? That messy British Inspector? Should I fix the Tenkiller Mage who's having a private conversation with the Inspector right now? Oh, and by the way, that Mage in the limo alone with the Inspector has a burn on her arm." Her voice rose in a rare fit of anger. "Do you know what else has a burn, Thomas? My lab has a burn."

Thomas's hands stilled. The swaddling towel around her face made AnnaLeesa look like a newborn. "But, you Charmed her. You Charmed SaLT."

She flung the towel to the floor. "Well, she burned my lab and now she's the tour guide for Inspector Thistlewaite, so maybe, just maybe, my Charm did not work." The only sound was the smooth hum of the long black car. In front, the driver was nodding along to a song, but she couldn't hear it through the soundproof glass. She set and adjusted her wig as she spoke, "Here's what we do. I will be in private meetings with the Inspector for the rest of the day. If possible, I will Charm her and the delegation. The Tenkiller Mage is a Taker. I thought to use her later, but the fire in my lab changed our timeline. I told Curtis that I will debrief the girl after her meeting with the Inspector, but you take her to the lab. Find out what she knows and what she told the Inspector. After I finish my meetings, I'll deal with the little arsonist."

"Got it." Thomas handed AnnaLeesa a jug of water, "You'll need this."

AnnaLeesa nodded, "I'll Charm the delegation into forgetting the existence of Topaz Tenkiller."

Chapter Twenty-Seven

"Bloomington Town was much smaller two years ago when Inspector Ricket visited. I am pleased to see that it has grown. My office submitted a request to tour a croft two months and four days ago, but we have yet to receive a response. I am sure it was an error, although Mayor Bennett does not seem the type to make errors. Can you tell me about your home, Miss Tenkiller?"

"They treat us great in Bloomington," Topaz answered, although that did not answer the question that was asked. She watched the control tower of the airport retreat in the distance from her position in the seat facing the Inspector and her Chief of Staff. Could she trust this foreign woman? Topaz had ten minutes before the limo reached Bloomington to decide.

"But your home?" the Inspector insisted, "What is the name of your croft? Do you miss it? Why did you leave?"

"Caesar Croft," Topaz thought of home, not the trailer with piss yellow insulation bulging from corrugated metal, but the land, "is red. The dunes, the sun, even the air is red. Sand does not clump together like it does here and the smell of Cedar and Sage cleanses things."

"It sounds beautiful. I understand that Caesar Croft is located in the state of Utah? That is an area that was settled by the Mormons in the 1800s, am I correct?" The Inspector did not wait for confirmation. "Tell me about your culture on the croft, dear. Do you adhere to the Old Ways? Is magic freely done?" The Inspector's breath smelled like chamomile and honey.

Topaz was silent. The film was a small bump in her pocket, but the decision loomed large. She had known this woman for less than an hour. Why did Thistlewaite care about Mages in America? If she gave this film to the Inspector, it was gone, that was it. The woman would get on her airplane and help Mages, or maybe leave everything the same in America.

"My mother taught me the Old Ways, as her mother taught her."

Topaz had so much to tell the Inspector, but her tongue would not untangle. Although kindly, this woman lived in a castle across the ocean. Topaz had never seen a castle or an ocean. She felt the miles slipping beneath the tires, but she could summon trust.

Behind the large spectacles, blue eyes sought Topaz's eyes. The Inspector held them. Her words responded to Topaz's unspoken question. "I'm just an old woman who is interested in preserving culture, especially those taken or exploited by others in power."

The car was silent. Topaz wanted to help her people, but could not bring herself to relinquish the film, the only evidence she had of the horrors visited upon that Mage last night. Her tongue strayed toward the empty spot at the front of her mouth.

Inspector Thistlewaite turned to the man next to her on the seat. He had not spoken, but had been observing the conversation carefully. "Mr. Neil, would you be so kind?"

The man's voice was deep and sonorous. "Miss Tenkiller, I am a Polygrapher. You have not lied to the Inspector, but you are avoiding a truth," Mr. Neil said.

"Canopus grace," Topaz responded. The sharing of magic gave one power over another. This decision was more momentous than that of sharing the film in her pocket. Topaz reciprocated his show of trust with her own, "I'm a Taker."

They both said, "May your magic die with you."

The Inspector's eyes flicked to her Chief of Staff. He nodded. It was done.

She trusted this strange woman. Inspector Thistlewaite was not a mage, she was from a foreign country, yet she respected the ways of Canopus. She reminded Topaz of a frizzy, fuzzy, impatient Curtis.

"Now dear, let's start over. In Britain, one with your power is referred to as a Conduit. Your kind has a long history of being exploited for your power. I am surprised the mayor has not used you in her experiments. We've not much time. The mayor is suspicious and I'll not get another opportunity to speak alone with a Canopian. Based on my inspection, I will have no choice but to certify America for another two years, unless I learn something to take back to the International Trade Federation." The car turned a corner and Inspector Thistlewaite swayed into her Chief of Staff. She gave him an injured look and righted herself. "I know this is terribly intrusive, but would you tell me about life on your croft?"

"Inspector," Topaz burst out, "Bloomington's fake. Canopians are captives of electricity, addiction, and poverty on the croft. The Old Ways are forbidden in Macbeth. There's a lab at the Bloomington Bus Terminal, shipments of bodies come from Macbeth trucks labeled, "Magic Milk." I found Canopian corpses and fake Magical chambers. They're trying to take our magic."

The Inspector patted Topaz's hand. "Oh love, I thought as much. Miss Tenkiller, can you prove this? It is possible for me to delay the certification process with what you have told me, but I suspect your persuasive Mayor will explain everything away."

Topaz handed the film container to the Inspector. "I took these last night." The Inspector and her Chief of Staff looked at one another. "I broke in and photographed bodies, the lab, phony magic chambers and then I set fire to it."

"Who is responsible? I understand why, people have tried to harness the power of Canopians for centuries, but who?"

"The mayor. Mayor Bennett is killing Mages for their magic. She's Canopian," Topaz said, "and a Charmer."

The woman turned to Mr. Neil and raised her eyebrows.

He nodded and said, "Unfortunately, she is telling the truth."

The seat made an offensive sound when the Inspector leaned back. "Girl, I dare not develop these pictures here. Bloomington is tightly controlled by the mayor. I shall take them with me to develop and I promise to help you. Is there anything else you can tell me?"

"I don't know what's happening to my brother on the croft. The mayor takes the letters Mages send and we don't get any letters from home. A "Magic Milk" shipment arrives tomorrow night. Maybe someone can check it out? The mayor was there for the last shipment."

The limo slowed and parked at the curb next to Memorial Park. Mayor Bennett was right about one thing; this park was where they worshiped. Topaz thought of the nameless ashes stirring on the stone memorial the night before. Where there was a mage and Canopus, there was magic and release.

The mayor's black car pulled in behind them.

"Miss Tenkiller, you have taken enormous personal risks to obtain this evidence. Are you certain that you are safe, dear? It would be quite the international incident," the Chief of Staff snorted and the Inspector rounded on him, "but I can protect her, Neil."

Topaz felt the knife on her hip and the ember of Tenkiller fire, not magic, but the stubborn courage that her family possessed. "I'll be fine. There's no way to connect the fire to me and, besides, she thinks I'm Charmed like everyone else."

The short British Team member opened the door and Topaz slid out.

Chief of Staff Neil disembarked after her. Before he turned to help the Inspector from the car, he leaned down to Topaz and murmured, "Leave a message on Randall's bulletin board if you need help."

Topaz kept joy off of her face as she stood with her back to the Inspector's limo. She scanned the park and raised a finger in greeting when she saw Curtis. He cut his eyes to the mayor's limo in a warning look. She would ask him later.

SaLT had mapped out locations based on the itinerary the mayor had provided, but Inspector Thistlewaite had already messed that up. Theoretically, Topaz knew the location of the rest of her team, with the exception of Franco. Who the hell ever knew where he was? The surveillance van parked near the post office undoubtedly held Delta and probably Greg. The surrounding buildings were low, so Jamal would be inside a nearby storefront. It appeared as if she and Curtis were the only security inside the park. Topaz was torn between excitement and worry and the burn on her wrist ached. The walkie pulled at her pocket without the balance of the film in her other pocket. The mayor had no idea who had set fire to her lab last night and Topaz had given evidence to the Inspector.

The golden morning sun glinted on the powder that filled in the wrinkles on the Inspector's face. The old woman slapped Mr. Neil's supportive hand away as they walked to the park, but she looked tired.

Thomas held the limousine door while Mayor Bennett flowed out in a slender pink suit with a wide belt. Topaz winced at the pressure on her barrier when the mayor walked past her. If she had a door, it would have splintered under the Charm jackhammer. When the mayor joined Inspector Thistlewaite at the Tenkiller Memorial, a man with a camera followed behind to document the moment. Luckily, the breeze had blown away any vestiges of ash.

Topaz scanned the area. There was not much cover and the street was empty at 9AM on a Thursday. Curtis's hands rested motionless at his side, but he flicked his index finger to the left and she turned to look. She almost collided with Thomas's aviator glasses and recoiled. Topaz could not get used to mirrored sunglasses, they still reminded her of Johnson.

Thomas stood uncomfortably close to Topaz as they watched the Mayor and Inspector talk in front of the Tenkiller Memorial, but she forced herself to remain where she was.

Thomas turned his head and spoke into her ear, "Tenkiller, right? How was the ride with Inspector Thistlewaite?"

"Fine, sir," she said. She was not used to such close proximity. She leaned away to check the sidewalk down the block. Mark stood outside the Bloomington Post Office holding a cup of coffee. She longed to be drinking bad coffee and singing bad songs with him.

"Did you discuss America? How about Bloomington?"

"Yes, sir." At his enquiring look, Topaz said, "Both, sir."

"What did you say?"

"About what, sir?" she asked.

"Specifically, what did you tell the Inspector about being a Canopian in America?"

His rough voice raised the small hairs on the back of her neck. Topaz forced her hand to remain straight at her side rather than bending to the knife sheath at her hip. She was supposed to be Charmed by his boss. Now, how did the Charm work? What if this was a trap and the Mayor's Charm actually did not last this long? Just be Charmed, she told herself.

"I told the Inspector how lucky I am to be here. That working in Bloomington is a wonderful opportunity and that the crofts are isolated, but... wonderful. She is right in this."

Canopus Balls, Topaz could not remember the exact words the mayor used. Maybe he saw something in her face, or perhaps he had planned it all along, but Thomas jerked his head toward the mayor's limo.

"I'll hitch a ride back with SaLT. You go in the limo to debrief Mayor Bennett. Then, take the rest of the day off. It seems the Inspector expects everyone to be on London time, so we will need somebody fresh to cover exceptionally early meetings. Understood?"

"Yes, sir," Topaz said.

Topaz understood that AnnaLeesa Bennett wanted to find out exactly what she had told the Inspector. She also understood that the mayor could not do anything to her now. The tiny black container of film rested in the Inspector's bag. The tiny spark of hope only needed a whisper of air to burst into flame. She had actually given evidence to a United Nations Inspector.

She took out her walkie to let Curtis know that she was riding with the mayor, but Thomas pulled her arm down.

"That won't be necessary," he said.

"But, sir, I—"

Thomas said, "No need to check in." He looked into her eyes as he deliberately tightened his fingers around the blistered skin on Topaz's wrist.

She gasped when the burn flared into pain. He knew. Topaz didn't know how, but Thomas knew she had something to do with the fire. She did not release the Walkie. She had to get help, tell Curtis

"Look down," Thomas said.

She knew what she would see before he moved his blazer to the side. The Galvanizer peeking out of his pocket made Topaz's hand on the Walkie grow slick with sweat

"Slip your walkie into my pocket. Don't try anything and I won't give you convulsions. Walk to the mayor's limo."

Jagged duct tape covering a light, leaking red and casting a hellish glow in the back of the bus. Her mother's red wig. Topaz's breathing quickened and her magic roiled in panic when she slid her Walkie into Thomas's pocket.

"Keep it together, Tenkiller," Thomas whispered.

What if she refused? Would he Galvanize her in front of the Inspector and photographer? The mayor would not want pictures of a convulsing Mage on the evening news. Even as her brain recognized the facts, her eyes were caught on the Galvanizer and her feet moved toward the limo. Her strength was liquified by the Galvanizer, as surely as her mother's evaporated with alcohol.

The Mayor and Inspector completed their circuit of Monument Park and approached the limos, the photographer trailing behind them.

Thomas opened the door and gestured. "Get in." Topaz hesitated and he whispered, "You will not make eye contact with Curtis or the Inspector."

He smoothly extracted her knife from its sheath as she slid into the Jean Nate-smelling limo. She slid over the seat and tried the other door, but it was locked. The mayor slid in the limo next to her and Thomas shut the door before Topaz could figure out a way to signal Curtis.

"Hello, Miss Tenkiller," the mayor said as she smoothed pink linen over her knees, "how is your burn?"

The force of the Mayor's Charm bowed Topaz's barrier inward, but it held. Topaz was unarmed and felt the walls of the limo pressing in. "Fine, thank you," she said.

"You have certainly become an integral part of the Bloomington Security and Logistics Team. Curtis values your contribution to the Close Protection Team. How are you relating to your American counterparts?" the mayor asked.

"Fine. Thank you, ma'am," Topaz said. Her mind raced to find a way out. The mayor knew that she set the fire and nobody knew where she was right now.

"Fine? Oh, dear, neither of us is right in this," Topaz turned to look at the mayor, but the other woman continued staring out the window. "Yes, I know, dear, or rather, I know that you know. In a crowd, it's imperceptible, but now that we're alone, I can feel my magic repelled by your barrier. I know you're a Taker. Why else would I risk the poisonous presence of a Tenkiller in my beloved Bloomington?"

"Death and life exists within," they said together. The mayor's voice was wistful.

Topaz felt shifting sands beneath her and gave up the slender hope that the ride with Bennett was a professional debriefing. The Mayor knew Topaz had caused the fire. Despite her terror, Topaz had questions. She knew that Topaz was not Charmed. What else did she know?

She asked, "How have you done it, pretended to be an Offcrofter for so long? Other than television, America has no ritual, no ceremony or joy of magic. I feel half alive here."

"Oh, I had such difficulties for the first few years. My whole body ached from suppressing my magic. Let's face it, dear, was your life on the croft really a full one? I know of your family, Topaz, your life was like mine. And you know why? Magic. That's why my father was a drunk and a rapist and why your family is dead or addicted."

The mayor's words battered Topaz's heart because she was right. Topaz said, "But, electricity and poverty have broken so many of us. It's only the Old Ways, Mayor Bennett—"

"Victoria, Tori, Snakeheart," the Mayor corrected.

A shiver trickled down Topaz's back, a drop of cold prescient water. Why would the mayor say her real name? She had a vision of Octopussy confessing her dastardly plan in the last James Bond movie. She tried again, "If you freed Mages, we could live full, good lives. Purple Canopus, it would improve the lives of offcrofters too."

"Ms. Tenkiller, may I call you Topaz?" Topaz nodded and the mayor continued, "It will never work. The fear of magic runs too deep. The only way to improve the lives of Mages in America is to make them just like Americans. Mages must be rid of their magic to integrate into society. I have lived both ways. Pretending to be American is better than celebrating an ancient genetic flaw."

"My magic is part of me as surely as my eyes or my fingers. I've learned there are kind Americans, not all of them hate and fear us. You can help change the rest of America's mind."

AnnaLeesa Bennett shook her head and tightened her lips. Girl to girl friendliness was replaced with mayoral efficiency, "Did you enjoy your ride with the Inspector?"

The consistent banging at her internal chamber stopped and the eerie quiet set Topaz's nerves on edge. She leaned against the door to distance herself from the mayor.

Mayor Bennett smiled, "Come now, it would be best if you told me the truth. What did you discuss with her?"

Topaz shook her head. She would not tell this woman anything. "Since we're asking questions, why did you try to have Curtis shot on our exercise?"

"Oh, that's easy," AnnaLeesa said. "He is protective of Mages, and SaLT in particular. Curtis, a few active-duty servicemen, and some vets meet at the VFW once a week and they have taken an interest in a few missing Mages. Mages go missing all the time on the croft and nobody cares."

A snarling beast flung itself at Topaz's barrier, jagged claws ripped at the material, slashed at the knots holding it in place. Topaz rushed to hold the bottom of her tarp down.

"It builds and builds until I have to set it free or I will die. My magic, like my father's, will not be denied or measured out in tiny fractions of that which I am capable."

Topaz moaned and clenched her eyes closed.

"I know it hurts." Dimples peeked from either side of AnnaLeesa's wide mouth. "I answered your question, now you answer mine. What exactly is your barrier? How are you resisting my Charm?"

Then Topaz felt it. The onslaught had weakened it. Her barrier bowed and a corner, the one where she had written the names of her family in black marker, lifted.

AnnaLeesa laughed, "A tarp? I should have known. Strong, yet flexible. So that's what happens when a Tenkiller and a Fareye unite."

Sand beneath Topaz eroded and pulled her down. She lost her footing and AnnaLeesa's Charm entered her Magical Chamber.

"What's your barrier?" Topaz was curious and she had lost.

"A chest in which I hide from my father. I keep the best part of me there."

The full force of the mayor's Charm flooded her chamber and rushed to Topaz's chalice.

"I heard you cry in your Magic Chamber," Topaz said.

A tear rolled down AnnaLeesa Bennet's face. She swallowed and said, "I'm sorry, Topaz. You welcome the chance to help your country. I am right in this."

Magic lapped throughout Topaz's Magic Chamber. The hot oven when she baked with her mother. Cuddling Coral in the top bunk. Hot cocoa on a cold day. Helping AnnaLeesa Bennett and her country was the warm thing to do.

Chapter Twenty-Eight

She drank cool water out of the green garden hose in the summer. Bees droned nearby. She loved the featherweight softness of a bee, the feel of its feet. They were her "Melissas," a term she must have read in a book. If she kept very still, one may land on her. Topaz had never been stung by a bee. Old smoke lingered in the air. Dad must have burned the garbage yesterday.

Cold penetrated to chill her thigh, hip, and arm up to her shoulder. To avoid waking fully, she went to her Magical Chamber, but that angered the bees. Topaz groaned, pushed onto her side, and raised herself onto one arm. She checked her hip to confirm what she already knew, her knife was gone. The car ride. The mayor had Charmed her. At least the film was safe with the Inspector. She now understood that America was not her enemy. Canopians were. Mages were their own worst enemies.

The dusky scent of smoke and ash lingered in the air, the smell of the fire she had set at Bloomington Bus Terminal. She must have lain on the cold green linoleum for hours, judging by how it had stiffened her bones. Topaz eased herself to a sitting position, and looked around while she stretched.

She was in a large storage closet; empty wooden shelves lined the walls and a string hung from a dim bare bulb above her.

Once she was Charmed by the Mayor, Topaz eagerly followed directions. She went into the closet and stood docile. After the promise of a meaningful discussion later, Bennett locked Topaz in the closet. Then a nightmare began.

Sine Wave Stimulation battered her magic. She had no idea how long she had been here, but wave after wave of electricity unrelentingly eroded her magic. Her tongue stuck to the roof of her mouth when she tried to swallow. Her futile fight against the mayor's magic and buzzing onslaught of electricity had cost her. She needed water now.

Topaz rose and dizziness struck her. She swayed, but held onto a shelf to stay on her feet. Hoping against hope, she turned the doorknob, but it was locked. The door was solid and she was weak. She was a prisoner.

This time when she tried to swallow, her throat stuck closed. There was no moisture to swallow and her eyes burned from dryness. Topaz's body was a husk, but it had to do one thing. She needed to write a message on the bulletin board. When she let Randall know where she was, he would tell SaLT.

When Topaz went to her Magical Chamber, the bees coalesced into a swarm of voltage. She reached through the pain for her magic. The sting hid it, separated her body from her center, from Canopus. Thrumming electricity licked at her fingertips and twitched her nerves. The SWS intensified.

She swayed. Dizziness made her feel weightless. Sweat slickened her hand. Topaz staggered and her hand slid along the edge of the shelf and it slipped from her grasp. Her legs would not hold her upright. She toppled to the floor.

Topaz rested her cheek against the linoleum. The world, her body, jittered. Pain pursued her fleeing magic.

"Oh, sweet Canopus, help me," she whispered.

Wave after wave of nausea crashed into her. She was going to die and leave her magic a Remnant. She had abandoned Mal. A sob hitched her chest. She rolled into a tight ball and cried.

* * *

The glare of light on her face woke Topaz. It quieted the Melissas and sent them back to their queen. Her throat was acidic, but no longer clogged with vomit.

She cracked her eyes open. The mottled linoleum under her was dry. Thank Canopus, she had not pissed herself. A wheezing chuckle escaped her. Topaz had been Galvanized and was going to be a science experiment, but she was worried about peeing her pants.

Oh Canopus, she was thirsty. She shook her head to clear it and her neck protested sharply. Her tongue throbbed, too big for her mouth. She lifted her head and pain twinged down to her back.

Only then did she see Thomas standing in the open doorway. Light from behind backlit him into a large threatening silhouette, but the Galvanizer in his hands was clear.

She scrambled to her feet. This time when Topaz grabbed the shelf, her hand held it.

No Melissas meant no SWS. She was dehydrated, but felt a little stronger. She weighed her chances against Thomas and his Galvanizer, but her best chance to make it out of here alive was magic. If she could get to her Magic Chamber and Randall's Board, Topaz could alert everyone about what was happening.

"You good to meet with the mayor?" Thomas asked. Topaz nodded tiredly and he gestured with the Galvanizer. "Speak up."

He could not see her clearly in the dark windowless room. Topaz mumbled, "Yes."

Light from the hall poured in when he squatted and reached to the side. There was a click and the Melissas drilled into her head. Topaz clutched the shelf to stay upright while the pain tried to split her in two. She clenched her teeth so she did not bite into her swollen tongue.

And then, it stopped. Soft mewling sounds escaped her, but Topaz remained upright. She rested her forehead on the sharp shelf edge.

"Anytime you act up, I juice the room just like that, got it?"

Topaz could not lift her head. She opened her eyes and croaked, "Yeah."

A wave of sick rose and she swallowed the hot liquid. She breathed shallowly for two or twenty minutes. When Topaz was able to open her eyes, the mayor was seated in a folding metal chair in the doorway. She had a white pillow under her, and, backlit by the hall light, looked like an angel in a slender ivory strapless gown.

"You wasted precious time resisting me this afternoon. Now, there will be no games. I am to host a welcome reception for the ghastly Thistlewaite this evening, so I don't have long. I am going to Charm you again, Topaz, you will tell me everything, then I will leave."

"SaLT will miss me," Topaz said thickly.

The tinkling laugh cajoled Topaz to join, but she remained the injured churl.

"Oh dear, being an outsider, a loner, has its drawbacks. Your roommate will not miss you because you are uncommunicative. Long lonely jogs are not conducive to friendship. SaLT will not miss you because you never really joined the team, did you?"

I'm a team player now, Topaz thought. She found the poor bruised muscle near her heart and fumbled to tighten the knots securing her tarp. A loud beep sounded from outside the room.

The mayor tick-tocked a finger back and forth and said, "Uh, uh, uh. If the 3M alerts me one more time, I will leave. Then Thomas will return with the SWS. He likes that." She shivered delicately, "It's no wonder you are woozy. Do you know that he left you in it for five hours? I wish he had not left it on so long, but, as you are still alive, there is valuable data to be collected. I cannot imagine how you must have felt, although Thomas and I do watch," she pointed at the door and said, "through there."

"Okay, okay, no more magic," Topaz panted, "please, no Galvanizer."

She glanced at the open door and the window in its center. The thought of the mayor and her goon watching her convulse was disturbing. Topaz was even more grateful that she had not lost control of her bladder.

"I am going to ask you questions and you will answer them quickly and honestly. Do you understand?" Topaz nodded and AnnaLeesa continued, "Did you set the fire here last night?"

"Yes," Topaz said. The mayor knew, anyway. A scathing voice at the back of her mind told Topaz it didn't matter what she did, the mayor was going to kill her, but Topaz had recently learned what hope was. She would not give it up easily.

"You jeopardized years of work. I am trying to help America. What on Purple Canopus possessed you to burn one of my sheds?"

Topaz said the words slowly and distinctly, "Fire Death."

"The Old Ways? When a Canopian dies, they're dead. Why waste precious magic by sending it to a mythical planet? We might as well be of some use while we're here. You tried to burn my lab down because you are an ignorant Mage. What did you say to the Inspector?"

Topaz had to avoid being Charmed, no matter what. Her only chance to help Canopians was the film. The mayor must not find out about the film.

"About how lucky I am to be in America. I told her that the crofts are idyllic, but I am grateful to be in Bloomington."

Topaz's legs no longer trembled and her head felt clear, but she leaned on the shelf and panted. If the Mayor moved out of the doorway for one moment, she could make a break for it. First, she needed water. She needed to replace what magic took from her.

Silk rustled when the mayor rose. The pillow dropped to the floor and she picked it up and dusted it off. "I thought we were having a nice truthful conversation, but I'll get Thomas."

"No," Topaz's hoarse cry echoed in the room, "we are, we will have a nice conversation. Don't get Thomas. Okay, I told the Inspector the truth about the crofts."

"Which is?" The mayor remained standing and folded her arms.

"We're trapped, penned up like animals. We fight for crumbs and hope it's enough to feed our children. Our minds and bodies are hungry. That's what I told her."

"You told her all that?"

"Yes, everything." Now that she started, Topaz could not stop talking, "that you're a Mage and Bloomington is a bullshit city." Her magic called, but Topaz refused to respond.

"I was in meetings with Thistlewaite all day. Why did the Inspector not mention any of this to me?" Bennett sank into her chair and held the pillow on her lap. "She would not believe the ramblings of a dissatisfied Mage, would she? She would need to corroborate these wild accusations." The mayor's eyes were far off as she worked through some internal problem. "I'll have her luggage searched while she's at the reception. Is it possible to search the saggy creature's person without creating an international incident?"

A glass container exploded hot pink glitter in her Magic Chamber. Cutesy pink fire raged, a beloved unhinged fire that frightened Topaz.

"Okay, Coral," Topaz whispered.

No more veneer of civility, she was pure Canopian Fire. Topaz wheezed as unpredictable fire streamed out of her body. It emptied her Magic Chamber, but it felt gleeful to let go.

The 3M beeped frantically.

Coral's cotton candy fire destroyed everything in its path, the shelves were alight, linoleum melted, the doorframe, it headed for Annaleesa Bennett's shocked open mouth.

Thomas tackled AnnaLeesa from the side. The metal chair tipped and clanked onto the floor, while the jet of fire slammed into the wall. Thomas hit a button on the wall.

Topaz's body clenched itself around piercing pain. She did not feel herself falling, but her cheek rested on the familiar linoleum.

Chapter Twenty-Nine

A sound brought her around and Topaz blinked awake again. Before she could make her uncooperative limbs straighten, Thomas wrapped a rope around her wrists and tied her hands in front of her. Topaz tried to wriggle away, but he pulled her back like a fish on the line.

Thomas grunted and said, "Jesus Christ, help me, Pete."

A slender man with red hair maneuvered a squeaky metal gurney into the closet. He grabbed Topaz around the midsection and lifted her. She flopped and kicked to unbalance him and the man dropped her onto the gurney. She started to rise, but Thomas jerked her hands so they stretched above her head and pulled her back onto the gurney.

"Don't worry, Pete, she's my puppet. Watch," he heaved the rope toward him, forcing her to sit up. "Do you wish you were a real boy, Pinocchio?"

Her arms felt like they were separating from her body. Thomas loosened the rope and she fell back. The ceiling was soot covered with white foam. They must've used fire extinguishers to put out Coral's fire. Although it was empty, Topaz Tenkiller instinctively sought the safety of her magical chamber. There was a loud beep.

"Hit it, Pete," Thomas said.

The Melissas filled her head and Topaz's swollen tongue filled her mouth, but she found space for the words, "Okay, no magic. Please."

"Are you going to try any funny business?" Thomas asked.

Too tired for any sort of business, Topaz shook her head and groaned, "No."

The electricity stopped. The Melissas stilled. Her body was weak, but her own again.

"I ask questions, you answer or I hurt you, understood?"

When she murmured, "I hear you," Topaz's lower lip cracked open. The rusty taste in her mouth reminded Topaz of the hose.

"We searched the Inspector's room during the reception, but didn't find anything. I don't think she believed your crazy rambling, but the mayor wants to be sure. I need you to tell me if the mayor has any reason to worry when that plane leaves in the morning. Is there anything you're not telling us?"

Crazy rambling. Topaz smiled and widened the cut on her lip. Blood left a warm trail down her face, lingered to cool, and dripped onto her blazer. The tan jacket now had a bright splash of red to complement the faded blotches of brown down the front. Curtis was going to be pissed that she ruined another uniform.

The rope bit into her wrists. Her tongue sought out the familiar empty spot in her mouth and her heart stuttered when she could not find it. She quelled her panic and felt carefully, painfully, with her sore tongue and found the gap right where it should be. She drew a relieved breath. Who was she without magic?

Thomas had said something important. What was it? Her brain sluggishly thought back. They searched the Inspector's room during the reception and didn't find anything. If the reception was over, it had to be after ten or eleven. Over 12 hours and nobody had missed her. It didn't matter. Thistlewaite had the film on her person or it was well hidden. As long as the Inspector's plane took off with the film. Topaz had won.

"Answer me," Thomas said.

A hissing sound made Topaz lift her head to look at Thomas. The tip of his whip struck her just above the hip, sank through the cotton of her shirt and bit into her skin. Topaz moaned and her body bucked.

"Pete, tie her legs, will you?" Thomas leaned over Topaz and his face obscured the light bulb. "I don't want you to hurt yourself."

Searing pain pierced her stomach, but Topaz refused to look away. Thomas's eyes were the color of the sky. Mages eyes were of earth, like Franco's. She smelled his coffee breath when he exhaled and straightened. It must be morning.

The man in the lab coat wrapped rope around her legs to fasten her to the gurney. He spoke to Thomas over her, as if he were wrapping a present rather than restraining a person.

"Don't injure her real badly. You used an excessive amount of SWS last night. Any damage to the exterior of the container can affect the integrity of the experiment."

"Define 'badly.' The Boss needs to know what she did."

"Look Thomas, the mayor said that this girl," Pete backed away, "is a Taker. She could be the answer to everything. We have fresh containers coming on the truck. What if the mayor can Charm her into Taking from a Remnant? Maybe she can Take more than one power. What if we keep her in a Shed and use her to store magic indefinitely? Imagine having a variety of magics to choose from and putting whatever we need in this girl. This little girl is what we need to win the Cold War, Thomas."

"Yeah, well, this little girl set fire to your Shed," Thomas lifted Topaz's restrained arms and turned her burned wrist toward Pete, "was alone with the Inspector yesterday, and almost killed AnnaLeesa with pink fairy fire last night. Look at this room," he gestured at the snowy looking foam that coated everything. "So, you'll pardon me if I don't give a shit about the integrity of the container."

Blood tickled her hip. Topaz's thoughts were sluggish from the Galvanizer induced convulsions, but the deep burning in her midsection awakened her mind. The future of her people depended on that film. She would not tell Thomas anything. Should she make up a lie? Would that satisfy him? From what they said, it must be Friday evening. Could she stall until the Inspector's plane left Bloomington in the morning?

"I know she's real dangerous. So, let's get her into a Shed and drugged right now. If we're successful at transferring magic, what she knows or doesn't know won't matter. She's the ultimate weapon to end the Cold War, to end all wars."

"The truck's not here yet. I have time," Thomas dangled the whip in Topaz's face.

Topaz had met men like him before. Men like him and Johnson liked to inflict pain. She had to keep him busy, withstand the torment until the Inspector's flight left.

"I'm sorry I told the Inspector about our crappy lives on the Croft," Topaz said heavily. She tried to sound contrite. Americans underestimate Mages, men underestimate women, and everyone underestimates the young, so maybe she could get out alive.

"What were you doing in the lab on Wednesday?" Thomas asked.

"I wasn't in the—"

It flashed too fast for her eyes to follow, but Topaz heard the whistle and then felt the slash of the whip. Blood striped her pants where it cut into her leg. Her body instinctively doubled over to protect itself, but the ropes restrained her. The pain cleared her head. Damnit, she forgot she had already told the mayor the truth about the lab.

"There was nobody here and I was looking for stuff to steal," Topaz said.

"Typical Mage. I knew it," Thomas said. "Why did you burn it?"

"I didn't mean to. I was trying to get the silver thing and propane spilled. I'm sorry," she added a girlish wheedle to her voice, "I don't understand what's happening."

"So, you're telling me you saw this lab on Wednesday and then were alone with a nosy inspector and didn't say anything about it?"

Now that he mentioned it, that did not sound rational. Why would she do that?

"I told her that the crofts were shitholes, but she didn't believe me. Why would she believe me if I told her I saw a lab with a dead body? Besides, I don't know what this place is, what would I say?"

"I don't believe you're that stupid." Thomas flicked his wrist and the whip rose like an angry snake. "So why don't you tell me the truth?"

Topaz flinched away. She would tell him every truth, except the film.

A buzzer sounded from another part of the building.

When Thomas shimmied the rope again, Pete said, "Thomas?"

"You're not that stupid, right?" Thomas raised his eyebrows at Topaz.

"Thomas, come on," Pete urged. "That's the delivery."

Thomas sighed. "Okay. You go out and meet Bob and I'll let the mayor know he's here."

They were going to leave her alone. Her bound arms were numb, but her mind and body no longer felt trembly. Topaz's heart leapt.

Thomas tucked the whip in his pocket and walked to the door. When he reached for the switch, Pete cleared his throat and said, "Umm, Thomas, SWS isn't good for the container. She's had a real lot since yesterday."

"What should I do, Pete? Give her a cup of tea? If we leave her alone, she'll use magic."

"We can't keep dosing her. If I'm right, part of the problem thus far is that the Containers are unhealthy as the result of trauma. Also, we've never had a Container that's conscious. Do you understand, Thomas?" Pete's voice rose and his words tumbled over one another. "We could lock her up in the Art Shed, maybe tie her real tight on the Death Bier. If it makes you feel better, maybe use the portable SWS real low, you know, even lower than the buses. While we unload, I'll identify a fresh Container. Later, the Mayor Charms her into taking its magic, and voila, a weapon to end the Cold War. We're watching history happen, man."

Purple Canopus, Topaz's heart stuttered.

"Fine, we'll put her in the Shed. We've got to be careful with her, Pete. Listen carefully, if the 3M goes off," Thomas motioned to the machine sitting outside the door, "you flick the SWS switch and shock the shit out of her.

Hey, Tenkiller," Thomas poked his finger into the cut on Topaz's side. She cried out and Thomas continued, "stay completely still."

It felt like a needle was being shoved into her bone. Topaz knew then that she would not escape. Maybe she had always known. That's why she did not try to alert SaLT or escape at Memorial Park. She had no intention of allowing this hall of horrors to exist. Her escape would be a glorious Fire Death when she destroyed the mayor and this lab. Her death would help others, just as Joseph and Lucille's death had inspired Mages. Franco, Delta, and Curtis would see to her Witching Hour Chants, thank Canopus.

Thomas maneuvered the gurney to push it through the door. "Get the Galvanizer, Pete."

Pete retrieved the weapon and pointed it at Topaz. "Ready?"

"No, idiot, you have to get the 3M too. It's over there somewhere." Thomas tapped Topaz's forehead and aimed his sky-eyed coffee-breathed face down at her. "Don't even think about trying anything. Pete can hit that switch faster than you can say 'Dead Girl.'" He raised his voice, "Got it, Pete?"

Pete struggled to lift the 3M, but kept the Galvanizer shakily trained on Topaz.

"Okay, you keep watch while I get her to the Shed. Then, I'll strap her in good while you go help Bob."

Thomas wheeled her out of the closet into a hallway, Pete close behind them. The man in the lab coat did not seem comfortable with the Galvanizer and 3M. A Fire Death now would kill Thomas and Pete, but Topaz would wait for Mayor Bennett.

They emerged into the lobby of the bus terminal. Thomas's voice echoed in the large space, "Come on, let's get her to a Shed before she tries any funny business."

Topaz wondered what business was funny. She ignored the jabbing pain in her neck and lifted her head to look at the streetlight shining enticingly through the plate glass windows. She was going to be Frankenstein's Monster, but it felt good to be out of the smoky closet.

She tried to see into the darkness outside in the forlorn hope that someone had come looking for her, but the glare from the streetlight cast everything else into shadow. If the truck was here, that meant it was Friday. She had not told Franco that she planned to get pictures of the bodies being unloaded, so he probably thought she had ditched him again, which she had. It didn't seem like anyone missed her. She had known it, but her heart still hurt.

Thomas pushed the gurney past the ticket counter while Pete labored behind them. Was the 3M that heavy? Greg didn't struggle when he carried it. When would the mayor get here? Would a First Death from here reach the Magic Milk delivery truck? She wanted to kill Bob, the offcrofter truck driver, also. He knew what was in the back of his truck and did not care. There was no way to be sure the fire would devour Bennett. Better to wait until the truck was unloaded so she could give the Macbeth Mages the Fire Death they deserved. Anyway, Canopus damn her for a coward, Topaz would rather die than endure another shot of electricity.

The gurney rotated and she faced a fireproof steel door. Both men were behind her. Topaz flinched at a loud thump and felt the looseness of the ropes around her wrist.

Thomas hissed, "Easy with that thing. It's saving your life right now."

She felt better each second as magic surged through her and repaired her body, its home. Offcrofters were frightened of her magic, but Curtis had taught her that her body was a weapon. Why make it so easy to escape and kill them? Were they testing her? Killing AnnaLeesa Bennett, destroying this lab, and freeing the Macbeth Mages with a Fire Death were her priorities, so she would stay on this gurney. Her tongue throbbed, but Topaz poked the empty space in her mouth.

Thomas spoke quietly, "Pete, I'm going to unlock the Research Room door now. Watch her. If you see one muscle twitch, Galvanize the Mage."

"Okay, Thomas. Do you want me to come closer or—"

"Stay out of her reach. Jesus, you act like you've never guarded a prisoner before." Thomas stood in front of Topaz and rattled through a set of keys.

"Well, actually—"

"Just joking with you, buddy." Thomas jammed a key into the lock and opened the door.

After the quiet closet and bus terminal lobby, Topaz blinked at the onslaught of sensory stimuli. Lights on metal stands were set up around the room. Loud fans in the corners of the room rustled blue tarps draped over the nearest small building. The chemical smell of fire extinguisher foam hit her nose followed by the smell of wet ash.

Thomas pushed her through the doorway. "Look what thou hath wrought. Luckily, Pete has the spare computers set up so he can still experiment on you." He tossed the keys to Pete, "Lock up and open the Art Shed."

Thomas pushed the gurney forward while Pete locked the door behind them.

Canopus Balls, they were obviously accustomed to dealing with dead Mages. Containers, they called them. She could slip her legs out now and escape, maybe make it back to the room before Joy got off of work. It wouldn't be too hard to escape Bloomington and go to Caesar. She thought of Mal's baby face and bowl haircut, but he was not that baby anymore. Just like Mal, the Macbeth Mages on the truck did not ask for this. They could not help themselves. She thought of Franco's stricken face when he recognized the truck from Macbeth. Of her mother's adherence to the Old Ways. Her place was here. She would honor her people with a Fire Death.

Thomas grunted as he wheeled Topaz over a bumpy area near the blue shrouded remains of a building. She looked at it as long as she could. She did that and could do it again any time.

Pete enthused behind them, "Oh God, we're doing it. A living container. If this works, we'll have access to unlimited money, power, whatever we want. I was thinking, maybe we can just keep her in there as a conduit. I mean, granted, that might not be real useful for all magics, but there are some ways...Hey, Thomas?"

"Pete, have your nerdgasm, but get up there and open the Shed," Thomas ordered.

"Do you think that there's a way to use her as a Container and combine magics? Like mash them up." Pete rushed ahead to unlock the door and went inside to fuss with things.

Thomas murmured to Topaz, "That guy's nuts. Two magics?" He stopped at the door of the Art Shed. "Welcome to the place of your eternal rest."

"What do you mean, eternal rest?" Topaz forced a tremble into her voice.

"Look," Thomas said, "Pete's batshit crazy. I believe in Leesa, but this is not going to end well, for you, I mean."

The clackety clack of heels and lemony scent of Jean Nate approached. "Oh, my doubting Thomas, the transfer is going to be absolutely successful and she will live here forever. Do you know why?" AnnaLeesa Bennet did not wait for a response, "Because our little Mage wants this to happen." She called, "Dr. O' Shea, be a dear and go help Bob unload."

Pete left the shed and Topaz heard the sound of a door closing behind her. Thomas pushed the front of the gurney into the Art Shed. The metal legs screeched as they folded. Thomas pushed the gurney along the floor and climbed into the building with her.

Topaz opened her mouth to say there was no way in hell she was going to stay here and help destroy her people, but AnnaLeesa spoke, "Do you know why she will do this, Thomas?"

"Why, Leesa?" Thomas's voice was strained as he lifted the gurney. The metal screeched once again as the legs lengthened so Topaz was even with the closest marble Death Bier.

"Because her family is on Caesar Croft. Her eldest sister abandoned them and her other one committed Fire Death suicide, but snipers have Topaz's father, brother, and mother in their sights at this moment. Admittedly, that trailer out in the dunes was difficult to locate, but the cedars offer cover for the soldier currently tracking Henry Tenkiller. This girl's younger brother and mother are much more considerate as they are both drinking at The Driftwood Lounge. The snipers are a phone call away."

Topaz raised her head to look at the mayor. "A soldier can see my mother right now?"

"Yes, don't think I can't reach someone at a bar. The snipers have a standing order; anything happens to me, your family dies. Be a good girl; otherwise, I'm afraid this is the Tenkiller's last rebellion."

Topaz suppressed the smile of joy, but could not control the tears that filled her eyes. "The soldiers can see all three of them right now?" Her mind sought to untangle the guilt she felt from causing her mother's death to the joy of knowing she was alive. "My mom too?"

"I don't bluff. Your concern is touching, but I know that we were both born of feral Mage parents."

Thomas separated the top of the gurney, slid it atop one of the two marble Death Biers and reinforced her restraints with nylon rope around Topaz's midsection and legs. She could move her neck and wiggle her bound hands, but ropes attached the rest of her body to the table.

Topaz had denied herself the luxury of imagining Crystal alive. Did this change things? She came all this way to help Mal and, if she were honest, Crystal. If she did what the Mayor wanted, would AnnaLeesa really leave her family unharmed? Could Topaz allow herself to be infected to save her family? On the other hand, Topaz could ensure the safety of the Mage people by destroying this lab. Topaz opened her eyes wide. Saving Canopians was saving Tenkillers. It was not one or the other. After they unloaded the Canopian corpses, she would end this lab and this woman by Fire Death. The Tenkillers were more than capable of taking care of themselves. Thomas was right, this room, with its vivid art, would be a good place for her eternal rest.

Mayor AnnaLeesa Bennett climbed gracefully into the Art Shed. Her silky powder blue blouse and skirt set looked like Monet against the Van Gogh wall. A phony blue rose to match her phony blue eyes was pinned to her cornsilk colored hair.

"Thomas," AnnaLeesa said, "be a dear and point that Galvanizer at her for a moment."

"Mayor, do you really need me to cover her? I should help Pete. He's probably on his third drink by now."

The sour scent of magic crept below the mayor's perfume and the Mayor winked to let Topaz in on the joke.

Thomas said, "You're right in this. I'll cover her with the G."

"I hope you have been treating her with more caution than your present response seems to indicate," the mayor chided Thomas. "Topaz, can you explain to him what a Taker does?"

Topaz did not want to ruin Thomas's last hour on earth, so she did not mention the utter lack of caution he had displayed all day.

"I can take power from another Mage," Topaz said.

"Be careful she doesn't take from you, Mayor," Thomas said.

"The SWS has been interfering with that, which is good. We need her empty so we can fill her with whatever Bob has brought us. Time for a booster." The silk of AnnaLeesa's skirt whispered when she crouched to be eye level with Topaz.

Acrid sweat heated and mixed with AnnaLeesa's perfume.

The 3M beeped and Thomas said, "Boss? She almost set you on fire yesterday."

"Turn it off," Bennett said, "It's just me."

An undertow of Charm lapped at Topaz's barrier. There was no 3M to detect magic now. The trouble was, she was out.

AnnaLeesa stroked Topaz's long hair back from her face. "It would be nice to have a daughter. You will stay here with me," she said. "I am right in this."

Topaz went beneath her heart and removed the stopper from the bottle that used to contain Coral's Fire. This time she was ready for the flood of Charm. As it seeped into her Magic Chamber, she filled the empty bottle and snapped it closed.

"You are right in this," the words escaped before Topaz had conscious thought. "We can be our own family."

Topaz heard a smoke-thick voice sing "You Are My Sunshine." Her mother was alive and had given Topaz the Old Ways and love. When she set the bottle on her window sill, Bennett's murky magic drifted like a jellyfish.

"I'm putting some medicine in your arm, dear. I don't want you to move and hurt yourself during the transfer, so I asked Pete to mix up a sedative." AnnaLeesa opened an alcohol pad and wiped Topaz's arm, "This is probably unnecessary, but I want what's best for you."

Topaz rotated her arm as much as her bound hands would allow so the mayor could reach the blue vein on the inside of her elbow, "Is that better?"

"Thank you, Topaz." The mayor smiled down at her, then called over her shoulder, "Thomas, go help unload the truck. As Pete always says, "Fresh is best."

"Sure, Mayor," Thomas gestured at Topaz, "but should I turn on the 3M so she won't try something funny? She wasn't Charmed that first time, maybe she's pretending now."

"You worry about the truck and I'll worry about magic. I have calmed Topaz's magic and this benzodiazepine will calm her mind and body." The mayor inserted a needle into Topaz's arm, taped it down, and injected a bit of orange liquid into the port. "Let me know what we have as soon as they're unloaded, please?"

The needle pushed ice into and up Topaz's arm. She needed to fasten her tarp so that ugly coldness could not enter her Magic Chamber. She tore herself away from the bottle of jellyfish. A Charm cannot erase love, even flawed love.

AnnaLeesa said, "You should be feeling relaxed now. "

The mayor's face split and there were two golden orbs floating next to Topaz. Two Mayors. One Mage and one American. It would be nice to be two people. A Topaz on the bench with Franco and another Topaz here helping the mayor.

"The medicine needs a few moments to take effect. I will leave you here for a moment while I go see what arrived on the truck. After I check on the boys, we will have a new power for you, won't that be nice?" The mayor took the Jean Nate with her, but the stench of magic lingered.

Is this what an American mother was like? Someone who told you what was best and made decisions for you? She had fastened her tarp tightly. Now,

Topaz snuggled into the gurney. She was always fighting against something; her father and religion, her mother and alcohol, Mal and addiction, Coral and sadness. Now, she was done fighting. Her family was safe and Topaz could accomplish something with AnnaLeesa. Fighting Russia and winning the Cold War. Just because she wasn't Charmed didn't mean the mayor wasn't right. Made perfect sense.

She was waiting for the dead Macbeth Mages to be brought inside. Why was she waiting for that? She had to do something. What was it? Oh yes, Fire Death. Why?

She looked at the "Starry Starry Night" painting. A Fire Death here would ruin this beautiful room, everything AnnaLeesa had worked for. How would a Fire Death help anyone?

Alive, she could free Mages from the shackles of ignorance. She took magic all the time, why not do it for America? AnnaLeesa thought Topaz was just a Taker, but she had more to offer. When AnnaLeesa came back, Topaz would tell her what she could really do. Taking three magics is much better than one. It would be nice to surprise the mayor.

"Death and life exist within," a voice whispered in her ear.

Chapter Thirty

She knew that voice. Topaz looked around, but the building was empty. Her tongue sought the empty spot in her mouth. "Franco?"

"Yup," he said. "I thought you stood me up. Thank Canopus you were only kidnapped, tortured, and drugged. Let's get the hell out of here."

"Hey, the mayor is right," Topaz said.

"Yeah," he said, "we only have a few minutes while they decide which dead Mage to make you Take from."

A knife sliced through the plastic ties to free Topaz's wrists and hands. The rest of her was still bound to the table, but now she could move her hands.

"Hi," Topaz waved at Franco, "I thought you were mad at me because I didn't bring you to the break-in. You're really beautiful."

"I can't take this shit," Franco said. The tape near Topaz's elbow was ripped off and the needle removed.

"Ow," Topaz yelped.

"Shut it," Franco said. A piece of gauze was placed between the needle and Topaz's arm and the port taped on top. "This'll make it look like you're still being drugged, in case she comes back. Now, I need to get you loose." Items rose and were discarded around the small room.

"Sorry, gorgeous," Topaz said, "no can do. I've been given ben...benzo...a sedative to soothe my troubled head, but AnnaLeesa's jellyfish Charm is so warm, I probably don't need it."

"For fuck's sake, stoned Topaz talks a lot. We have to get you out of here," Franco said. A water bottle appeared in front of Topaz's mouth. "Drink."

The bottle tipped and Topaz swallowed. Water wet her dry mouth and throat, then chilled her stomach and cleared some of the fuzz from her head. She was able to hold the bottle with her freed hands. A scalpel sawed at the ropes around her waist, with little effect on the thick nylon.

"Don't you worry about the ropes," Topaz said, "I have a plan."

"Could you whisper and suck your stomach in a little?" The scalpel rubbed furiously against the rope and then flew across the room. "Damn it, this isn't working. What's your plan?"

The small building was crowded with the scent of smoke, Jean Nate, and magic, but underneath it all was the clean cotton of Franco. She inhaled his sunny scent. "My Fire Death."

"You are high, if that's your plan. Nope, no Fire Death."

"You have to go," she said, "They'll be back and turn on the 3M any minute," she said.

"Not without you," Franco said.

The knots moved frantically. Topaz felt the warmth of Franco's hands as he tried to untie the knots.

Topaz went to her Magical Chamber. The only magic she had left was AnnaLeesa Bennett's murky Charm, but Randall's Bulletin Board hung on the wall. There were increasingly frantic messages scrawled on it.

AoK? Aok?

What happened? Where are you?

Evidence? Do you need help? Answer!

Insp left. with evidence????? I'm Extracted by Res. will ck here for info!

She scrawled, "Insp has film. tell holder & Ken– snipers on my family."

What else did she need to take care of? Tell Randall to let Mal know she loved him and hoped he understood? Forgive her mother? Stop judging her father? Thank Curtis and Delta? Tell Joy to marry Mark? Topaz cleared her throat. There was something stuck, something that made it thick and her eyes scratchy and watery.

She spoke to the invisible Franco, "I've never known anyone like you. You have to leave, Franco. Go to Caesar and see if my family is safe. This lab…it has to be destroyed or they'll destroy us. Bennett has to die and the Macbeth Mages from the truck deserve to go to Canopus. Death and life exists within."

"You do like me," Franco said. "Fucking Canopus, you think I'll let you do a Fire Death after that? Good Mage women are hard to find."

The door from the lab to the Research Room opened. Pete whistled Olivia Newton John's "Let's Get Physical" as he pushed a gurney into the room.

Topaz whispered, "They finished unloading. Leave and go to my family, don't make this for nothing, Franco."

He pressed the bandage against the loose port and turned the zip ties so it looked like Topaz was restrained. The smell of laundry on the line disappeared.

The gurney clattered and screeched over wires as it approached. Pete poked his head in and looked around. He looked at the gurney, and then at the floor, then back at the gurney. "How the heck am I going to fit this in here?"

She opened her mouth to tell him that the gurney would fit up his ass, but remembered she was supposed to be sedated. She drooped her eyes. The Mayor and Thomas would be back soon. Then it would be time.

"We've never done this with a real live subject before, you know." Pete stepped in and took a silver flask out of his pocket. He drank deeply before he said, "Thus far, most of the magic has been lost in the extraction process, you know? We got a real fresh Container today, Kismet, right? So, you are going to Take," he tucked the flask into his pocket and leaned out of the shed. He picked a clipboard up from a mound resting atop the gurney and consulted it, "Charlie Tootall's magic. Then we will see if you can make yourself bigger. It's not fancy, but easily observable. First, I have to figure out a way to get him up into the Shed so I can hook you two up, oh my, hook you up, that sounds interesting. Thomas usually does this part. Hmmm...I wonder where he went," Pete said.

He stepped down out of the Shed and shouted, "Thomas?"

There was no response. Pete grumbled as he wove through cables and wire to the lab.

When she heard the lab door close, Topaz sat up to look out of the shed door. Her eyes fell on the gurney. The clipboard had caught and bunched the covering and the top of a pale face was exposed. A slash of black brows, thick lashes, and high cheekbones reminded her of Franco.

"Charlie Tootall, I will give you a Fire Death," Topaz told the dead Canopian.

She was ready. When AnnaLeesa, Thomas, and Pete returned, she would free this Mage and them. That was enough. If a life of purpose was not possible, a death with purpose was honorable.

Chapter Thirty-One

A bolt of lightning zipped from the ceiling to the computer table. The computers sparked and smoked, then the wires and cables that led to the Shed made popping sounds. Little fires ignited around the room. Burnt plastic competed with the scent of smoke and magic.

Thunder boomed. Through the open door of the Shed, Topaz watched sheets of rain descend onto the Research Room floor. Puddles formed and dissipated the burnt electronic ozone scent. Then, as abruptly as it began, the rain stopped.

The door to the lab clattered open and Thomas walked into the Research Room.

Topaz lay back to appear drugged. She had to have AnnaLeesa Bennett near before she did the Fire Death. Beneath her lashes, she spotted a dark hand on Thomas's shoulder.

Jamal pushed Thomas forward and motioned toward the wall with a gun. Thomas narrowed his eyes, but obediently sat on the wet concrete with his back against the wall.

Topaz grinned and Jamal jerked his chin toward her in his characteristically effusive manner.

"Jamal," Topaz shouted, "watch out for the mayor."

The maniacal beeping of a 3M and shrieks of, "I am right in this," grew louder when Greg opened the door from the lab. He pushed AnnaLeesa Bennet through the open door. Her heel caught on a colorful bouquet of cable and her shrieks changed to howls when she fell into a puddle.

Thomas started toward AnnaLeesa, but Jamal cocked his gun and said, "Don't move." Thomas subsided back against the wall.

Greg leaned down and jammed his Galvanizer into AnnaLeesa's temple and the 3M quieted. "I told you not to say that again. Get up, move over there." When he gestured with the Galvanizer, AnnaLeesa's wig tilted down over her face.

She straightened it and moved over against the wall.

Seeing Topaz, Greg smiled. Then his eyes widened and his smile faded. He pointed his Galvanizer at AnnaLeesa with two hands and spoke through clenched teeth, "I changed my mind. You tortured a member of SaLT? You messed with my family. Please, tell me I'm right in this. Come on!"

Topaz called, "Guys, the redhead—"

"—is right here," Franco said. He pushed a rolling chair in from the lab. The scientist had so much duct tape wrapped around him and the chair, he looked like a silver mermaid. Franco smirked at Jamal, "I told you I didn't need a gun." He flexed his muscles, "I got these guns."

"Where's the driver?" Topaz asked.

"How about a thanks, Mage," Jamal muttered.

"We waited until he left and then got these three. Franco did a sweep, but is there anything else we should be worried about?" Greg asked.

"Nope. Hey, could someone untie me?" Topaz called. Franco started forward, but Topaz eyed the Macbeth Mage corpse next to her and called, "Not you, Franco."

"I saw him when they unloaded," Franco said. He spun Pete's chair toward Jamal, moved the gurney out of the way, and went to untie Topaz.

Their eyes met. Franco and Topaz said, "May your magic die with you."

"Look what I found in the lab," Franco held up a giant pair of shears and cut the ropes around Topaz's waist and feet. "I don't want to know what they used them for." Topaz started to rise. He said, "Easy," and helped her.

The blues, yellows, and whites of "The Starry Night" swirled. Franco stayed close as Topaz stepped down from the Shed and crossed the puddled cement floor.

The guys looked at her expectantly. Greg, in his backwards "Huskies" cap, grinned while he bent over to press his Galvanizer into the skull of a terrified and silent AnnaLeesa Bennet. Jamal's gun was an extension of his arm steadily pointed at Thomas. This destructive rainstorm had to be caused by Delta. And Franco, Franco had never really left her.

Topaz wondered what Curtis thought of all of this. She would miss him. She understood and respected his allegiance to America. This seemed like a coup and it was unfair to expect someone to betray his country for her. Why were they looking at her?

She cleared her throat and said, "Thank you." Topaz blinked rapidly to keep tears from filling her eyes. "It's hard without Curtis here to guide us." Topaz paused. She had no idea what she was going to say next.

"What do you mean?" Greg asked, "They're doing Perimeter Security."

Curtis too? The whole team had come to help her. This time she could not contain the tears. She turned away so they would not see her cry.

Jamal said, "Oh, for god's sake."

Greg sniffed and responded, "I know just how she feels, okay?"

Franco whispered in her ear, "Dumbass." Then he raised his voice, "Okay, let's secure the prisoners. The door on that little artsy shithole has a strong lock. Tie Thomas to the Death Bier and lock him in there. Where should we put that piece of shit?" He pointed at AnnaLeesa Bennett, who was silently weeping.

Topaz swiped at her eyes and took a deep breath to dislodge the lump in her throat. She thought briefly of the mayor's internal chamber, a hiding place from her abusive father. Then she thought of the closet where she had been kept for days, but she could not do that to another Mage.

"How about the smaller lab next door? We can put the redhead in the closet where they kept me. It's smoky and bloody and perfect."

* * *

Greg turned off the SWS and they found five Mage corpses in the Coolers. They used Bic Lighters, but SaLT gave each Mage his or her own Fire Death. Delta created a brisk wind to blow the smoke away. Topaz could not find anything suitable to use for Soul Baskets, so she dumped pencils, paper clips, floppy disks, gum, and other detritus out of five metal desk drawers. Maybe it was time for Bloomington to have its own Soul Basket.

The team lined the five drawers neatly at the base of the loading dock. SaLT sat and waited for Canopus to rise. The black SaLT Van was backed up out of sight under the overhang.

"Somebody has to fix this soup sandwich," Curtis said.

He, Jamal, and Greg were leaning against the wall of the terminal. The Mages were uncomfortable being near where so many Canopian corpses had rested, so they sat on the steps.

"Sir, I want to help the people in Macbeth. Do I have your permission to go over the hill?" Franco asked.

Topaz looked at Greg. Greg said, "A 'soup sandwich' is an impossible situation and Franco wants to leave without permission."

"I'd like to go over the hill, also," Topaz said. She looked over at Franco, but it was too dark to see his expression. Was she asking him or Curtis? "I mean, if that's okay."

"I'd like permission to help these little pussies who won't use a gun, sir," Jamal said.

Delta, Franco, and Topaz looked at one another. It was sacrilegious to even speak of guns near the ashes of Canopians.

"I'd like permission to get away from this bag of dicks, but somebody has to stay and explain what happened at the bus station from hell. Permission granted, you three," Curtis said. "Delta, Greg, what say you?"

"TL, it would be helpful if a Mage was here to help explain, also. Topaz told me of a way we can communicate using magic. Assuming you want to communicate with this band of hooligans, sir?" Delta's question begged for reassurance that she was doing the right thing.

"I wouldn't have it any other way," Curtis said. "Delta, I know you have my six and I've got yours. I, honest to Jesus, sincerely appreciate it. Greg?"

"I'll pop smoke with the hooligans to handle the Galvanizer and 3M. I'm assuming we're going to strategically acquire the SaLT Van?" When Curtis smiled and nodded, Greg continued, "In which case, I drive." He looked around, but nobody challenged him. Then, Greg said softly, "I have a lot to learn from my Mage Family."

"That's it, then. Me and Delta are Latrine Queens while you four go Elvis. I give you my blessing, but Uncle Sam has not, and will not. Best be sure before you go AWOL."

The group was silent. Topaz thought of warm campfire scented blankets and a man who taught her to trust offcrofters.

Franco nudged her and said, "Isn't that Canopus?" He pointed at the purple planet.

The other five members of SaLT rose and picked up an ash-filled drawer. Topaz tapped Curtis on the shoulder as he went down the stairs. When he turned around, she said, "Please, Curtis, come with us. I need you."

"I'll be more useful here. Between the film you gave Inspector Thistlewaite and what's here at the terminal, people will be looking for answers. Authorities in America twist things the way they want and we believe them. Someone has to stay and tell the truth and explain the truth and tell the truth again. I still have a few friends who'll listen."

"Am I running away, Curtis?"

"No, Gem, you are not running. You're doing what's best for your people. I'm doing my best to stop my people from being asshats. SaLT is on its most important mission, yet. Don't screw it up."

"Yes, sir," Topaz said. She followed Curtis down the stairs.

This time when purple Canopus silver beckoned, Topaz's family shouted the joyous farewell, "May your magic die with you."

Acknowledgments

To My Husband, John, for the gifts of love and uninterrupted time, and coffee, lots of coffee.

I hate to ask for and accept help, but when writing a book, it cannot be avoided. Luckily, I'm pretty good at "thank-yous." There are many people to thank for this book.

My children, the little time-suckers, always encourage me. Their pride is the reason I get up at 4:30AM to write. Mom and Sasha are my best friends. They have leveled forests to print and read everything I write, and they claim to like it. Family is the best.

It took all of my courage to let anyone see my work. Lesley and Jack, both friends and teachers, were generous and kind readers. They were not related to me and they actually liked my book. I still didn't dare call myself a writer, but I pretended and joined a few writer's groups.

Linda, John, and Jim are true friends and make me a better writer. Thanks Anne, Judith, Cathy, and Robyn for the great writing sessions and endless homeless meal prep. Kindness always wins!

I appreciate the teachers who have mentored me and those students whom I have mentored. You all have taught me.

My three dogs, three cats, and eleven chickens give me absolutely unconditional love, but my turtle hates me. May every animal find a forever home.

About the Author

Julie Colacchio has taught Creative Writing, Literature, and Public Speaking at the high school and college level for over 20 years. She grew up on the Uintah Reservation in Utah, but now lives in New York with her husband, three children, and 18 rescued animals.